GUILT IS MIDNIGHT BLUE

JOSALYN MCALLISTER

EBURNEAN
BOOKS

EBURNEAN BOOKS

Published by Eburnean Books, an imprint of Emberworks Creative, LLC.

www.eburneanbooks.com

www.emberworkscreative.com

GUILT IS MIDNIGHT BLUE

To Shelly Biggs, my Alpha One Reader

ONE

Cash slammed the truck into drive, causing the wheels to spin and splatter mud all over Billy. He saw steam coming out of his brother's ears in the rear-view mirror, but he didn't stop to apologize. Not this time. He had steam enough inside his own head. He drove towards town, not really having a final destination in mind. There was the bar and the diner, but Billy would find him in either of those places. And Cash needed to think before he could talk to his brother again. Frustration simmered in his brow for twenty minutes until he hit main street.

It was a tourist trap of a town, nothing but antique shops and boutiques. There were a couple of Appalachian Trail outfitters, but Cash would spend money he didn't have if he stepped into one of those. He scanned the signs going down the road and flipped a U-turn, when he got to the end of the shops. He then started scanning the other side of the street. It had to be somewhere no one would look for him, somewhere his brothers would never go.

The old mill caught his eye. It had been a dilapidated old building for a long time, but about five years ago someone had fixed it up and turned it into a shop. Underneath an ancient sign reading "Red Gap Mill" was another, more modern sign: "Chocolate and Books." Perfect. Billy only read at a fourth-grade level, a source of mortification for him, so he avoided books at all costs.

Cash drove to the end of the street before he pulled into one of the forty-five degree angle parking spots lining both sides of main street and ignored the parking meter. Parking meters were for tourists. He parked relatively close to the bar. If Billy went looking for him in there, he probably wouldn't make it out in a timely manner. He walked back up the street, ignoring the disapproving glances people shot at him and his mud-covered boots and pants. His shirt had a big hole in it too, he remembered now. Right across his lower back like a tramp stamp. He stomped his feet a few times and dried bits of concrete littered the sidewalk underneath him. When he got to the door of Chocolate and Books, he stopped, looking down at his messy appearance. What if they threw him out because of his dirty, holey clothes? It wouldn't be a new experience.

He peered through the glass in the front door and didn't see anyone. The place appeared deserted, there wasn't even anyone at the front register. After thinking a bit, Cash decided to risk it. He pulled the door open and cringed when a metal bell attached to it started ringing. Cash reached up and grabbed it so it would stop, muffling the sound with his hand. No one came running out from the back. Relaxing, he took a few steps into the store. He inhaled deeply, trying to pinpoint the store's pleasant kind of smell. It smelled like chocolate and something unfamiliar to him. He chuckled at himself. Books - the smell must be books. He couldn't see any chocolate from where he was standing, just shelves and shelves of books.

Books were stacked on the floor and piled up on end tables. There were ten sets of main bookshelves creating four aisles to walk down, inviting you to come peruse the books. On top of each shelf, books were stacked even higher. Cash shook his head. It was surely a fire hazard. An inspector would have a fit if he ever stopped by.

At the end of one of the rows was an overstuffed chair with a tower of books right next to it. Cash looked down at his mud-caked jeans and resisted the urge to sit down in the chair. His house had never had furniture so inviting in it. Cash walked down one of the rows of shelves. He wondered how you were to find anything that you wanted because there were no labels or signs anywhere to tell you what kind of books were shelved where. In fact, he saw a copy of *The Cat in the Hat* right next to *A Tale of Two Cities* and *The Prince*. It didn't seem organized at all.

After taking a few steps down what felt like a tunnel of books, he caught a glimpse of a bright open space. He walked tentatively towards the light. When he emerged from the stacks of books, the effect was nothing short of magical. The entire back of the building was encased in glass with the arched ceiling of a conservatory. The view of the North Georgia mountains made his breath catch in his throat. The gigantic wheel that used to grind grain into flour spun in the river's current with hypnotic regularity.

Nestled within the space was a bakery counter displaying various confections and rows and rows of chocolates. There was a little coffee menu as well. Overstuffed chairs like the one in the front were everywhere, and the brick wall to his right housed a large wood-burning fireplace. A chess table sat nearby, set up with a game in progress. His jaw actually dropped. It felt like the book tunnels were a portal to another world. A secret clubhouse.

"Hello there!" a cheerful voice called out. He looked around but didn't see anyone. For an instant he wondered if the disembodied voice was another part of the shop's magic. "Don't you just love the cooler weather? I'm so happy every year when I can finally light a fire again." Then movement caught his eye from the direction of the voice. A tall forty-ish woman got up from lighting the fire. Her posture made him think of a queen, but her manner still held a certain openness.

"I..." Cash stammered, "I didn't see you there."

The woman looked down at her stone colored cardigan and khaki pants. "Oh yes," she laughed, "I suppose I'm a bit camouflaged." She came towards him with her hand out. "Welcome to my shop," she said, reaching to shake his hand. "I'm Miss Hazel, Hazel Randolph Dean." She didn't even blink at his dirty pants and holey shirt.

"Th... thank you." Cash wasn't normally a stutterer, but he was overwhelmed by the experience, so different from his normal life. He didn't talk much normally. He glanced at his dirty hand, hesitant to put it in hers, but she reached out and took it anyway. He'd heard of the Randolph family. They built Red Gap Mill hundreds of years ago, then the town of Red Gap grew up around it. They didn't exactly own the town now, since the mill hadn't been in operation for over a hundred years, but they were still well-liked and well-respected. Everything his family was not.

"And you are?" Miss Hazel Dean asked.

"Oh, sorry ma'am, I'm Cash. Cash McCleary."

One of her eyebrows raised ever so slightly. His surname did that to people. "Well, what can I do for you, Mr. McCleary? You seem to be in search of an escape."

"Well, I..."

Her eyes lit up, and she raised a finger "I know just what you need," she said.

He followed her to the counter where she'd started concocting some kind of beverage. "This is my famous escapist hot chocolate, on the house," she told him. "You just set yourself down wherever you like and I'll bring it over to you."

"Yes, ma'am." Cash mumbled automatically. He didn't want to ruin any of the nice furniture by sitting in it, but it didn't seem like Miss Hazel Randolph Dean would take no for an answer.

He made his way back over to the fireplace and found a chair tall enough that he could rest his whole head on the backrest. He could have easily fallen asleep if he hadn't been so mystified and curious. He tried to take in everything he saw with big round eyes.

"Here you are," Hazel Dean brought over a gigantic mug of hot chocolate with fat, square, chocolate-swirled marshmallows on top.

"Thank you, ma'am."

She nodded with a big smile lighting up her face. "Now all you need is a book."

"I'm not much of a reader, ma'am," he apologized, putting his hand around the mug and feeling the ceramic burn his fingertips slightly.

"Nonsense," she said. "That just means you haven't found the right book yet." She tapped her finger against her chin, scrutinizing him with thoughtful eyes. "Perhaps..." she trailed off and walked away. Cash got the impression that she was just as likely to disappear forever as she was to return.

He sat staring into the fire and sipping his hot chocolate, turning his argument with his brother over in his mind. He often disagreed with Billy, but he usually kept his opinions to himself. Billy was the oldest and the decision-maker for their family and their business. He had been ever since their dad died. Normally Cash was willing to go along with whatever terrible ideas Billy had because he figured it didn't make much difference either way, but this was different. This time, Billy was going to get them into serious trouble and Cash felt that it was his duty to say something, to protect their younger brothers. Eugene was still in high school, and he had his whole life ahead of him. Cash didn't see how he could let Billy mess that up. At least not without speaking his mind first.

"This one," Miss Hazel Dean materialized in front of him. He jumped and would have spilled the hot chocolate on himself had there been any left in the cup. "Oh, I'm sorry," she said. "I didn't mean to startle you."

"That's alright."

"Here," she offered, holding out a small paperback towards him. "This is what you should read."

He hesitated, then set his hot chocolate down on a nearby end table and wiped his hands off on his pants before taking the book from her. The cover read *To Kill A Mockingbird* with a subtitle saying, *a novel by Harper Lee*. A black tree with spring green leaves sprawled across a burnt orange background. "How do you find anything in this place, Miss Hazel?" he asked, overcome with curiosity.

"Oh, you noticed my shelving methods?" She smiled. "I like to think of this as more of a book preserve than a bookshop. I rescue books, and then I find their perfect owner. They have a way of calling to me when the person they belong to walks in the door."

He nodded, though he had no idea what she was talking about.

"It's a lovely book. I think you'll really enjoy it," she said.

He looked back down at the book cover and opened it to the first chapter. *When he was nearly thirteen, my brother Jem got his arm badly broken at the elbow...* Cash looked back up to thank Miss Hazel Dean, but she had already disappeared again. Cash continued reading, chuckling every once in a while at the antics of Jem and Scout. When he finally looked up at the grandfather clock that stood sentinel at the end of one of the rows of books, he was surprised to see that it was already after two o'clock. He looked around to find Hazel Dean.

"Miss Hazel?" he called quietly. He hadn't noticed anyone come in, but there were four more people engrossed in books scattered across the room now. He got up, carrying his empty mug back over to the counter because he didn't know how else to clean up after himself. He carried the book carefully in both hands. "Miss Hazel?" he called again. She didn't answer. He wandered down another book tunnel back towards the front of the store. He needed to get home, Eugene would be coming home from school soon and Billy would either be mad or drunk or both, so Cash wanted to be there as a buffer.

He reached the front of the store but still hadn't found Hazel Dean. His heart heavy with regret, he carefully lay *To Kill A Mockingbird* next to the cash register. He really wanted to know what happened to Jem and Scout and Atticus and that sweet Calpurnia. He wished that he had grown up with a Calpurnia. Maybe Billy would have turned out a little differently. Or maybe if their father was as noble as Atticus Finch. He looked back at the book one more time and had his hand on the door handle when Hazel Dean appeared from one of the book tunnels.

"Where do you think you're going without that book, Mr. McCleary?" she asked.

"Oh ma'am, thank you very much for the book ma'am," Cash didn't know how to explain. "I really enjoyed it - I did - but I can't bring it home with me."

"And why ever not?" she asked.

"Well, you see, there's five of us and Eugene is still in school and Virgil has a couple of kiddies that he has to support... The budget's a little tight, and my brothers would skin me alive if they found out I spent hard cash on a book. They wouldn't understand..." He glanced back at the book on the counter again.

Miss Hazel Dean's face softened. "Mr. McCleary, you have more of a right to that book than I do. It wants to go home with you, don't you see? I can't charge you for it. It wouldn't be right."

Cash blinked at her. "Excuse me, ma'am?"

"It's yours, Mr. McCleary, it chose you. I wouldn't let money stand in the way of such a thing."

"I couldn't just take it, ma'am. McClearys don't accept charity."

She tapped her chin. "Why don't we call it a free sample?" she said finally, "You take the book on the condition that you'll be coming back here when you're finished with it to find another one."

"Perhaps I could do some work for you?" He gestured around the bookshop. "I'm in the construction business. I would be happy to build you some shelves or help you out with any maintenance..."

Hazel Dean smiled. "Alright then, I'm sure I can find you something to do. Here you are, sir." She picked up the book and handed it to him.

"Thank you, ma'am," he said.

"Of course," she replied, nodding in acceptance.

"Really, thank you," he repeated, then headed out the door.

* * *

ONE EVENING IN LATE SEPTEMBER, Hazel Dean had a feeling that something was wrong. Her skin prickled into goosebumps and she felt a little dizzy. She had to steady herself on the bookcase, gripping one of the shelves for a moment while regaining her balance. She moved towards the front of her shop.

Hazel didn't usually hang out in the front of the shop. She wasn't concerned about inventory control and preferred to be either in the stacks or the cafe, helping her customers. Hanging out by the cash register made her feel like she was in it for the money. The front was empty, but that was no surprise. One of the book clubs had scheduled a meeting later, but none of them would be there for fifteen minutes at least.

She took reluctant steps towards the front counter, looking

around warily. Everything seemed to be in place. Perhaps the front window was a little dirty. She pulled out some window cleaner and was in the middle of scrubbing when the boy came in.

For a split second, she thought it was Cash McCleary, but his face was obscured by the waves of inky blackness that fell from him. She narrowed her eyes, trying to see through a fog of color that she knew was invisible to everyone but her.

All her life, people's emotions appeared before Hazel's eyes in a colorful haze surrounding them. Her Grandma told her that it was because she had been touched by an angel as a baby. Over the years, Hazel had learned to tune out the over-whelming colors and sights. Now, she didn't notice it so much unless she paid more attention to it or someone was feeling a very strong emotion. This boy was awash with emotion.

"Are you Miss Hazel Dean?" asked the boy in a small voice.

"Yes sir," she affirmed, a note of concern tinging her voice. Hazel examined his mostly smooth face and took in his gangly proportions. "Are you Cash McCleary's little brother?"

The boy's eyes widened in surprise, and the deep black color around him lightened slightly. "How did you know that?"

"Well, you look just like him, don't you?" And he did. He had the same sandy-brown hair and straight, narrow nose. Something in the eyes as well, reminded Hazel of Cash. "What's your name, child?"

The young man flinched when she called him child and stood up straight, but he didn't make eye contact when he spoke. "Eugene."

"Well, what can I do for you, Eugene?" Hazel asked. She tried to sound upbeat even though the cloud of blackness was filling the space around him and she was sure that something was terribly wrong. She had never seen anyone's emotions take up so much space.

Eugene reached into his backpack and pulled out the copy

of *To Kill A Mockingbird* that she had given Cash the week before. He held it out to her. Hazel made no move to take it. She raised an eyebrow at him.

"My brother..." Eugene started, turning the book around and around in his hands. "-He wanted you to have this." He tried to hold it out to her again.

Hazel smiled. "Your brother and I worked out a trade for that book. It belongs to him."

Tears brimmed over in Eugene's narrowed eyes. He tried to take a breath, but a sob erupted from his throat.

"What happened to Cash, Eugene?" Hazel asked, fighting her instinct to fold the boy up in her arms like one of her own sons. She settled for reaching through the cloud of darkness that surrounded him and putting her hand over his. The manifestation of emotions had never harmed her in the past, but sometimes, like now, she felt like they might.

"He died," Eugene choked out. "He's gone."

"Oh, you poor boy," Hazel said, squeezing his hand. Her throat tightened. Tears threatened to spill onto her cheeks, but she blinked them away. "Can you tell me what happened to him? I understand if it's too painful to talk about."

Eugene pressed his lips together, and Hazel didn't think that he would tell her. She rubbed his hand. "That's okay," she said.

"He was shot," Eugene blurted out, louder than he had spoken previously. Hazel's hand dropped his and flew to her mouth.

"What?" she gasped. "When?"

"Two nights ago. He..." Eugene's voice cracked, revealing torture inside. Despite her aversion to his black cloud and her fear of acting inappropriately, she reached out and hugged him.

"I'm so sorry. He was such a sweet young man," she murmured. "You poor, poor boy. I'm so sorry." He sobbed into her shoulder until the bell rang on the front door and someone else came into the store. He jumped, but she held on to his hand still.

It was Hazel's friend, Nora, surrounded by her usually rosy glow. "Is everything okay?" she asked, her eyes darting between Hazel and Eugene.

"Yeah," Eugene said, hiccupping and wiping his eyes with the heel of his hand. "Yeah, I have to go. Roy and Billy will wonder where I've got to. Please take the book, ma'am." He shoved the book into Hazel's arms. "He wanted to you to have it. He told me before he..." Eugene couldn't choke out the final word.

Hazel nodded, hugging the book to her chest. "Please come see me again sometime," Hazel said.

Eugene's face was blotchy and red. He had a trail of mucus running across his face from where he wiped his nose with his sleeve. He looked painfully young, all of five years old. "Maybe," he replied, sniffling. He attempted a smile at her before he walked out the door, taking the black cloud with him.

TWO

"What was that all about?" Nora asked.

The world around Hazel spun. She attempted to straighten her posture but felt too dizzy. "He lost his brother."

"Oh, how sad," Nora said, taking Hazel's arm and guiding her towards the cafe. "Is he a friend of Jeremiah or Elias?"

"No," Hazel shook her head slowly. "I don't think so. His brother was a new customer. He was returning a book." Hazel felt the corner of *To Kill A Mockingbird* digging into her arm. Eugene's grief-stricken face filled her mind. She felt like she couldn't breathe.

"Are you okay?" Nora's forehead wrinkled.

Hazel could only nod. The image of Eugene in her head morphed into an image of herself as a little girl, equally grief-stricken. She remembered standing in the aisle of the chapel in front of her parents' caskets. Eugene had already lost both of his parents as well, now his big brother was gone too. Hazel was glad that Nora had taken her arm, she felt shaky and weak.

"Well, let's distract you. I came to help you set up for book club."

Hazel leaned on Nora more than she wanted to as they walked down an aisle of books to the cafe. Hazel collapsed into a chair. She took deep breaths, willing her heartbreak to ebb into the background.

Nora started arranging some of the chairs into a circle. "What kind of delicious goodies did you save for us today?"

"There's a chocolate mousse cake in the walk-in fridge," Hazel was surprised that she sounded so much like her normal self.

"Oh, my favorite!" Nora squealed, hurrying to find the cake.

Hazel rubbed her forehead. "Look, Nora, would you mind taking over book club today? I just need to go and check on a few things."

Nora stopped short, her aura tinging an anxious lime. "Is everything okay? Are your boys alright?"

"Yes," Hazel managed a smile to calm her anxious friend. "I'm just worried about that little boy, Eugene, and his family. I won't be able to focus on the discussion. You're more than capable of running things. Just lock up when you're done." She stood up and patted her pockets down, searching for her keys.

"Will you be okay?" Nora asked.

Hazel located the keys in the last pocket she checked, in an apron that she had forgotten she was wearing. She handed the keys to Nora and hung the apron on a hook in the bakery. "Yes, I'll be fine. I'm going to go straight over to Jason's office, so no need to worry about me."

The wrinkles in Nora's forehead disappeared, and she nodded. She looked back towards the fridge. "Oh good. I'll call you tomorrow."

"Thank you." Hazel gave her friend's hand a distracted squeeze, then made a beeline to her car to drive to the courthouse where her husband's office was. As the area's district attorney, he should be able to tell her more about what happened to Cash. She barely noticed the brightly colored leaves raining down on her car as she drove down Main Street. People smiled and waved at her, but all she offered back was a half-hearted lift of her hand. Her grandmother would have been horrified by her lack of manners.

"Gran, if you're looking down on me right now, I hope you understand," Hazel murmured under her breath. Less than ten minutes later, she pulled into the courthouse's parking lot. She had made it there purely on autopilot.

"Hello Mrs. Dean, business or pleasure?" Danny, the assistant with many hats, greeted her from reception, but she only gave him a tight smile and hurried towards her husband's office.

"Wait! Mrs. Dean!" Danny called after her. She ignored him, continuing down the hall and bursting into Jason's office.

"-don't think there's enough evidence..." Jason snapped his mouth shut when he saw Hazel. "Hazel, I'm in the middle of a meeting with Captain Tate."

Captain Tate, better known to Hazel as Uncle John, was standing in the middle of the room with a red face and clenched jaw, the air around him pulsing neon orange.

Hazel was still shaken by the news of Cash's death, and the look on Uncle John's face didn't comfort her. It wasn't the environment she had been seeking when she fled from her bookshop. Hazel's eyes pricked with unshed tears. She bit her lip and blinked. "I'm sorry," she said. "I'll wait." She backed out of the room.

She closed the door and stood in the hallway, uncertain how long Jason would be.

"You liberal-minded, West Coast, bleeding-heart!" Uncle John began yelling as soon as she closed the door behind her. It sounded like it might be a little while. Unable to face Danny's perpetually cheerful demeanor, Hazel sunk to the floor and leaned her back against the wall. This part of the courthouse wasn't usually busy, and no one passed Hazel as she inadvertently eavesdropped. She couldn't hear Jason's responses, but she could hear Uncle John's raised voice.

"When are you going to do something about this?!"

"I know what happened!"

"You're ignoring the evidence!"

"Good enough?!"

After a few minutes, it got quieter and she could no longer hear John's outbursts. Hazel gazed up at him when he stepped out into the hall. He jumped a little when he saw her sitting outside the door. Then took several deep breaths. Hazel watched the neon orange around him break up and dissipate into a faint amber. He held out a hand to help her up.

"Sometimes I wonder what your daddy might say about that husband of yours," he muttered.

Hazel attempted a smile, but her voice was shaking. "He'd say that he was a good man that stood by his principles and he would be tickled that he didn't give in to a bully like you."

Captain Tate chuckled. "I suppose he would. But that man of yours sure is a pain in my butt."

Hazel nodded, attempting a laugh again, but it came out a little more strangled. She was still on the verge of tears.

"Are you alright darlin'?" Uncle John gripped Hazel's shoulder, then bent over to look her in the eye.

"I just... lost a friend."

"Lost? Someone died?"

Hazel didn't want to talk to Uncle John about it. John wouldn't like the idea of her tangled up with the McCleary family. On the other hand, he would know all about what happened. She opened her mouth to speak when Jason stepped out of the office.

"Oh," he said. "You're still here."

"Just talkin' to my honorary niece," Uncle John said. "Do I need permission from you to do that?"

Jason rolled his eyes and ignored John. "You can come on in now Hazel."

Uncle John gave Hazel a gentle squeeze. "I'm always here if you need me," he softly reminded her, then turned and gave Jason a hard glare before he walked down the hall towards the back of the building where the police station was housed.

"What was that all about?" Hazel asked as Jason ushered her into the room.

Jason ran both hands through his hair, adding comical height to his hairstyle. "Captain Tate is irritated with me because I don't want to prosecute the people he arrested in connection to the semi-truck robberies."

"Oh," Hazel said.

"I just don't think he has enough evidence against them. It would be a waste of resources at this point. I told him to collect a little more evidence and then I'll prosecute. You know Hazel, the last thing I want to do is to prosecute innocent people."

Hazel had a hard time focusing on what Jason was saying. She slumped into a chair across from his desk.

"Your Uncle John... Are you alright, Hazel?" He cut himself off and sat in the chair next to her.

"Jason, have you heard anything about what happened to Cash McCleary?"

Jason winced. "How did you hear about that?"

"I met Cash a week ago or so when he came into the bookshop." Her voice was shaking. Jason reached out and took her hand. She squeezed it. "He was agitated. I could tell. He had muddy orange waves rolling off of him in a kind of zig-zagging, manic motion. He was jumpy. I made him a hot chocolate and got *To Kill A Mockingbird* out of the stacks for him. Today his little brother came in to return the book and tell me that he had been shot." Hazel bit her lip and took a deep breath to keep her voice from breaking. "He was just such a nice young man. He'd clearly had some hard luck, and I thought I could be his friend, or help him somehow. Now he's just gone. Just like that. I won't be able to rest until I know what happened to him. And that poor little brother of his, Eugene. He was beside himself. My heart is breaking for them, Jason."

Jason scooted closer to her and put an arm around her. "Oh Hazel, you are a sensitive soul." He smiled at her, but she was too upset to feel the glow of his love. "This business is a little grisly. I don't want to upset you more."

"No," she disagreed, leaning into him. "I need to know."

Jason nodded reluctantly. "Cash worked a construction operation with his brothers. Well, the oldest four anyways. Youngest one's still in high school."

"That must be Eugene," Hazel said. "He's the one that came into the store."

Jason nodded. "They're not much more than unskilled labor, but between the four of them they knew enough to do most of what they needed to do to meet a passable standard. Recently they've been working with a man who is building one of those glamping hotels east of town. He's a stranger here; no one knows much about him. Name's Chris Mills. You must have approved his plans in the city council, you might remember him."

While sitting on the city council, Hazel approved a lot different construction projects. She tried to remember a Chris Mills. She thought of razor-sharp incisors and slicked back hair but couldn't be sure she was thinking of the right person.

"The four of those boys were down working on the hotel a few nights ago when it happened. Cash was shot once in the head with what we think was a rifle. The bullet is missing, went right through the guy and is believed to be in the woods somewhere. Cash's brothers tried to race him to the hospital, but by the time they got there Cash was in a deep coma and died sometime in the next few hours."

"So, it was an accident?"

"The remaining McCleary brothers, other than Eugene, made statements to the police that they saw Wallis Trudgeon running away from them in the direction that the shot was fired."

Hazel gasped, her hand flying to her mouth. "The feud? After all this time?"

Jason shrugged. "It seems to play in somehow. The police went over to Trudgeon's to search the place, see if they could find a rifle. We'd have to find the bullet or some casings at the crime scene to be able to match them for sure."

"Of course, Wallis Trudgeon's going to have a rifle in his house. Everyone in town has a rifle in their house. This is ridiculous. It's the twenty-second century for crying out loud. The feud." She rolled her eyes and took a breath. "What will they do when they find it?"

Jason shrugged. "With three eyewitnesses? People have been convicted with less. They could arrest him. They might just bring him in for questioning. Depends on how dear old Uncle John is feeling. I don't know, Southerners seem to put a lot of stock in things like feuds."

Hazel shot him a look. Her husband seemed to distance himself from Southern culture or pretend to be a local depending on the situation.

Danny stuck his head into the office. "Hey Jason, they found a rifle at the Trudgeon place. I guess Wallis wasn't exactly cooperative. They've arrested him and are bringing him in now. Also, I brought you another piece of the cake you liked so much."

Jason glanced at Hazel, his pallor turning a deep navy. "Oh, uh, thanks Danny. Ummm, you can just put it on my desk. I'm sure Mrs. Dean would like to try it."

"Hi Danny," she smiled at the receptionist weakly. The boy had graduated from college recently and was trying to earn money to go to law school by working at the courthouse and police station as a receptionist/assistant. She liked him, but still wasn't feeling quite herself.

"Well, I'd better go. I've got more paperwork for this case than I've ever seen before in my life. A grisly murder right here in our very own town. Who would have thunk it? I can't believe the luck I'm having. This will look great on my law school applications."

Jason reached across the desk for the cake and offered her a forkful. She shook her head. "I thought you had sworn off sugar. How long did you last?"

"A full four days! I would have kept going, but Danny made the cake himself for Judge Prousts' birthday. I couldn't say no." He put the fork into his own mouth. The navy emanating from him deepened slightly.

Hazel shook her head indulgently. "I want to see him."

"Who? Not Cash, I don't think that's a good idea."

"No, not Cash," she said. "I want to see Wallis Trudgeon."

Jason laughed. "You want to see the murderer."

"I'm not joking, Jason," Hazel said solemnly.

He stopped chuckling and looked at her with his eyebrows raised. "I don't think that's a good idea either, Hazel."

"All I know is how upset Cash was the other day, and it didn't feel like a feud kind of upset. It felt like a family kind of upset. Besides, I'll know. Just by looking at him, I'll know if he did it. I can just watch him walk down the hall."

Jason swallowed and set down the cake. "You want to get one of your... readings on him?" he asked. Jason had enough experience with Hazel's gift to take it seriously, but it always made him turn an uncomfortable chartreuse color when they talking about it.

"It can't hurt," she said, crossing her arms over her chest.

"They're not always that clear though, right? I mean, you said before that I have a different angry color than Jeremiah or

Elias, right? How will you know if the color you think means 'innocent' actually means 'guilty?'"

"I'll know," she said. "It's not *that* vague. You know, color families and all that. Your worried color is a deep forest green, and Elias' is a pale green and Jeremiah's is more of an army green, but they're all green. The tricky bit is when there are layers of different feelings. But I've been navigating these colors for a long time, dear. I think you could say I'm a bit of an expert."

"Alright," he said, leaning back in his chair. "But then will you come home with me, and we'll go to Elias' football game tonight?"

"I wouldn't miss Elias' football game." Hazel didn't know whether to be proud or mortified of her son's success as a defensive lineman. "But if I think Trudgeon's innocent, then I have to find out what really happened to Cash."

"We can't just leave that to the police?"

"Please," Hazel rolled her eyes. "Like you said, eyewitnesses, murder weapon, ancient feud. Even as the DA, you don't have *that* much discretion. I don't think they'll feel really motivated by 'my wife has a feeling Trudgeon's innocent.' You know Uncle John thinks that my color thing is just a bunch of fanciful nonsense."

"Alright," Jason shook his head. "But you better stay far away from anything dangerous, you hear?"

"I can't imagine what would be dangerous about it."

Jason furrowed his eyebrows at her. "Seriously? We're talking about a murderer. Murderers are inherently dangerous."

She shrugged. "I've never felt unsafe in my hometown. But I'll be careful. I promise."

"I'm going to hold you to that," Jason said, pointing his fork at her before picking up the plate of cake again. "Now, will you please eat some of this cake, Hazel? Otherwise I'm going to eat the whole thing and I'll really be off the wagon."

Hazel reluctantly took the fork from him and put it in her mouth. "Wow, so Danny can bake. He's going to make someone a great husband sometime."

"No, Hazel," Jason groaned.

"What?" she grinned. "I don't have anyone specific in mind." The idea of getting to the bottom of what happened to Cash renewed her good humor a bit. The chocolate cake and playing matchmaker for Danny helped too.

"I don't remember this going very well the last time you tried to set someone up."

Hazel waved a hand. "They were older. Danny is all young and innocent. What about my friend Shana's daughter?"

"Shana has a daughter?" Jason mumbled. He had turned his attention to his computer and started working again. Hazel knew he wasn't paying attention to her anymore but continued to chatter about possible girls for Danny until she heard his footsteps in the hallway.

Danny stuck his head in the door again. "They're here!" he called.

Jason turned to her. "I'm going to go down there. You stay here and leave the door open. You'll be able to see him as he walks down the hall."

Hazel nodded, and Jason disappeared out the door. Hazel got up and stood in the doorway, looking both ways down the hall. Hazel hadn't spent much time hanging out at the courthouse before. If she wanted to see Jason during a workday, she usually just met him for lunch. When the police brought in an arrest, did they just use the front door? Or was there a special entrance for them? Within moments, her questions were answered when two policemen appeared with a handcuffed man pushed out in front of them. It was dark in the hallway, and Hazel wasn't able to make out any of their features until they got quite close.

From what Hazel had gathered about her gift over the years, the stronger someone was feeling an emotion, the more color they had hanging around them. Eugene, earlier that day, had the darkest black cloud she had ever seen around a person. Most of the time the people around her had faint colors or no color at all. They weren't feeling any particular emotion very strongly. The better she knew someone, the easier it was to discern and interpret their colors. Jason was right. It was easy to misinterpret for people she didn't know. But Hazel didn't want to think about that. This time, she knew, she'd be able to tell.

Wallis Trudgeon kept his eyes on the ground as he walked down the hall. She could see a dark cloud all around him. It encompassed half of the policemen on each side of him. As he got closer, she could see that it was a very, very dark blue color, almost black but not quite, and around the edges was some yellow. It perplexed her. When he was steps away from the door, she saw that he noticed her feet. She was about to retreat back into her husband's office when he glanced up at her. The look on his face is what made up her mind.

"It wasn't him." Hazel declared when Jason returned to the office moments later.

"Hazel..."

"No, it wasn't him," she insisted.

Jason looked at her, a blanket of dark, hunter green covered his chest and his eyes widened. It was the same face he made both times she told him she was going into labor. "Well, love," he said. "If Wallis Trudgeon didn't do it, who do you think did?"

"I don't know," she said. "But I'm going to find out."

THREE

Hazel thought she had plenty of time to drive by the construction site where Cash was killed before Elias' football game, but halfway there she realized she was quite wrong and had to turn around. She thought perhaps she could get a feel for things, maybe notice something that the police had missed. She would have to head out there another time.

She drove through Chick-Fil-A, picking up nine chicken sandwiches. One for her, three for Jason and Jeremiah, and five for Elias. When she got to the high school, the stands were empty with the exception of the marching band, who were just settling into their section. Carrying her bag of sandwiches, a gigantic flannel blanket and her purse, she found the perfect spot in the empty stands. The place that Elias knew to look for them each game. Then she got out her phone.

In stands at our spot. Got your lucky sandwiches. Come and get them.

It didn't take long for Elias to respond. B right there

Hazel sat in the empty stands, waiting for her family and watching the marching band warm up. She wrapped the blanket around herself. It was cold for late September. She rummaged in her purse for some hand warmers she knew she had in there somewhere but ended up pulling out Cash's book. It glowed the pretty green that it had been before Cash came into the shop. On that day it had turned the exact same muddy orange chevron that was coming off Cash in waves. That's how she had known he needed the book. Now she wasn't sure what she would do with it, probably just re-shelve it at the shop.

She opened the book, and an envelope fell out into her hands. "Mrs. Dean" was scrawled across the front of the envelope in sloppy writing. She gasped. The envelope blazed a vibrant crimson with gold right at the center. For most of her life, people were the only things that showed colors. A couple weeks after she opened the book shop, she noticed the spines start to glow faintly with mismatched colors. It bothered her, so she began to reshelve them, so they wouldn't clash with each other. As she reorganized her shelves, the books began to glow with deeper and more vibrant color.

Hazel remembered the first time a book's color had changed to match a person's color. Nora had come into the shop looking exhausted. Hazel hadn't seen her before, but Nora explained that her husband had insisted she get out for a few minutes while he took care of their new baby. As she was talking, Hazel noticed *Big Little Lies* on the shelf behind her turning from its usual stormy sea color to the dusky purple that Nora wore. Hazel instinctively handed it to her and gave her a cookie. Nora read for an hour straight. Hazel watched as Nora's color went from that dull purple to a beautiful rosy peach. When she tried to buy the book, Hazel had refused to take her money. It felt wrong to take money for the books that changed color for their perfect reader.

Hazel began to flip through the pages of *To Kill A Mockingbird* and noticed that Cash had highlighted some lines and made a few notes in the margins. She smiled. Apparently he had planned on keeping the book after all. A red pencil outlined a few of the most famous lines in the book in dark, decisive lines.

"I wanted you to see what real courage is, instead of getting the idea that courage is a man with a gun in his hand. It's when you know you're licked before you begin, but you begin anyway and you see it through no matter what. You rarely win, but sometimes you do."

"It was times like these when I thought my father, who hated guns and had never been to any wars, was the bravest man who ever lived." Next to the highlighted section, a big 'yes!' was scrawled in the margin.

She bit her lip and blinked back tears. If she was going to find Cash's true killer, she couldn't get so emotional, couldn't tear up every time she was reminded of how alive he was just days before. She continued flipping through the book.

Occasionally, she was interrupted by a friend or acquaintance as they hiked up the bleachers. She was greeted with "Hello, Miss Hazel," or "Hi, Mrs. Randolph." Hazel was never fully able to shed her maiden name. One person sat down with a determination to discuss a sidewalk initiative she was reviewing as a member of the city council.

"I really can't discuss it, Tucker," she repeated multiple times, before Tucker eventually gave up and left her to her book. Hazel turned back to Cash's notes.

Wish we had a Calpurnia.

Wish we had a Miss Maudie. Hazel almost choked. She would have loved to have been that boy's Miss Maudie.

'Waylon Gibbon' was written next to a paragraph describing Boo Radley. Hazel didn't recognize the name. It seemed that Cash had identified people in his life that correlated with quite a few of the characters.

There was one phrase that Cash had scrawled over and over again throughout the book. 'Brave like Atticus'.

Hazel closed the book thoughtfully. She guessed that there was something in Cash's life that was giving him a bit of a moral dilemma. Atticus Finch must have inspired him to do what he thought was right. She wondered if he was able to act on his new resolve before he died. Or maybe he did, and that was why he died. The next step was to figure out what Cash wanted to be brave for. The best way to do that was by talking to his brothers.

"How are you feeling, darlin'?" Uncle John sat down beside her, shaking the bench slightly. She hadn't noticed his approach and jumped a bit.

Hazel smiled at him. "I'm fine."

"You seemed so sad earlier - you said a friend of yours passed on?"

"A new customer at my bookshop," she explained vaguely.

"Ah," John nodded. He wasn't a reader himself.

"It was unexpected," Hazel said. "He died before his time."

John reached out and put an arm around her. "I'm sorry to hear it," he offered. "God rest his soul."

"Thank you," she replied.

"Hey Mom," Elias greeted her, plopping down next to her on the bench. "Hi Uncle John."

"Hey!" John broke into a broad grin. "There's our boy! You're going to crush 'em tonight, yeah?" He slapped Elias on the back.

"Yes sir," Elias said seriously. He grabbed the bag of sandwiches and started inhaling them.

John watched him with admiration. "The coach is okay with you eating all that before the game?"

Hazel laughed. "These are clandestine sandwiches. A few games ago, Elias didn't feel like he got enough food at the team dinner and ran to get a few chicken sandwiches before the game. Then he had eight sacks. He talked me into bringing the sandwiches now before every game."

"How does he not hurl all over the field?" John asked.

Hazel and Elias shrugged in unison. "I'm just hungry," he said.

"Don't you have to be getting down there?" she asked. "I know you're not allowed to be up here."

"Alright, thanks Mom," Elias said, wiping his hands on his football pants.

"You're an inspiration," John told him.

Hazel pointed to her cheek. He kissed her and started running down the bleacher seats. The bleachers shook and made a big clanging noise each time his foot hit. People jumped out of his way. When he reached the bottom, Jason appeared and gave him a big back-patting hug. Hazel offered a chicken sandwich to John. He shook his head.

"Hello, Captain Tate," Jason nodded. He took Elias' spot next to Hazel and grabbed the Chick-Fil-A bag.

"Jason," John nodded. Hazel found the coolness between John and Jason comical.

"What do you have there?" Jason asked Hazel, motioning to the book she still had clutched in her hands.

"This is the copy of *To Kill A Mockingbird* that the customer I told you about returned," Hazel said, raising her eyebrows. She hoped Jason understood that she didn't want John to know about her interest in Cash's case. "He wrote me a nice note."

"Is that your customer that passed away?" John was too astute for Hazel to keep him completely in the dark.

"Yeah, that's the one," she said. She tucked the book and envelope back into her purse, noticing how the inside now radiated crimson and gold.

John looked at her with narrowed eyes. The air around him turned a dark purple where it was light blue the moment before. He was thinking. Hazel looked at Jason, willing him to change the subject.

Jason looked down at the field. "How's our boy?" he asked.

It worked - John's color lightened. "Well, he just ate five sandwiches in about five seconds flat."

Hazel chuckled. Elias and Jeremiah were the only things that Jason and John could talk about with warmth.

Music started blaring from the speakers, and the cheerleaders got up to perform their dance routine.

"Where's Jeremiah?" Hazel asked.

"Here I am, Mom," Jeremiah plopped into the seat next to Jason and grabbed the bag of food from Jason. "Hi Uncle John! Hey Dad. Mom, did you manage to save me anything? Or did Elias eat it all without noticing?"

"There's some there for you," she said, smiling.

"Hey there, son," Jason said, giving him a rough shoulder pat. "How was school?"

"Could've been worse," Jeremiah shrugged, unwrapping a sandwich.

"How was that eco depot thing?"

"Aca deca, Dad," Jeremiah said, rolling his eyes. John laughed uproariously. Hazel knew that Jason mispronounced the nickname for academic decathlon just to be funny, but she didn't think that Jeremiah or John realized that.

Jeremiah continued talking with his mouth full. "It was fine, I guess. I don't really get why they're not letting me do much. I know more than anyone else there, but politics, I guess. No one wants admit a freshman in the smartest person in the room."

Hazel's eyebrows went up. Before school started, she had worried about Jeremiah, but his confidence had only increased in the last couple months.

"What about that girlfriend of yours?"

"What girlfriend?!" Hazel whipped her head around, looking from Jason to Jeremiah.

"Hazel, look at this good-looking kid," John said. "Of course, he has a girlfriend."

Jeremiah's face turned red and Hazel noticed a gray sheen

cling to him. "I don't have a girlfriend. Relax, Mom. Dad just saw me talking to Jennifer Henderson."

"Oh," Hazel murmured. Hazel didn't have time to worry about her fourteen-year-old having a girlfriend.

The announcer came on the loudspeaker to announce the teams. The players rushed onto the field, growling and spitting and roaring. It was a rival game between their high school, The Miners, and the next closest school, The Pipers. The visitors brought bagpipes, and they were so loud that nothing else could be heard, although that didn't stop the announcer from attempting to identify the starters on each team. Hazel strained to hear Elias' name and cheered as loud as she could, but she didn't even hear herself.

Hazel was uncomfortable with Elias' position on the foot-ball team. When Jason wanted to sign him up for a pewee league ten years earlier, she had consented on the condition that he would be a quarterback. She should have realized with Jason's genetic gifts that it wouldn't be in the cards. She especially didn't like that his main job was to hurt other kids. She always ended the evening feeling like she needed to send apology letters to the opposing team's moms.

But tonight Elias hardly had anything to do. One of the Miner's other defensive lineman was playing with so much aggression that the beleaguered quarterback was on the run the whole game. She worried that the Piper's quarterback would be seriously injured and prayed for him to throw the ball out of bounds every play.

"Who's that kid?" Jason asked Jeremiah, pointing to the Miners' left tackle.

"Oh, that's Eugene McCleary."

Hazel dropped her coffee. Some of it leaked out and burned her leg before she could right it again. She caught Uncle John looking at her with furrowed eyebrows.

"McCleary?" Hazel's voice was high and unnatural, but Jeremiah didn't notice. John, however, caught her eye.

"Yeah," Jeremiah went on. "He wasn't at school today, so I'm surprised they let him play. I thought there was a rule that said if you miss school you can't participate in athletics that day. Anyways, the quarterback on the Pipers is a Trudgeon, so I'm sure Eugene wants a piece of him because of the whole feud thing."

"Oh Jeremiah," Hazel's shoulders sagged. "Really? Kids your age are still talking about that feud?"

"It's a thing, Mom," Jeremiah talked like she was a complete idiot whose family hadn't lived in their small town for generations. "The McClearys and the Trudgeons hate each other. They always will. It's just the rule." Jeremiah threw a thumb in the direction of John. "The law's the only thing that keeps them from killing each other."

Hazel made a strangled noise, but Jeremiah didn't notice because the bagpipes had started to play again. Hazel tried to glance at John without his noticing, but he was looking right at her. His mouth pressed into a thin line.

"Okay," Jeremiah yelled over the noise. "I'm going to sit in the student section now. Thanks for dinner, guys." He clapped his dad on the back and gave his mom a kiss on the cheek, then clambered off down the bleachers to join his friends.

Jason scooted closer to her and put an arm around Hazel while she bit her lip and blinked, trying to smile so John wouldn't notice how shaken she was. The sound of bagpipes and cheering fans drowned out whatever Jason was trying to whisper in her ear.

* * *

AFTER THE GAME, Hazel claimed she had a migraine from all the bagpipe music. John nodded and kissed her on the forehead.

"You know I'm always here if you need anything," he told her. Hazel smiled at him.

"I know. Thanks, Uncle John," she said, squirming. John had some deep running prejudices, having lived in Red Gap his whole life. One of them was about the McClearys and the Trudgeons. Hazel assumed he had to be connected to one clan or the other somehow, as most people in town were, but he didn't like either group. He warned Hazel her whole life not to go near any of them. Aside from hiding her suspicions that John had arrested the wrong man, Hazel didn't want him to know that she had befriended a McCleary.

"I'll round up Jeremiah and drive him home," Jason told her. "We'll be back a little before Elias."

Hazel drove herself home and got ready for bed. Her mind was spinning. Of course, Hazel knew all about the feud. She had grown up in Red Gap, after all. Her family had been in the area almost as long as the McClearys and Trudgeons. The feud began sometime around 1800. The story was that the two families originally had a business venture together. The McClearys thought the Trudgeons had swindled them out of their fair share of the profits. The Trudgeons claimed that someone in the McCleary clan had stolen the innocence of a Trudgeon daughter. After a couple hundred years, there was enough wrongdoing on both sides that the malice ran deep. Due to intermixing with other families and outsiders, it was less obvious nowadays who was a McCleary and who was a Trudgeon. People who had been friends for years were known to find out about their friends' ancestry and never speak to them again. Hazel had inherited her family's ambivalence about the issue and tried to be a peacemaker by changing the subject whenever it came up.

As far as Hazel knew, Cash and his brothers were the last remnant of the patriarchal line of McClearys still living in Red Gap, whereas the place was full of Trudgeons. Maybe that's why Hazel had assumed the feud had died down. She had been shocked to hear her son talk about it as a fact of life. It didn't sit right with her. If Wallis Trudgeon was falsely convicted of Cash's murder, it would cause even more of a rift in Hazel's town. She couldn't let that happen.

As she got ready for bed, Hazel dug out the letter Cash had written her.

MRS. DEAN,

I DON'T THINK I'll ever be able to thank you for handing me To Kill A Mockingbird last week when I came into your store. To be honest, the only reason I walked in at all was because I was trying to escape an argument with my brother and it seemed like the last place he would ever go. But your kindness and that book have changed my life, and I'll never be the same because of it.

I was in a pickle when I stepped into your store. My brothers and I have had to get on by ourselves for near on five years now. I was sixteen when my dad died. Billy, he's the oldest, was mostly grown up, out of high school and working, anyways, and so he set about providing for us, but there are five of us and I think the pressure got to him. We all pitched in, getting odd jobs where we could and helping to raise our littlest brother Eugene. Anyways Billy did the best he could, but out of necessity, I think he got to a place in his mind where the end justified the means, if you know what I'm saying. As long as we had enough to eat and money for heat, he doesn't mind if a job isn't strictly legal.

We could never ask anyone for help or seek government support because they would have split us up as fast as looked at us. That just *didn't feel right. We were mostly on our own anyways before Dad died.*

Anyways, all this rambling is just to say that the jobs Billy's had us taking didn't sit right with me and we had argued about it and I was unsure of what to do. He made some persuasive arguments, and Virgil and Roy seemed to feel he was right. But when I read about Atticus and how sometimes you know you're licked before you start and you have to try anyways so you can look at yourself in the mirror, I knew what I needed to do. I'm not sure what's going to happen, but I know that I'll be doing the right thing. I'll at least be one family member Eugene can look at and be proud of, just like Jem was sure proud of his Daddy.

Hopefully, my decision will set my family on a new path, one of self respect and pride. And I have you to thank for it, Mrs. Dean. I don't know if I'll ever give you this letter, but I needed to express my thoughts and gratitude. Thank you, ma'am.

Cash McCleary

HAZEL REELED. Could it be possible that Cash confronted his brothers, and they killed him over it? She tried to remember what Eugene had told her about when Cash died but couldn't remember if he had said he was there when Cash was shot. If the brothers were in collusion, they could easily have pinned the shooting on a Trudgeon. But how could they do that to their own brother? It didn't make sense.

Tears sprang to her eyes. It had been such a long, long day.

She felt a strong hand grip her shoulder and Hazel jumped in shock. She hadn't heard Jeremiah and Jason come in. "Are you alright, love?" Jason asked. "What are you reading?"

"Is Elias home yet?"

"Not yet, but he's got half an hour before curfew, so no reason to worry yet," Jason spoke gently, like she might shatter if he was too loud. "What do you have there?"

"Cash wrote me a note before he died," she said, handing it to him. "His brother gave it to me today."

Jason looked over the note. "Oh, Hazel. This is really nice. Your bookshop really helped him."

Hazel nodded, tears falling onto her cheeks. "I know. I just can't believe he's gone. I hope it's not my fault."

"How could it be your fault?" Jason asked, incredulous. He reached over with one hand and began to scratch her back lightly. Something that often helped her relax when she was feeling worried.

"What if he's dead because he stood up to his brothers?"

"You think his brothers are responsible for his death?" The air around him turned a dull brown, which is how Hazel could tell he was shifting into work mode.

Hazel shook her head. "I don't know. It's possible."

Jason sat mindlessly rubbing her back as his eyebrows came together and his eyes narrowed. "Do you really think they're capable?"

"I don't know," Hazel shrugged. "I don't know them at all."

"But you're going to look into it, aren't you?" Jason's brown darkened into his hunter green, worried color.

"I'll be safe, I promise."

"Sure, you will," he said, sarcastically. "You are great at taking care of yourself." He glared at the letter in his hand. Hazel took it back from him, gently. It was still glowing that gold and crimson.

"Well, I think the McClearys could use a casserole in their time of grief, don't you?" Hazel smiled.

Jason grimaced. "If you really think so. Can you take someone else with you? Maybe Nora? Or Uncle John would be great."

Hazel laughed at the idea of showing up with a casserole and the captain of county police ops. "Not John, obviously. I'll ask Nora, but she's got those little kids."

"Maybe I should come with you," he said.

Hazel reached for Jason's hand. "I think that if I show up with a big guy like you or John, my pretense of bringing them dinner will be shot. I'll make them cookies. No one has ever been upset with someone for bringing them cookies."

"I guess you're right."

"I'll call you when I'm on my way back. There's nothing to worry about."

A door slammed downstairs, and they heard Elias call, "I'm home!"

"We're up here," Hazel said. They heard Elias' heavy tread on the stairs before he came into their room to say goodnight.

"Good game, son," Jason grinned. "That was a big win."

Elias shrugged and kept his eyes on the floor. "Didn't do much. Eugene was too fast."

"The poor boy," Hazel murmured. She craned her neck to be able to make eye contact. "You keep an eye on him, Elias. His family situation is dicey."

Elias nodded and handed them his phone for the night. "Goodnight," he said, backing out the door.

Jeremiah passed him on his way in to say good night too. He reluctantly handed them his phone. "I'm the only person in the world who has to turn in his phone to his parents at night," he grumbled.

"Sure you are," Hazel chuckled. "I love you, goodnight."

"Good night," he grumbled, slumping out the door.

"I love you, Hazel," Jason yawned, settling into bed.

"I love you too," she said, kissing him goodnight.

Hazel set Cash's letter on her nightstand. It wasn't long before she could hear Jason snoring next to her, but she lay awake, her thoughts racing. Ever since she talked to Eugene, she kept thinking about her parents. She hadn't been there the day of their accident, but she could hear the screech and crash of the truck all the same. She could feel their claustrophobia and panic, their desperation. "I love you baby," her mom cried out, pain tinging her voice in this fake memory. "I'll always be with you." She chased fake and real memories of her parent's faces, a kaleidoscope of pain and fear and joy and love, until she fell asleep.

FOUR

Hazel spent the morning in her bookshop finding the perfect recipe to take to the McClearys. Cookbooks were almost always a sunny yellow color, so they were easy to find in the shop. She went to the market during lunch, then spent the afternoon cooking. She didn't usually use the shop kitchen to cook actual meals, but these were special circumstances. Bringing a casserole to a family who had lost someone was a time-honored Southern tradition and the perfect excuse for chatting up the McCleary boys. She also baked up a batch of her peanut butter fudge cookies because surely the boys could use some chocolate at a time like this.

After finishing up the baking, she settled at the front desk to do a little research on the computer. Luckily the local paper had an online archive, because otherwise, she wouldn't have found a thing. Technology wasn't her strong suit.

She had stumbled on a few articles that helped her get some background on the family.

Tragic Death in the Community

Aubrey McCleary, nee Reeves, wife of Dakota McCleary, died Wednesday at her home. She was twenty-five years old. She died in childbirth from severe hemorrhage after attempting to deliver her breach baby at home. The midwife in attendance was able to save the life of the baby, who they named Eugene. When asked why his wife didn't attempt to deliver the baby in the hospital, McCleary said, "Those doctors are only after hard-working folks' money. They don't know nothin' I'm not going to give them a red cent. Our four other babies were born at home without any trouble at all." Unfortunately, this time, that wasn't the case. However, the midwife referenced two other unsuccessful pregnancies. The details on that are unclear. Aubrey Reeves McCleary is survived by her husband Dakota McCleary and her five sons. Billy aged eight, Cash aged five, Virgil aged four, Roy aged three, and Eugene aged zero.

HAZEL FELT A PANG OF GUILT. Why hadn't the young couple been on her radar? Her grandmother had taught her that, as the founders of the town, it was their responsibility to be aware of people who may be in need of a friend. She tried to remember Dakota McCleary from high school but didn't have any images to go with the name, and she couldn't remember any anecdotes about him. Hazel wished she would have befriended Cash's mom. Maybe things would have turned out differently. That was back when Hazel's grandmother was still alive. She had probably noticed them. It made Hazel smile to think of her grandmother reaching out to Cash's mom with a word of friendly advice or some encouragement.

Hazel did some math. Aubrey had been seventeen when she married Dakota. Cash was twenty-one this year, which made Eugene a year older than Jeremiah. Roy was only a year older than Elias, so he should have graduated the year before. Billy, the oldest and default patriarch of the family, was twenty-four years old. Hazel clicked her tongue. He was way too young to have to bear the burden of responsibility for his four younger brothers. Three now.

Hazel took a deep breath and continued to sift through the newspaper articles that had come up in the search.

She saw about fifteen blurbs in the crime beat section, though none were dated before Aubrey's death.

Dakota McCleary (32) and Vance Moore (45) were charged with disturbing the peace at a local bar last Saturday. Eyewitnesses say that McCleary had been drinking for the better part of the evening when a Tennessee Vols fan made a derogatory comment about the Georgia Bulldogs. The two men got into a shouting match and began to shove each other. The police arrived on the scene before any serious injuries were sustained. Both spent the night in jail and will be required to pay a $400 fine or spend ninety days in jail. Moore is just passing through town.

Two or three articles came up that looked like this:

Dakota McCleary (35) and Pistol Trudgeon (32)
were both charged with assault and disturbing
the peace after a fight at a local bar.
Witnesses at the scene claim McCleary saw
Trudgeon enter the bar and immediately got up
to confront him, telling him he wasn't
welcome in that specific bar. Trudgeon asked
if McCleary owned the place, whereupon the
men began to hit each other. The eyewitness'
accounts are conflicting as to who threw the
first punch. The bartender called the police,
and they arrived a few minutes later. In the
interim, the two men took the confrontation
outside where they were still fighting when
they were arrested. Both men were taken to
the hospital. Trudgeon was treated for some
missing teeth and a gash on his face that
needed stitches. McCleary suffered a broken
finger and nose. They face six months in
prison or a fine of $1000.

HAZEL DEDUCED that the death of his wife had driven Dakota to
drinking. He had been left alone to care for five young boys.
Hazel wondered where the family involvement was. Usually
these old clans were fiercely loyal and devoted to their kin and
would have considered it their duty to help Dakota out. She
shrugged to herself. Maybe they had, and things would have
been even worse otherwise.

THE MOST RECENT article that Hazel found was Dakota's obituary.

Dakota Ray McCleary

Passed away on Friday morning at two am at
the county hospital. He died of liver and
kidney failure due to toxic levels of alcohol
consumption. He was forty years old. He is
survived by his sons. Billy, Cash aged
sixteen, Virgil aged fifteen, Roy aged
fourteen and Eugene aged eleven. In lieu of
flowers, the family asks for donations to
their family trust for the boy's future
education.

HAZEL WONDERED why Billy's age wasn't listed in the article, then it occurred to her that he must have been over eighteen. Old enough to take responsibility for his brothers and become their legal guardian.

She got out her phone, and although she knew it was futile, called Nora to invite her to go to the McClearys.

"Oh my," Nora said. "You're a brave woman."

"What's so brave about taking a bunch of hungry boys a casserole?" Hazel was irritated by her friend's unwitting refrain of Jason's concern. "Unless you think they're so hungry they'll eat me as well," Hazel laughed overly hard at her bad joke but Nora didn't even giggle.

"Those McCleary boys are bad news," Nora argued. "Always fighting and getting into trouble. They have been ever since they were little."

"You mean ever since their mom died and they haven't had a wholesome feminine influence?"

"I guess..." Nora said. "But sorry, I can't come with you. I've got all my kids here and I'm not taking them to that place."

"No, of course not. I just promised Jason I would ask. I told him you wouldn't be able to."

"Good luck, Hazel. God bless you for being so sweet."

Hazel felt a twinge of guilt. Providing a meal for Cash's family was a secondary motive. Her primary one was to discover if they killed him. "Have fun being a wholesome feminine influence," she said brightly.

Nora laughed and hung up.

Hazel set the casserole inside a cardboard box, then wrapped the plate of cookies in tin foil and balanced them on top. She carried them to the car and set them on the passenger's seat. As she settled into the driver's seat, she pulled out her phone to call Jason before she left.

"Hello?" Jason answered on the first ring.

"Hey babe," she said. "I'm headed over to the McCleary's now."

"You made them something delicious?" Jason's voice had a little wobble of concern in it.

"Yes, I made chicken and biscuits. And peanut butter fudge cookies."

"Those lucky sons of guns," Jason said.

"Hardly," Hazel's voice was dry.

Jason sighed. "You're right. I'm sorry. Did you find anything interesting in your search?"

"I found a bunch of stuff about the dad on the crime beat. I can't tell if it was a blessing for his kids that he passed or not."

"How sad." Hazel could hear the concern in his voice. "How long ago was that?"

"About four years ago. The oldest, Billy, was only twenty at the time. But he was old enough that he could become the others' official guardian and they could all stay together at home."

"That's good," Jason pointed out. He had an older brother back in California that he worshipped. Being raised by him, instead of their vain mother and workaholic father, would have been his fantasy as a kid.

"Yeah." Hazel wasn't so sure that it was good. "I just don't know where the extended family is. Usually there would be an aunt or a grandmother or at least a cousin that would step up and help out."

"From what I've been told, the McClearys are dying out around here," Jason said dismissively. "Maybe there isn't anyone."

Hazel twisted her lips. "Maybe. But what about the mom's family? It seems like someone should have taken an interest."

"Uh oh," Jason groaned. "I know that tone."

"What tone?" Hazel asked. She put Jason on speaker so she could punch in the McCleary's address on her phone.

"You're taking an interest."

"Someone's got to do it!" Hazel started the car.

Jason chuckled. "Call me when you get out of there," he reminded her.

"I will."

"Alright, I'll let you go so you can concentrate on driving."

"Yes, yes. I love you!"

"I love you too. Good luck." Jason hesitated another moment before he hung up the phone. Hazel smiled. He was such a worrier. She wasn't afraid of a bunch of adolescent young men. Besides, she was bringing them food. Everything was going to be just fine.

HAZEL THOUGHT she knew Red Gap pretty well, but her GPS told her to turn in a spot that she didn't even know was a road about fifteen miles out from Main Street, on the opposite side of town from the high school. The trees reached up and over the road, blocking out the beautiful blue sky. Sunlight escaped through small patches of the canopy, leaving the road dappled with light. An occasional red or orange leaf floated down from the tops of the trees, flashing with color as it alternately passed through light and shadow.

The road had once been paved, but it was poorly maintained. Hazel bumped down it, hitting multiple potholes for another five miles before the GPS told her to turn into a long driveway. Hazel hesitated. Although there wasn't a locked gate, there was a large no trespassing sign nailed into a post and another sign on a tree that said, "Keep Out." She glanced over at the box full of cookies and foil casserole dish. Who would turn away a well-intentioned woman with a home-cooked meal to offer? Surely not a group of boys who had barely known a mother. She nodded her head once, then pulled into the driveway. It was even bumpier than the road, and she threw a hand out to brace the casserole so it wouldn't go flying across the car.

The car crawled along until she was within view of the house, then she stopped. She was staring at the archetype of ancestral poverty. It was an old house, a sturdy one made of split wooden siding. The house itself appeared to be in pretty good shape. It was a patchwork of materials, any attempt to match repairs to the original construction was abandoned. However, the roof was intact without creeping moss and none of the windows were broken. There was a large front porch with several battered La-Z-Boy recliners sitting on it. It would have been homey in a bachelor kind of way if it wasn't for all the garbage. Ten rusted out cars sat on one side of the driveway, blocking a mound of old rusty farm equipment that looked like it had just been thrown in a heap. Old furniture crowded around the front of the house. Piles of scrap metal and various construction materials were strewn haphazardly about the yard.

Hazel got out of the car and went around to the passenger's side to grab the casserole and the cookies. She was just about to slam the door with her hip when someone yelled at her from the porch.

"Who are you and what do you want?" the belligerent male voice demanded.

She blinked up at the man standing on the porch and wasn't all that surprised to see a gun pointed at her. People in North Georgia tended to be a little territorial. "I'm Hazel Dean," she said, looking into his face and ignoring the gun. He had a smoky gray haze all around him. It looked like a cloud of cigarette smoke, but several shades darker. "I brought you a casserole."

The man, who Hazel guessed was Billy, narrowed his eyes. "Why would you do that?" he asked, his voice more confused than angry.

Hazel didn't think that Billy was really planning to shoot her, so she took a few steps towards him. "You lost a family member, sir," she said, attempting a firm but respectful tone. "It's the neighborly thing to bring a casserole. My sons go to school with your Eugene."

Billy lowered his gun and scratched his head. "Well, alright then, I guess." He stood on the porch staring at her with dead eyes but made no move to take the food from her. Her unexpected arrival had prompted momentary exertion, but grief had glazed him over again. She climbed the porch steps.

"Would you like to eat it tonight?" she asked. She tried not to search his face, looking for resemblance to Cash. She didn't want to stare. He seemed to have Cash's straight, pointy nose, but on Billy it reminded her of a rodent. Patchy facial hair covered his smooth white face and his hair was shoulder length, pulled back into a greasy ponytail. "It'll freeze okay if you've already got plans for dinner."

"Ummm, no... we ain't got no plans," he said.

"Well, I'll just go in and put it in the oven for you then, alright?"

Billy just nodded numbly, still making no move towards her or the house. She walked slowly past him towards the front door, trying not to make any sudden moves. When she edged into the house, she almost choked on the stench of alcohol. The boys needed a meal, if only to soak up some of the alcohol in their blood.

The gray haze that settled over the porch and around the house became a cloud of midnight blue and black inside. Hazel didn't want it to touch her, but she had no choice if she was planning on preparing a meal. She had never seen someone's color extend so far from their body before. Presumably, the inky darkness was a physical manifestation of the brothers' grief. They appeared to be wallowing in it.

"Go on then," Billy said from behind her. She was blocking his way into the house as well. She took a deep breath of fresh air and then plunged in. She tried to hold her breath so she wouldn't have to breathe in, but she knew she'd be there too long for that to be an effective strategy. Especially if she was planning on talking, which was the whole point of the visit. The kitchen was on the other side of the living room from where she stood. She made a few strides across it and realized that there were two sets of eyes on the couch, watching her. It was hard to see them within the inky drifts of emotion that filled the room.

"This here's Miss Hazel Dean," Billy said in monotone. "She brought us a casserole."

The eyes blinked, but nobody said anything. Hazel looked at Billy with expectation. He shook himself, remembering his manners.

"That there's my brother Virgil and my other brother Roy."

Hazel smiled. "Pleased to meet you, Virgil, Roy."

Still no one said anything.

"Is Eugene here?" she asked, hoping to see his familiar face.

"No ma'am," Billy said. "Eugene went to school today."

"I have a son who's on the football team with him. He played quite a game last night," Hazel tried to sound conversational.

"Closest we can get to avenging our brother," Billy said, "is to beat up them Trudgeons in a football game." He slammed his shotgun down on a rack by the front door. Hazel flinched at the harsh sound.

She continued walking into the kitchen to find a place to set down the casserole and cookies. Billy followed on her heels. The counters were devoid of clear space, but Hazel used the foil casserole dish to push some dirty, smelly rags out of the way. The kitchen was mostly full of old dirty dishes and spoiled food. The darkness was getting to her. She started to feel agitated, irritable. She set to work cleaning the kitchen and preparing the meal to give her hands something to do. In the midst of her cleaning, she noticed a beautifully carved wooden fox sitting on the windowsill in front of the sink.

"What a charming fox," Hazel said. "Did one of you carve him?"

"No, ma'am. That was a gift from a friend." Billy glowered. Hazel realized that her time in the house was limited and decided to dispense with the niceties.

"I was so sorry to hear about Cash," she said. "He was a good man."

"God rest his soul," she heard Virgil and Roy mutter from the other room. The kitchen was a separate room from the living room, but it was close quarters and there was a cutout in the wall between the two spaces. Virgil and Roy weren't cut out of the conversation.

"Are there funeral arrangements in the works?" she asked, preheating the oven.

"Yes'm," Billy said.

"I see." She rummaged through the cupboards until she found a relatively clean plate to set the cookies out on. No one stopped her or offered to help.

"I heard that your brother was killed by one of the Trudgeon clan because of the feud?" she made it sound like a question, hoping they would tell her what they told the police without her specifically asking.

"He sure was," Roy jumped off the couch, speaking for the first time. "We was all workin,' mindin' our own business when that Wallis Trudgeon came out of nowhere and shot our boy Cash." Roy was pacing around the room making manic hand gestures. "We all heard the shot and turned 'round and there was Cash lyin' on the ground dyin' and Wallis Trudgeon was runnin' right off into the woods."

"So you didn't see Cash get shot?" she asked.

"We just as well as did," Roy shouted, taking her question as a contradiction. "There's no way to 'isscontrue the evidence."

"Yes, yes," she said, trying to soothe him, although she felt like yelling back at him. Her skin was tingly, and she tried to brush the cloying blackness off, although she knew that it wouldn't do any good. Was she being influenced by their emotions or was it all in her head? "I'm sure you're right." The oven beeped, and she put the casserole in to cook. In the very back of the cupboard under the sink she found some dish soap and set about to washing each dish she could find in as hot of water as she could stand, even the ones in the cupboards.

"What exactly are you doing here, anyways, Miss Hazel?" Hazel turned her head towards the door while her body still faced the sink. She could see Billy standing in the entrance with his eyes narrowed, staring at her with cold dark eyes.

"I told you," she said, trying to keep the snap out of her voice. "I brought you a casserole. I was worried about y'all."

"You don't even know us," he said.

"I told you, Eugene goes to school with my sons," she

paused, then decided to push her luck. She turned off the sink and wiped her hands on the front of her pants before picking up the plate of double fudge peanut butter cookies and holding it out to him. He glared at them before taking one. "Also, I met Cash the other day when he came into my bookshop. It must have been last Monday," she said slowly. "He seemed very upset." She turned back towards the dishes and began drying them with the least offensive towel she found. She tried to keep an eye on Billy while she worked.

Billy's eyes jumped towards her. "Is that right?" he said, the casual tone of his voice contradicting his intense stare.

"Yes," she said, concentrating on the plate she was drying. "He told me he was embroiled in a moral dilemma."

"A moral dilemma, huh?" Billy maintained his disinterested tone and was studying the cookie she gave him like it might turn into something else if he didn't watch it closely enough. "Did he say what about?"

"Oh no," Hazel said, "he didn't give me any specifics, but that's why I gave him *To Kill A Mockingbird*. It's a good book for someone who is having a moral dilemma."

Billy took a bite out of the cookie.

"I do have the book with me," Hazel went on. "I'd like to give it to you all. He wrote some lovely notes in it, I thought you might like to have it."

"We're not much for readin' around here, Miss Hazel," Billy said with ice in his voice.

"No?" she said. "That is a shame. Reading has a way of helping you solve your problems."

"Our only problem," Billy growled, slamming the half-eaten cookie onto the counter with one fist. "Is that the Trudgeons are still out there... and that they won't be satisfied until there aren't any McClearys left on God's green earth."

Hazel decided it was time to go. She turned off the sink and turned, wiping her hands on her pants instead of touching any of the towels in the filthy kitchen. Billy stood between her and the door.

"And," he continued in a low voice. "That our *neighbors* don't seem to understand that."

"Well, sir, I can assure you that I was only trying to help. Wallis Trudgeon is currently in jail facing charges for murdering your brother. That's how justice works in this country. We don't hold whole families responsible for their individual members' behavior. Now if you will excuse me." She pushed past him, using a forearm to push him out of the way. He grabbed her hard by the wrist of her other hand. She cried out in surprise and pain as he pulled her around to face him.

"We don't need any more charity, Miss Hazel Dean," he snarled in her face. She could smell the liquor on his breath and struggled not to gag. "We don't want to see you coming 'round here again."

She twisted his arm free of his grip, refusing to rub it with her other hand. "I have no intention of ever coming 'round here again." She marched towards the door. "Enjoy the cookies," she yelled at the other two men. "The casserole comes out of the oven in a half hour." She slammed the door and ran down the steps down to her car.

Her keys were elusive, hidden in one of the eight pockets in her pants or coat. Her heart raced. She glanced back up at the house. No one was out on the porch or in the doorway watching her. She relaxed and took gulping breaths of fresh air, not tainted by the anger and grief suffocating the McCleary house. Then she began a calmer search for her keys.

When she finally found them, she unlocked the door and opened it. Before she climbed in, she noticed a dark cloud coming from around the bend in the driveway and knew that it was Eugene coming home from school. She had never seen anyone else carry such a black cloud with them. She noticed that Eugene's grief looked more like a rain cloud and less like the smoke his brothers were marinating in. It had more depth to it too with more colors: gray, black, midnight blue and deep purple. It looked like a bruise on his soul. She left her car where it was and walked out to meet him.

"Hello Eugene," she called.

Eugene froze in his tracks. "Miss Hazel? Wha... What are you doing here?" he stammered.

"I brought some dinner," she said.

Eugene glanced nervously at the house. "That wasn't a good idea, Miss Hazel. My brothers aren't the friendliest folks."

"Yes," she grimaced. "I noticed." She rummaged through her bag and dug out Cash's copy of *To Kill A Mockingbird*. "I'd like to give this back to you," she said. "Cash put some great notes in it. He was a good man. You were lucky to have him for your brother."

Eugene's face crumpled with grief. "He was the best of us," he said, his voice strangled.

"I'm surprised you made it to school today," Hazel put a hand out, as if she could steady him. "My son Jeremiah told me you weren't there yesterday."

"I was suffocating here," he said, his restless eyes darting to the house. "I had to get out."

Hazel smiled and nodded. "I understand. I think you know my son Elias too, right? You're on the football team together."

"Sure, I know Elias," he said. "Quiet guy."

"Yes, that's him," Hazel smiled. "We watched your game last night, seemed like you were playing a lot more aggressively than usual."

Eugene just shrugged and shifted his weight to his other foot.

"I'm sorry," Hazel said, "I don't mean to pry. Billy said none of you would want the book, but I thought you might like to decide for yourself?"

Eugene swallowed, his over-sized teenage Adam's apple bed

up and down noticeably. He wiggled his fingers at his side for a few long seconds, then finally reached out his hand. "Yeah, I'd like to have it," he said quietly.

Hazel carefully placed it in his hands. "You better hide it from your brothers," she said. "I think Billy would probably light it on fire if he found you with it."

"Yeah, and probably me too," Eugene said, stuffing the book into his backpack.

Hazel raised her eyebrows.

"Not really," he mumbled. They walked together towards her car.

"You're welcome at the bookstore anytime," she said. "And if you ever feel like coming home with Elias for dinner, we'd be happy to have you."

Eugene stared at his feet and shrugged. "I don't know."

Hazel smiled. "Just keep us in mind. You tell Elias 'I'm coming home with you.' He won't even blink, I promise."

"Yeah, alright," Eugene said, still staring at his shoes.

Hazel got into her car. "I'll see you around, Mr. Eugene," she said. And began the nine-point turn she would need to make to turn around and drive up the driveway instead of backing out. When she could finally see the house in her rearview mirror, Eugene had disappeared into it. Hazel couldn't bear the thought of him being swallowed by the smoky anger. She bit her lip and blinked hard as she drove away.

FIVE

Hazel inadvertently skidded a bit when she pulled onto the highway from the dirt road. She was in a hurry and took the turn too fast. Her heart jumped in her chest as she course-corrected. Her heart pounded with the surge of adrenaline. Now that the boys had a meal in the oven, they would be stuck at home for at least an hour. Hopefully that's all the time she would need at the construction site where Cash had been shot.

Everyone had heard about the new boutique hotel going in on the outskirts of town. As a member of the city council, she had seen and approved the general plan and location of the hotel. She hadn't been to the building site herself, but she knew that Nora had taken her little boys out to watch the construction vehicles in action when they were excavating the foundation.

She grabbed her cell phone and put it in her lap, pressing the button to activate Siri. "Call Nora," she commanded.

"Calling Sephora," Siri answered.

"No, no, no, you ridiculous machine. Call Nnnnnnora."

But Siri was already dialing the cosmetics store in Atlanta.

Hazel slammed the red circle on her phone with her peripheral vision, then risked glancing at her phone for a second to find Nora's contact the old-fashioned way.

After four rings, Hazel almost gave up, but Nora finally answered.

"Hello? Sorry, I couldn't find my phone," she spluttered. "How did your visit go?"

"It went okay," Hazel said. "They're not doing very well over there."

"I can imagine," Nora murmured.

Hazel skipped to the point of her call. "So, remember when you took Harley and Jamie out to look at the bulldozer and stuff? Where was that exactly? Is it right off Highway 76?."

"Isn't that where that kid you knew died?" Nora was never one for subtlety.

"Um, maybe."

"Why do you want to know where it is? Isn't it like a crime scene or something?"

"Yeah, I just thought maybe that I'd go look around and see if the police might have missed anything, you know."

Nora's voice transformed to a tense whisper. "So, it *is* the actual scene of a crime?"

"I suppose, if you want to look at it that way." The characterization made Hazel uncomfortable. She just thought of it as the place where Cash died, and if she wanted to find answers, that's where she needed to go.

Nora was silent on the other end. Hazel could hear her kids yelling vaguely in the background. It came through pretty clearly over her car's speakers.

"Nora?"

"Yeah, I'm here. I just... So are you investigating the murder? Are you Miss Marple now or something? And didn't the police already arrest the guy who did it?"

"Um, yes they did, but..." Hazel sighed. Nora was a dear

friend, but she had never told her about the whole 'seeing people's emotions as color' thing. "It just doesn't feel right. It wasn't him."

Nora was silent again, but the background noise was gone. It sounded like she had gone into another room. "I don't know, Hazel. don't you think it's a little dangerous to investigate a murder?" Nora's voice had an odd, echoey quality.

Hazel paused, confused by the sudden change in Nora's voice, then she laughed. "Did you lock yourself in the bathroom?"

"It's the only place it's quiet in my house!" Nora exclaimed.

"Just wait until they're teenagers. They'll never be home and it'll be quiet all the time."

"I can't wait," Nora sighed.

"You'll miss them."

"So people keep telling me," Nora remarked dryly. "Aren't you worried that there may be some kind of bad guy waiting for you at the building site?"

Cash's brothers were at home, presumably eating her delicious chicken 'n' biscuits. Who else would be at the construction site? She highly doubted that this Chris Mills character was a local. "No, I don't think so."

Nora sighed. "Okay. It's right off 76 you can't miss it. There's a big 'coming soon' sign with a pretty drawing of the hotel. But Hazel, please be careful."

"I will," Hazel promised, then ended the call. It didn't take her long before she saw the sign and slowed to pull into the turnoff.

The site was perfect. The place was one turn before the exit for the Appalachian Trail pickup, and the drive through the trees wasn't too windy or steep. When she got to where the hotel was going up, it opened into a crest on a hill overlooking the mountains piling up around it. Sunrises would be lovely from the guests' windows, and the views of the dusky mountains in the evening would be breathtaking.

The foundation for the hotel had been poured, and the framing was up, but that was all that had been done so far. Hazel wondered if they would be able to finish the exterior walls before the weather turned for the worse this year, as winter seemed like it might come early. Surely Mr. Mills would want the hotel ready for the spring rush, which started as early as April.

Hazel knew she was at a crime scene, but she couldn't help but think that it would be a wonderful place to spend a getaway weekend with Jason.

"Curses," she said aloud to herself. "I forgot to call Jason. Hey Siri, call my husband."

Siri understood her just fine this time and dialed up Jason. The phone rang until she got his voicemail. She hung up and punched in a text.

McClearys went great. Am at crime scene now. Call you when I'm done.

A text didn't seem like the right way to tell him that they pulled a gun on her. Being from Los Angeles, he still didn't understand some things about the rural South. She put her phone back in her bag and looked around.

Hazel didn't see anyone, although there was a trailer nearby, presumably the construction office. Perhaps Chris Mills was inside doing paperwork. She got out of her car, climbed the steps to the door and knocked. There was no answer. She knocked again and counted to sixty before deciding that it was empty. The windows were too far off the ground for her to be able to look through them, so she walked over to the foundation.

She walked around the skeleton hotel, trying to imagine where the brothers were when Cash was killed. It was blocked off by police tape, but she ducked underneath it. She figured as long as she didn't touch anything, it wouldn't matter. She wouldn't leave footprints. It had been muddy a few days before, but it had dried up now.

It looked like the ground floor framing had been completed. In the front would be a lobby, a spacious room with a fireplace framed into it. She noticed the fireplace was framed to be double-sided, so she assumed the room on the other side would be a dining room and the kitchen would have to lay beyond that.

A poured concrete elevator shaft rose into the sky, indicating that another story would be framed on top of the ground level.

There were two hallways leading from the lobby, one with four tiny rooms branching off it and a room bigger than all the others at the end. The other hallway connected eight good sized suites that ran along the back of the building where the view would be. She walked back over to the smaller hallway and tried to figure the purpose of each room. The plumbing was in place for a small bathroom and she assumed another would be a utility room. The biggest room must be for staff, a staging area of sorts. Another room was probably an office for the hotel manager.

Hazel stood in the half-finished doorway of the smallest room, considering what would be so small. After studying it for a bit, suddenly the wood crosspieces she thought were temporary supports were the beginning of a stair frame. Had this been where the boys were working when Cash was shot? She looked around. She could vaguely see the woods through the layers of wood framing, but it would be a tough shot to hit someone who was working in this little room. It felt enclosed, protected from the woods where Cash's brothers claimed his killer appeared and disappeared from.

She looked down at the floor; the concrete was white and gleaming. Watching her feet, she walked back into the hallway and through the rest of the hotel. Cash hadn't been shot inside the structure. Surely the concrete would have some kind of stain if he had bled on it, even if someone had attempted to clean it up.

She sat on the edge of the foundation. Billy had never actually said that they had been working on the hotel when it happened, just that they were at the job site. She walked around the perimeter, trying to imagine where someone would sit down and have a drink or eat their lunch. Maybe they'd go back to the truck? She walked back towards her car, examining the ground for any trace of tire tracks. Luckily, the rain earlier in the week meant it had been muddy a few days previously. Ridges of truck tires sunk in the mud on the other side of her car, closer to the woods and the trailer. The tracks ended abruptly and then there were boot prints, but so many and in such a variety of directions it was impossible to piece together what might have happened. The tracks could even have been from before Cash was killed. She followed the perimeter of the heavily trafficked area, noticing a trail of footprints going off into the woods in one spot, perhaps because there wasn't a port-a-potty on site. Hazel wondered if that was some kind of code violation.

The hairs on the back of Hazel's neck prickled. Hazel expected a cool breeze to envelope her, but nothing happened. She froze, scanning the woods ahead of her slowly. Something, or someone, was watching her.

"Hello?" she called. No one responded, but Hazel heard a rustling beyond the tree line. Hazel figured she must have scared away a deer. She shook off her shivers and turned back towards the hotel.

There was so much that didn't add up in the McCleary brothers' story. She couldn't detect any signs of violence anywhere at the construction site. No blood, no trampled foliage, no slipping tire tracks from a truck trying to drive too fast on soft ground. Did the McCleary's give chase to Wallis Trudgeon through the woods? Hazel couldn't imagine Billy letting Wallis get away into the woods. The man she had just met would have chased Wallis down and attacked him. Hazel wished she had read the police report before she made this trip.

She came full circle and was facing the trailer again. The light of the setting sun glinted off the window, so she side-stepped into a shadow to avoid being blinded. It didn't help like she thought it would, so she took another step back, squinting at the window. It was broken. Hazel's eyebrows furrowed as she walked over to the trailer. The window was broken, and the frame below it was damaged, the wood punctured and splintered. She got out her phone and snapped a picture of it.

Turning around to look up the road, she headed back towards the steps that led to the trailer door and tried the handle. It was locked. Could the broken window be an attempted break-in? She pulled a credit card out of her bag and tried shimmying it between the lock and the door frame, but it was a deadbolt so that old trick wouldn't work.

She went back to look at the broken window. It didn't look like a break-in. The glass was still jagged and sharp, and it wasn't big enough to get more than just a hand through the window.

Hazel got in her car and drove it over to the trailer, right underneath the broken window. Then she got out and climbed on top of it. She could just barely peek over the frame. Avoiding the broken glass, she peered into the trailer. There was a desk right underneath the window, covered in a disorganized mass of paper, a half a dozen filing cabinets, an old beat-up couch, and a coffee pot. The position of the window made it impossible for her to see the far right of the room. She leaned over as far as she could and got out her phone to use as a flashlight, but she couldn't make out anything else.

Suddenly, *Every Breath You Take* by the Police started blaring out of her phone. Hazel shrieked in surprise and lost her footing on the top of the car, falling down her windshield and onto the hood with a loud bang. Awkwardly rolling onto the ground, she pulled her phone out and answered it.

"Hi Jason," she panted, cursing herself for thinking it was hilarious to assign him that song for a ring tone. She tried to sound casual and unhurt, but she landed hard on her butt and it smarted.

"I was in a meeting and I just got your text. You went where?" Jason demanded. His voice was shaking with either anger or concern, Hazel couldn't tell which one and he probably couldn't either.

Hazel checked the time. She had been at the build site for forty-five minutes. "I just wanted to see the construction site." she explained, leaning on the car to get to her feet. "Sorry, I lost track of time. I've got to get out of here."

"Yes, get out of there! What are you thinking? You went to the *crime scene*?"

Hazel flinched. When he said it like that, it did sound kind of stupid. She didn't respond.

"I'm coming to get you," he said.

"What?" she cried. "Don't be ridiculous, I'm just driving away now."

"You'd better be!" Jason was still yelling. "Do you have any idea how serious this is? They could charge you for obstruction of justice or interfering with a police investigation or some other such nonsense."

She snorted. "You mean *you* could charge me."

"I could be *instructed* to charge you. Do you know how embarrassing that would be?"

Hazel bit her lip. He had a point. She knew she hadn't thought her trip to the construction site through. The timing had just seemed perfect. She knew all the McClearys would be at home, no one would know she was there. There weren't any cops around. She was sure that Jason was overreacting. "Jason, no one is going to arrest me for snooping. I could say I had to check on something for city council. It's not that big of a deal."

"You need to get out of there, quickly and before anyone sees you," Jason ordered, ignoring her attempts to downplay the situation. "Damn it Hazel, you really didn't think this through."

"I'll be home in twenty minutes," she replied, getting into her Corolla.

"Fine." Jason ended the call.

Hazel started her engine and drove slowly, bouncing down the dirt road and picking up speed once the street was paved again. When she got to the turn onto the highway, she was surprised to see a truck turning in as she was pulling out. Billy McCleary was slowing down to make the turn towards the hotel. Roy was looking out the window and stared right at her, his face slack until his eyes blinked in recognition. He called to Billy and Virgil, who turned in their seats to look at her as well.

She had just enough time to see Billy's face contort itself into an expression of disgust and anger before she stepped on the gas and sped all the way home.

SIX

"Are those for me?" Jason appeared in the kitchen and reached around into the mixer to take a fingerful of cookie dough.

Hazel glanced at Jason. The night before had been taxing for both of them, and they hadn't really spoken that morning before he left for work. In the past, they hadn't had much occasion to fight. Jason had an easy-going personality and had mostly given in to Hazel's stronger opinions throughout their marriage. The only other time Hazel could remember him putting his foot down was when Elias was born and he wanted a more traditional role, being the sole provider for his family. Hazel thought he was being a bit old-fashioned but didn't really mind, as long as she could use her trust fund to maintain her ancestral home, so they struck a bargain.

Later, when the kids were in school and she wanted a new project, Jason had thought using her trust fund to turn the old mill into a bookshop was a great idea.

"I just don't understand why you need to be so involved in this," he had vented the night before. "Can't you just let someone else figure it out?"

"Who?" Hazel had spat back. "Who else is going to figure it out?"

"I don't know," Jason said. "Anyone who isn't my naïve and overly trusting wife?"

"I'm not naïve and overly trusting!" Hazel protested.

"You are when it comes to Red Gap. You can't accept that there is anyone who lives here who isn't a saint."

"That's ridiculous," she argued. "You don't understand, you grew up in a big city on the West Coast. No one in your town had lived there for more than twenty years. The people here have had relationships with my family for generations. I know everything about them—the bad and the good."

"Now that's ridiculous," he rolled his eyes. "You can't judge someone based on their family's temperament."

"Ha!" Hazel barked a humorless laugh. "Shows how much you know."

"Shows how much you know? Really? What is this the fifth grade?"

Jason's insistence that she stay away from anything involving Cash's death was only the second time that they had to work something out. Unfortunately, this time Hazel had a strong opposing view.

They hadn't come to a consensus. They had gone to sleep feeling vaguely frustrated and misunderstood.

"You are welcome to some cookies if you want some." Hazel said, speaking slowly and firmly. Hazel wasn't going to let Jason's emotions dictate her behavior. He made some good points, but she wasn't going to drop the case. She decided now wasn't a good time to point out that he was trying not to eat sugar. "But they're also for Trudy Trudgeon."

Jason froze with his finger in his mouth. "Trudy Trudgeon? Is that a good idea?"

Hazel returned her attention to scooping balls of dough onto the cookie sheet. She figured that if she was more open with Jason about what her activities were, he would be less worried. "It seems to me that if you were in jail, it might be nice for someone who believes you're innocent to bring your family something delicious to eat."

Jason considered it for a few minutes, sucking all the bits of dough off his finger. "I guess there can't be any harm in that," he said quietly, giving her a small smile.

Hazel beamed at him, recognizing the peace offering. "It's just taking a meal to a young mother who could use a little help."

"Are those for me?" Jeremiah's freakishly long arms were suddenly reaching around Hazel to get to the mixing bowl.

"You're just like your father," Hazel mumbled. "No, they're for a family in need."

"Ugh, of course they are," Jeremiah pouted. "Mom, when are you going to figure out that I'm in need? Why does Dad get some? Is he in need?"

Hazel threw up her hands. "Alright, alright. I get the idea. I'll make a second batch."

Jeremiah cheered.

"What's up?" Elias could be seen in the mudroom setting down a backpack, a gym bag, and a football. He was dripping in sweat.

"White chocolate cranberry pecan cookies!" Jeremiah called.

Elias came into the kitchen smiling and attempted to give Hazel a hug.

"Aghhh!" she shrieked in mock disgust. Elias loved to try to hug her when they were sweaty and gross. "Get away from me and go shower. Dinner's in fifteen."

Elias turned to head upstairs, chuckling. Jeremiah had found a spoon and helped himself to more cookie dough, then wandered out of the kitchen as well.

Jason didn't leave. He leaned against the counter, digging his own spoon into the dough. "So we didn't talk much about what you learned at the McCleary's yesterday. Did you find anything out?"

Hazel looked at him sideways, trying to tell if he was upset or if she was walking into a trap. "Are you sure you want to talk about this?"

Jason sighed and put down his cookie spoon. "I'd rather know what's going on." His phone began the ring. Hazel recognized the ringtone he had reserved for his mom. His countenance darkened and changed to a brownish orange. It took Hazel a long time to realize that the brown was created by the underlying forest green anxiety he felt for his mom. The orange, she thought, was irritation or wariness.

"I'm sorry," he said. "I really need to take this."

Hazel nodded. They'd learned over the years that it was better to take his mom's calls the first time.

"Hi Mom," Jason said.

Hazel could hear Jason's mother's voice over the phone from where she was standing. It had that overly bright quality that they'd come to dread even more than the sluggish low tones. The only thing worse was when her voice was slurred from whatever substance she had been abusing most recently. Jason was quiet. Hazel couldn't make out any specific words, just that Cindy was enthused about something.

"Oh, Mom. Really? Are you sure this is a good idea?" he said.

Cindy spoke again. Her voice came through in rapid bursts. Jason looked at Hazel with big eyes.

"Please be safe," Jason pleaded finally. He listened for another several minutes.

"Alright Mom, I love you." He hung up.

"What did she say?" Hazel asked. Hazel had only met Jason's mom on a handful of occasions. She vacillated between concern for the troubled woman and exasperation for her because of how much drama she added to Jason's life.

Jason sighed, the orange disappearing and giving way to pure dark green. "She met another guy," he said, the eye roll audible in his voice. "He's some kind of artist. He's really talented. She wants to give him money." Jason collapsed into a chair, rubbing his face in his hands. "I don't know how to respond when she calls me like this."

Hazel walked over and rubbed his shoulders. "I know," she said. "But you're such a good son. You offer her so much unconditional love. You're so good at forgiving her for all the trauma you went through as a child. I think you handle her perfectly. With kindness and understanding, but from far away."

Jason reached up and put a hand on Hazel's. "Thanks," he said. "I'm so glad that I found you."

Hazel smiled. "Me too. I mean, I'm glad I found you... you know what I mean."

"So, tell me about the McClearys," he repeated.

"All I can tell for sure is that they're hurting. I don't know that I've ever seen such strong emotions. But I think they're hiding something too. They were just so defensive. It didn't feel right."

"So do you think one of them did it?" Jason stared at the ground.

"I don't know," she said.

"What about the crime scene?"

She hesitated again, but he looked unemotional. The brown work mode haze surrounded his head. Hazel couldn't help but smile a little. One of the things that first attracted her to Jason was how consistent his behavior was with his emotions. Most of the time, being able to read emotions made dating difficult. But Jason was different. "I didn't find a thing," she admitted. "Not even a bloodstain, let alone any bullet holes."

Jason nodded. "I looked through the reports. The McClearys told the officers that the wound didn't bleed much before they got him to the hospital, and that Trudgeon had only taken one shot. The doctor at the hospital said that very little initial bleeding could be consistent with the entry point of the bullet."

Hazel shivered. It felt odd to be talking about Cash this way. "It still feels a little suspicious, doesn't it? I mean, why did they drive him to the hospital themselves instead of calling an ambulance?"

"They told the officer that they didn't have reception at the construction site."

"Interesting," Hazel said, pulling a cheesy chicken, rice and broccoli casserole out of the oven. "I didn't have that problem up there."

"Maybe they have a worse service provider than you."

"Maybe," Hazel said. She didn't buy it. "Let's feed our boys before they drop dead of calorie expenditure."

She went to pick up the casserole, but Jason stopped her and pulled her into a big hug. "I'm so glad you're okay," he murmured in her ear.

"Me too," she said, hugging him back. A tension in her chest released when Jason wrapped his arms around her. They were okay. When he finally let go, she picked up the casserole and carried it to the dining table. "By the way," she said over her shoulder. "Billy McCleary saw me leaving the construction site, and he didn't look too happy."

Jason groaned, his hand flew to his forehead. "Hazel!"

"Supper time, boys!" Hazel called up the stairs. Elias and Jeremiah came barreling out of their rooms, effectively ending the discussion.

After dinner, the boys settled on the floor in front of the TV while Jason sat on the couch and turned on Jeopardy. It had become a ritual of sorts in recent months. The boys always kept their faces glued to their phones, but they both called out answers once in a while. Instead of disappearing after dinner, they had made a habit of heading to the living room. Hazel knew that time like this with her boys was fragile, so she did everything she could to maintain it. Including dessert.

Hazel set a batch of cookies on a plate and brought them in to the living room. Before she could even set them down on the coffee table, Jason, Elias and Jeremiah had each grabbed one, murmuring 'thank you ma'am.' Hazel watched as a glow of contentment, each in a different sunny color, settled on her men. Thoughts of Eugene McCleary stuck in her mind, and she felt a pang of sadness for him.

"I thought y'all should know that I invited Eugene McCleary to come on over for supper whenever he liked."

They all turned to blink at her.

"I told him to come on home with Elias after practice."

Nods bobbed around the room.

"Yes, admiral! Turns out this once-named "Bad At Love" singer is good at music," Alex Trebek said from the television.

"Bon Jovi," Jason said.

"Nope," eye-rolled Jeremiah, "Halsey."

"Halsey," one of the contestants said.

"Correct."

"Bon Jovi has two names, Dad," Jeremiah explained as though his Dad was senile. "you've got to look for the clue in the answer. It's the key to Jeopardy."

Hazel took their renewed interest in the show to mean they accepted her invitation to Eugene.

"Now, why didn't I think of that?" Nora said. "Their daughter is in my son's kindergarten class."

Nora had called Hazel the next morning to ask about borrowing some books for her kids that afternoon, but Hazel told her she was closing the shop to take a meal to Trudy Trudgeon.

"It doesn't look like Wallis will be out of jail anytime soon," Hazel said. "Why don't you bring them something next week?"

"I will..." she said. "Just let me know how it goes with you today first. The Trudgeons make me nervous."

"What?" Hazel laughed. "Why?"

Nora got quiet. "I'm actually a Trudgeon. On my mother's aunt's side. My mom told me to stay as far away from any Trudgeons or McClearys as I could possibly get to avoid getting entangled in the feud."

Hazel pressed her lips together. "Your mother's aunt by marriage was a Trudgeon?"

"Well, not exactly. She was a Trudgeon on her father's uncle's side."

Hazel stifled a laugh. "So you're wary of feud entanglements because you are related to the Trudgeons in a roundabout way through two different marriages?"

"I know it sounds crazy when you say it like that," Nora snapped. "But I just don't want to cause any problems or make anyone feel uncomfortable."

"What are the chances you also have some McCleary relations?" Hazel asked.

"Not good, I wouldn't think," Nora said. "The McClearys are cursed. They haven't had a female born in their line for five generations." Nora lowered her voice conspiratorially, even though they were having a private phone conversation. "That's why a lot of them keep leaving town. You don't think it was really a feud killing, do you? Do you think Wallis did it? Everyone was talking about it at the bus stop this morning."

"No," Hazel said emphatically. "No, I don't think he did it."

"Well, the McCleary boys are framing him for murder then."

Hazel took a deep breath. Nora was ten years younger than

her, and most of the time it didn't make a difference. Just some-times her immaturity came through, like when she revealed her love of gossip.

"I think that's overstating it a little bit."

"Why would they say they saw him do it if he didn't?" Nora asked.

"That is the question, isn't it?" Hazel said, more to herself than to Nora. "Either way, I'm going to let you go so I can close up the shop and take food over to Miss Trudy."

"Alright. Oh, by the way, I made some more bookbags. I noticed you were running low. I'll bring them by the shop soon. Good luck with Trudy."

Hazel groaned and thanked the Lord that her Red Gap aris-tocratic ancestors had seen the wisdom in marrying outside of their hamlet each generation. Only one of them ended up staying and living in their ancestral home, while all the others went out into the world. Hazel's aunt and uncle and cousins lived all over the country, but she had been the one to stay behind. She went to the University of Georgia, where she met her husband while he was in law school, then she dragged him and her useless master's degree in English Lit back to Red Gap. They lived with her grandmother until she died, then the house became theirs. Before her parents died, the Randolphs had been an old money family that actually had no money. Her ancestors owned the mill that turned the community into a town, but the money had disappeared when the mill became obsolete. All they had was the house and a good reputation. Until Hazel got the settlement from her parents' accident. Her grandmother taught her good breeding and an aristocratic responsibility to be an example of upstanding behavior in her community.

Hazel hefted a phone book onto the counter and opened it to the M section, searching for McClearys. She found not a single entry, not even Billy's household.

Turning more pages towards the Ts, she found two full pages of Trudgeons. She remembered Ryker Trudgeon and Vince Trudgeon from high school, but Wallis was too young for her to have known and his parents would be too old.

She shut the phone book and gathered the casserole and cookies she had made for Trudy. The Trudgeons and the McClearys had been around and feuding for hundreds of years, but it seemed to her that the Trudgeons had come out ahead. As far as she could tell, Billy and his brothers were the last remnant of the clan in the area, whereas the Trudgeons still made up half the population of Red Gap. Sure, loads of people like Nora would have a tenuous connection to the McClearys, but they just didn't have a strong presence anymore.

So why would the McClearys want to blame Wallis for Cash's death? Hazel hoped that Trudy Trudgeon would give her some answers.

* * *

Hazel didn't have any trouble finding their modest home as it was listed in the phone book. It was in an older but cheerful neighborhood with well-kept yards and wreaths on the doors. Hazel pulled up in front of the house and climbed the steep driveway with her offerings. She balanced everything in one hand so she could knock, not wanting to wake up any napping babies.

The door opened up, but the storm door remained closed. "Can I help you?" The girl who answered the door was younger than Hazel had imagined. She was struck with the thought that the girl was probably closer to Elias' age than her own. She smiled. The girl had a haze of orange around her, but it wasn't an angry orange like Jeremiah often exhibited. More of a harried orange. Hazel remembered her days as a young mother.

"Hello, Miss Trudy Trudgeon?" Hazel asked.

"Yes, that's me," she said, eyeing Hazel's packages. "You're not a reporter, are you?"

"No," Hazel hadn't thought about how to introduce herself ahead of time and now regretted it. "I'm Hazel Dean," she said. "My husband works down at the courthouse and so when Wallis was arrested and I heard that he had a wife and children at home, I just wanted to help out. I brought you a casserole and some of my famous white chocolate cranberry pecan cookies. And a few books, I own the Books and Chocolate shop downtown and I couldn't help pulling some of my sons' old favorites for your kiddos. I have-"

"We don't need your charity ma'am," Trudy's eyes were hard. "Thanks for your kind words, but..." She began to close the door.

"Wait, Trudy," Hazel called out, stepping towards the storm door. "I believe your husband is innocent."

Trudy froze, and after a beat, the door opened back up. "You do?" Trudy asked, her eyes brimming with tears.

"Yes, I surely do. I knew it the moment I saw him down at the courthouse after he was arrested. He didn't kill that boy."

Trudy opened up the storm door. "Come on in," she said.

Hazel followed Trudy through the house to the kitchen. The front room was devoted to kids' toys and there were two toddlers playing quite happily with blocks and obnoxious mechanical music toys. The house was a 1950s style rambler without the newer open floor plan, so the kitchen was walled off from the living room except for a cutout that allowed Trudy to see into it.

"He didn't do it," Trudy said. The orange that surrounded her darkened and turned to a rich, deep blue.

"I know he didn't." Hazel affirmed.

"Two of my day care kids canceled on me," she sniffled, scrubbing at the counter with a rag. Hazel admired her ability not to break down into sobs. She set the food she brought down on the sparkling clean countertop. "They're not planning on coming back. I know it's because they think he's guilty. They think my husband..."

"They'll be back," Hazel promised. "I'm working on the investigation. My husband's the prosecutor. He knows your husband is innocent too." Hazel bit her lip, probably an exaggeration, but she just kept talking. "Does your husband have an alibi?"

Trudy's eyes spilled over. "No, that's the problem," she said. "He said he was going out with some friends after work, but the friends claim that he never came to the bar they were supposed to meet at." Her voice broke into a sob. She dropped the rag and wiped at her eyes with the back of her hand. "I don't know where he was," she cried. "I'm so glad you're convinced he's innocent, Miss Hazel, because I was doubting it myself." She sat down in the chair and the sobs came.

"Oh, dear," said Hazel, opening the bag of cookies. "I wish these were more chocolaty." She held one out for Trudy, who took it but continued to cry. Hazel sat with her for a few minutes and let her cry before she renewed her questioning.

"I know you have lots of family in the area," she probed. "Have they been supportive?"

"No ma'am, I'm afraid my mom is all I have, and she's not really in a position to..." Trudy's face darkened. "Wallis hasn't been on speaking terms with his family for some time."

Hazel blinked. "Is that so?"

"Yes, they didn't approve of his... career choices."

Hazel detected the hesitation in Trudy's voice and decided to push. "And what does he do for a living?"

"He's a physical therapist." Trudy tilted her chin upwards in a gesture of pride and defiance.

Hazel chuckled slightly. "I'm not sure I understand his family's objection to that."

"Oh," Trudy breathed, collapsing into a chair. "I don't really either. It was before we were married. From what I can gather, they offered to pay for Wallis to go to medical school, but he didn't want to. They said it was because he was lazy, and he said it was not worth the money to pay for schooling."

"I see," Hazel nodded.

"It was a big deal too, the falling out," Trudy went on without any encouragement. "He's the heir, you know, the oldest son of the oldest son, of the oldest son."

Hazel nodded again, although she was confused. Since when did the Trudgeons have any kind of estate to bequeath upon their progeny?

"We don't talk about them," Trudy said. "It makes Wallis angry."

"Has Wallis ever spent time with the McCleary boys before? Maybe they went to school together or something?"

Trudy frowned and shook her head. "Wallis wasn't on good terms with his family, but that doesn't mean he started spending time with the McClearys. Wallis graduated before any of those boys started high school. I can't imagine how they would even know each other." She collapsed into a chair and then glanced at the clock hanging in the kitchen and jumped right back up. "I have to meet the bus! My kindergartner will be getting home." She rushed towards the door. "I've got to get the others into the stroller."

"Why don't you let me sit with them while you meet the bus?" Hazel asked.

"Would you?" she said, her eyes shining. "That would be nice, thank you." She slipped on shoes that were sitting by the front door and headed out to meet the bus.

It had been a long time since Hazel had spent time with two-year-old children. She dug the books she had found out of her bag and sat down on the floor. "Does anyone want to read a book?" The kids ignored her until she pulled out *The Monster at the End of this Book* and started reading in an exaggerated voice. Then, their interest was piqued, and they came and sat close to her, looking at the pictures. Hazel wondered idly if she should add a kids' story time to her list of events at the bookstore.

Trudy's uncertainty about her husband's innocence concerned Hazel. Remembering the note that Cash wrote her, she wondered if Wallis was somehow tied up in things. Hazel was sure that he wasn't the killer, but he could be a part of whatever clandestine activities Cash referenced. But it didn't make sense that he was working with the McClearys. The animosity between the two families was real enough, and she couldn't imagine members of the two different clans voluntarily working together. Nora's reluctance to take a meal to the Trudgeons was enough evidence of that.

Hazel's eyes wandered around the room, and she was surprised to recognize an item sitting on the mantle. A carved wooden wolf, eerily similar to the fox she had seen at the McClearys the day before. Billy had said that it was a gift from a friend. Was he lying, or did Billy and Wallis have a friend in common? Hazel audibly squealed with excitement, startling the babies playing around her. They looked at her with wide eyes.

"Sorry," she said, blushing. "Just found a clue."

The door opened again. "Thank you so much for your help," Trudy said, ushering a little person into the house. "Miss Hazel brought us some cookies!"

The girl looked up at Hazel through dark lashes. "Well, aren't you adorable?" Hazel said. "Would you like a cookie?"

She nodded.

"Well, come on then," Hazel took her by the hand and led her to the kitchen, pulling a cookie from the bag and handing it to her. She glanced down at the little girl and then back up at Trudy. She had a lot of questions to ask about Wallis but it didn't seem like a good time to do it, in front of his daughter like that. It said something about a man if his wife thought it was possible that he could be a murderer, but it wasn't something you should discuss in front of the man's child.

"Can I come back and visit you again?" she asked. "I'd like to ask you some more questions about your husband so I can figure out what really happened."

"What about the police?" Trudy asked. "Are you working with them? You said your husband was the prosecutor..."

"Unfortunately, the police are satisfied with the physical evidence." Hazel gently pulled on Trudy's arm, so they were a few feet away from where the little girl was devouring her cookie and lowered her voice. "The wounds were consistent with the type of gun they found in your husband's car. There are three eyewitnesses that put him at the scene of the crime. They even found dirt in his tire treads that they can match to the build site where Cash was shot."

Trudy nodded, her face ashen.

"But he didn't do it," Hazel assured her. "I know he didn't." Hazel didn't stop to consider why she was so sure. She just was.

Trudy smiled tearfully at her. "Thank you," she breathed, hugging Hazel around the neck.

Hazel patted the girl on the back. "You poor thing," she murmured. Trudy was hanging onto her for dear life, and eventually Hazel had to gently pry herself away.

"I'll be back soon," she said, gathering her bag and heading towards the door. "By the way," she said, pausing as though it was an afterthought. "I noticed your beautiful carved wolf, it's lovely. Where did you get it?"

"Oh, that was a gift from one of Wallis' patients," Trudy said. "It is beautiful, isn't it?"

"Yes, it really is," Hazel turned to go, "thanks for the visit."

"Thank you for coming. I'm sorry I wasn't very friendly when you first knocked."

"I understand," Hazel waved it off. She balanced the now

empty box she had brought the food in on one hip and opened the door with her other hand. She pushed through the storm door but turned back when another question occurred to her. "Do you know anyone by the name of Waylon Gibbons?"

Hazel was in an awkward position, holding the storm door open and also managing the box, so she could see Trudy well, but she noticed the blue that had surrounded her since she started talking about her husband shifted to a brassy yellow.

"No, I've never heard of him," she replied. Hazel caught a glimpse of the space around Trudy turn a deep shade of midnight blue before she closed the door.

SEVEN

Hazel knocked on Nora's door, her fear of nap time prevented her from ringing the bell. The door didn't open. Hazel knocked again and stepped back to look at the house. She thought she saw a flash of movement in a window.

"Nora," she called quietly. "Nora, it's just me. I don't care if you're braless or anything. I need your help."

Nora opened the door. "Why would I be braless?" she asked at a normal volume.

"I never wore a bra when I was at home all day with little kids," Hazel said. "And then I would hide and pretend not to be home when anyone came to the door."

Nora laughed. "That is so you," she said. "Nowadays young mothers are encouraged to get dressed even if they aren't leaving the house, so they don't feel all frumpy."

"Huh," Hazel said. "It never occurred to me to feel frumpy."

"Of course, it didn't," Nora shook her head. "What can I do for you? Do you want those book bags?"

"Oh yes, that would be great." Hazel had been wary when Nora first asked about selling book bags at her store, but they had been a hit from the start. Now the place wouldn't be the same without them.

"Come on in, I'll grab them."

Hazel followed Nora into the house. "Do you know anything about Wallis Trudgeon and his family?" she wondered nonchalantly.

"Wallis Trudgeon's family?" As anticipated, Nora's gossip antennae were alert.

"Yeah, like his parents' names..."

Nora sat down on the couch. "Well, of course. Wallis is only a little younger than me. I think he was a sophomore when I was a senior."

Hazel collapsed onto the couch, squishing a large stuffed frog underneath her.

"He was in the marching band that year," Nora continued. "I think I have a friend who is a cousin of his on his mom's side. They're Bolings. Solid people, not that bright but real nice." She thought for a moment. "His mom had one of those names with the extra syllable at the beginning and an extra capital letter like DeNeece or LaBelle... what was it?"

She got up abruptly. "I'll just got text my friend and ask her. My phone's in the other room. Hold on."

"You're the best, Nora!" Hazel called after her. She discovered Nora's three-year-old daughter, Emma, peeking at her from behind the couch. Hazel pressed herself into the cushion to avoid detection and crept closer. Then she jumped up, craning her neck over the back of the couch to see Emma below her and yelled "Boo!"

Emma squealed with laughter and delighted shrieks. Hazel hopped around the couch and grabbed Emma, tickling her to keep the adorable shrieking going. When she noticed the little girl gasping for air, she let go.

"Oh, no, the baby's not asleep, is he?" Hazel said, realizing that she had hyped up Nora's kids.

"No, he's having tummy time," Emma said. Hazel peeked under the coffee table and saw the bald baby on the other side, gurgling and bringing his hands together in front of him.

"Oh dear, he'll be crawling soon," Hazel cooed. She wanted to pick him up and squeeze him.

"I know," Nora came back into the room, phone in hand. "Don't remind me. My friend says Wallis' mom's name is LaShay Trudgeon and you might be able to catch her at work."

"Where does she work?"

"She's a hairdresser at Hair to Please." Nora's eyes sparkled. One of Hazel's snobberies was getting her hair done down in Athens at a fancy salon.

"I guess I could get my hair done," Hazel ran a hand through her long, low-maintenance style.

"It doesn't have to be a cut," Nora said. "You could have her do an up do or something. Tell her it's a special occasion."

"You look a little over excited there."

"Just please, please take a selfie for me before you wash it out."

* * *

BEFORE SHE COULD THINK TOO much, Hazel found herself in a chair at Hair to Please, looking at LaShay's reflection in the mirror in front of her.

"You're lucky we had a cancellation," she said, smiling. "Otherwise, we'd never be able to get you in so last minute. What am I doing for you today?

LaShay's own sense of style was not as over the top as Hazel had expected. LaShay's hair was cut in a tasteful bob, appropriate for a woman of her age. The color was silvery purple, which flattered her more than Hazel would have thought. The same color seemed to cling to her all over, and she sparkled like tiny Christmas lights.

Hazel smiled, her eyes twinkling. She liked LaShay already. "I'd like to surprise my husband with a new look, but I'm nervous about doing anything permanent."

LaShay smiled and nodded, picking up a strand of Hazel's hair as if to test out its weight. She tilted her head to one side. "What if I just cut off an inch or two? Could you live with that?"

Hazel bit her lip. It would be worth it if it gave her any new insights into Wallis' innocence. "Okay," she nodded doubtfully.

LaShay squealed. "Oh, I love this kind of project," she said, expertly wrapping a cape around Hazel's neck. She sighed as she gently pulled Hazel out of her chair and guided her towards the shampooing stations in the back of the salon. "I could use the distraction. I've had the worst week."

Hazel wondered if she was referring to her estranged son's imprisonment. "Glad to help," she said.

"You live around here or maybe you're on a romantic getaway?" LaShay's voice sounded hopeful, but Hazel couldn't see her face at this point because she had leaned back into a sink and was staring at the ceiling.

"Oh no, I live here. I usually get my hair done in Athens, but I couldn't wait today." All strictly true.

"I see," she said. "Well, I'll do the best I can to make sure you become a regular customer."

"I would love that," Hazel said, again honestly.

LaShay began to wash Hazel's hair, and Hazel felt her shoulders relax. Investigating Cash's death had produced some tension.

"Have you lived here long?" LaShay asked conversationally.

"All my life," Hazel answered.

"Oh, me too," LaShay said, "but you're a bit younger than me. Did you go to Gap or Millcreek?"

"I went to Gap, graduated in '92. I have two boys there now."

"Do you? My oldest graduated in '06 and my last graduated two years ago."

"Oh wow, how's being an empty nester?"

"It's not so bad. All of my kids are local, so I still see a lot of them. Come home for laundry and all that. Okay, I'm wrapping a towel around you. Go ahead and sit up."

Hazel dragged herself to a sitting position, wishing that she could have had her hair washed for another twenty minutes.

"Are we doing color today?"

Hazel blanched. She had gotten her color fixed up about four weeks previously. "Ummmm..."

"Maybe something a little edgy?"

Hazel's interest was piqued. "I don't know. Do you think that I can pull it off at my age?"

LaShay snorted. "You're younger than me."

"Yes, but yours looks so great because of your gray."

"What if I just do something on the tips? If I do a dark blue, it won't be super obvious with your dark hair. And you can always trim it off if you hate it."

Hazel smiled in spite of herself. She scrunched her eyes shut. "Alright, let's do it."

LaShay cheered. "You'll love it. I promise. I'm going to turn you around so you won't see it until the end."

"Okay," Hazel said. She realized that she had become distracted about her hairstyle and dropped the ball on steering the conversation towards Wallis. She was going to have to be awkward. "So do you have any grandkids?"

LaShay was behind Hazel, so she couldn't see her face. "I do."

"I can't wait to have grandchildren," Hazel said enthusiastically. "I've heard it's even better than having your own kids. Is that true?"

LaShay was quiet for a moment. "I wouldn't really know. I haven't spent much time with my grandkids."

"Oh," Hazel feigned innocence. "Did they move away?"

"No, they're here in town." LaShay was quiet for another

few minutes, and Hazel patiently waited in silence. She clasped her hands together hard under the cape to keep herself from saying anything.

"It's my oldest son that has the babies," she went on eventually. "We don't talk to him much anymore."

"Oh no, I'm so sorry." Hazel said. She thought about the sweet toddlers she met when she saw Trudy and felt genuinely sad for LaShay. "That's terrible."

"It is," LaShay nodded. "We had a falling out years ago, before he got married, and he hasn't ever forgiven us."

"Oh, LaShay," Hazel murmured, feeling the need to pat her hand. She resisted because LaShay's hands were filled with scissors and a comb.

"It was our own fault," LaShay went on, her color darkened into a deep, solemn blue. "We thought tough love was the way to go, but now he's got his life together and figured there's no place for us in it."

Hazel almost nodded but realized that might mess up her haircut. She decided Hazel must not know that Wallis had been arrested. "I have two boys. A freshman and a junior this year."

"Do they behave themselves?"

"I think so," Hazel said with a stiff mini shrug. "They don't tell me much."

LaShay laughed, but her veil of blueness didn't lighten. "Ain't that the truth. My girls wouldn't stop talking. I'd have to shut the bathroom door in their face sometimes. But my boys, getting any information from them was a feat."

They fell into silence. The only sound was the scissors snipping and the low murmur of two idle stylists in the back room. Hazel felt bad that when LaShay started cutting her hair, she was that twinkling light purple, and now that dark gloom hung about her.

"I don't mean to pry..." Hazel said. "But..."

"Why aren't we on speaking terms?"

Hazel nodded.

"Watch yourself," she said. "I'm done cutting, but I'm moving on to color now."

LaShay didn't say anything else, and Hazel thought that she wasn't going to answer the question, but after another minute, she slumped in the chair next to Hazel.

"You need to sit for a few minutes while your color sets. I'll just sit next to you here and we'll have a little chat. You worried about your boys Miss Hazel?"

"Sometimes," Hazel said, but she was thinking about Eugene.

"My boy, Wallis. He's our oldest. We were so young when we were raising him. We made a lot of mistakes. The biggest one was not being more involved in his life. We weren't well-informed. I had little kids when he was in high school, and they took up all my energy. I figured if he wasn't complaining, he was fine." She leaned back in the chair and looked up at the ceiling.

"We didn't know who his friends were or where he was a lot of the time. Then he started to get irritable. He'd snap at us and the littler kids. He kept odd hours and slept through school in the morning. That boy would sleep all day if we'd let him, then he'd be out all night. His eyes started to look sunken and dark.

"I remember one day he dragged himself out of bed around noon looking for food and when he reached up in the cupboard for something, his shirt came up so we could see his stomach. He looked so skeletal, it scared me. I suddenly noticed that his clothes were hanging off him." She shook her head and Hazel noticed her eyes were shining with unshed tears.

"I'm sorry." Hazel squirmed. "I didn't mean to ask you to relive something painful."

"No, it's okay," she said. "I take a lot of comfort in knowing he's okay now."

"How do you know that?" Hazel wondered.

"I'm getting to it," she smiled. "In any case, it took us way too long to figure out that he was into drugs. We panicked. We didn't know what to do. We were so worried about his example to the other kids. We were so angry with him for being so stupid."

"That's understandable," Hazel said.

LaShay gave her a half-hearted smile. "Maybe, but it wasn't right. We threw him out. We told him if he was going to make choices like that, he would have to do it far away from us and our family." She shook her head and barked a mirthless laugh. "Our family, like he wasn't a part of it."

"Of course that's not what you meant," Hazel said.

"Was it not?" LaShay said. "I'm not sure." She shook herself and blinked, her eyes coming to rest on Hazel. Her smile looked a thousand years old. "It was a long time ago. Doesn't matter now. He left, and we didn't see him for years. One of my nephews told us he had moved to Atlanta, but that he wasn't doing well there either. Poor Wallis, I still don't know what drove him to it."

"I'm sure it wasn't your fault."

"That's nice of you to say. Anyways, when Wallis got married and moved back to town, he connected with my sister-in-law and her family. He told them he had gotten cleaned up and made a new life for himself. He got some kind of medical certification and married a sweet girl. But he told them that he didn't want to see us. He'd never forgive us for abandoning him when he needed us the most." LaShay's voice cracked. Hazel was impressed that she had been able to keep her composure for as long as she did. Forgetting her hair, she jumped up and put her arms around LaShay.

"You did the best you knew how," she soothed.

"Oh no, your hair!" LaShay squeaked. "I've got to rinse the color out." She rushed Hazel over to the washing station and busied herself unwrapping strands of hair and rinsing them out.

"Have you ever reached out to Wallis after he moved back to town?" Hazel asked.

LaShay shook her head. "No. My husband thought about it a couple times, but we don't want to get his sister in trouble for feeding us information about Wallis' family. They're pretty close, and that's better than knowing nothing like we did for so long."

"Maybe you should reach out. You, you're his mother. He has little ones now, he might understand why you did what you did. But even if he doesn't at least you can apologize. He'll be able to see how sincere you are."

LaShay bit her bottom lip. "Maybe... I'd sure like to see those babies."

"They won't be babies forever," Hazel reminded her.

LaShay nodded. "I know," she whispered. "I could tell him how proud I am of him for making a good life for his family. I've been wanting to do that for years. Julianne told us that Wallis has even saved up enough to invest some money into the new hotel that's going in."

Hazel froze. Confronted with this woman's pain, she had almost forgotten the reason she was getting her hair done in the first place. "The one by the trail over off 75?"

"Yes, I hear it's going to be beautiful and super modern."

"How did he get involved with that?" Hazel asked, trying to sound casual.

"Actually, that's why Julianne thought it was interesting and told us about it. The man who's building the hotel was Wallis' sponsor when he was going through rehab and stuff. I think his name is Chris. I guess he's like a mentor to Wallis or something."

LaShay was talking about the hotel the McClearys were building. Chris must have been Chris Mills, the man who had hired them. The hair on Hazel's arms stood up. She almost jumped out of her chair and out the door. But she allowed herself to be led back to the salon chair to have her hair styled. "Sounds like he's really gotten things figured out," Hazel said. Her throat tightened, imagining how LaShay would react when she found out that Wallis was in prison for suspected murder.

LaShay nodded, her countenance turning to a rosy yellow. Hazel decided that LaShay was the kind of person whose base emotion was happiness. "Now, no peeking," she told Hazel, turning her decidedly away from the mirror.

Hazel grinned at her.

LaShay laughed. "The hairdresser usually takes on the therapist role, I'm afraid I've talked your ear off today."

"I don't mind at all. I'm glad to know you, LaShay."

LaShay smiled "I think I'll take your advice and reach out to Wallis."

Hazel smiled, praying that the renewal in their relationship would be a blessing for all of them.

EIGHT

Hazel fussed with her hair in the mirror of her downstairs powder room. Her boys would all be home soon, and she was nervous about their reaction to her new look. She stared at the mirror, trying to like it. At least LaShay hadn't cut too much off, so the next day she could style it like she normally did. Hazel wasn't usually one for mousse. She told herself it was just the lighting in the bathroom that was washing her out, not the color in her hair.

After exchanging cell phone numbers with LaShay Trudgeon, she had rushed home to look up Chris Mills on the Internet. He was the connection between the McCleary boys and Wallis Trudgeon.

Unfortunately, Hazel's internet stalking skills left a lot to be desired. She only had one social media account, Facebook, and there were about five million Chris Mills listed. A Google search yielded the same results.

Hazel wandered back into the office and slumped into her high-backed office chair. She stared at the computer screen, thinking perhaps if she stared long enough, the Chris Mills she was looking for would stand out with a bright red glow or something. But it was no use. People's colors never came through in pictures.

She heard the back door open and close. "Jeremiah?" she called.

"Yeah Mom," Jeremiah walked through the office where Hazel was sitting on his way to the kitchen but stopped when he saw his mom staring blankly at a computer screen.

"... Whoa," Jeremiah said.

"Yes?" Hazel responded, feeling self-conscious.

"What did you do to your hair?" Jeremiah shed a backpack, a coat, and a trombone case next to her on the floor.

"Put your junk in the mudroom, please," Hazel said automatically. "I felt like a change," she answered his question.

"Why?" he asked bluntly. "You looked fine before."

"Does that mean you think I look ridiculous?"

Jeremiah scrutinized her. "I guess you look *okay*," he shrugged.

Hazel groaned. It wasn't exactly a rave review. "Take your stuff to the mudroom." She put her elbows on the desk and stared at the screen some more. Jeremiah ignored her request and disappeared into the kitchen.

A minute later, he reappeared in the doorway with a double-decker peanut butter and jelly sandwich.

"Take the food out of the office," she said without looking at him.

"Why are you looking up dudes on Facebook and changing your hair? Are you going to leave, Dad?"

"What!?" Hazel laughed. "Of course not. Your dad and I are madly in love."

"You guys are pretty gross," Jeremiah mused, taking a huge bite of the sandwich.

"Out of the office!"

Without moving his feet, Jeremiah leaned over so his head

was in the hallway. "The food is out of the office," he said with his mouth full.

Hazel groaned and pushed him out the door. "I'm doing a little research to try to help out someone who may be in trouble."

"Is this about that McCleary murder?"

Hazel looked at him sharply. "What do you know about that?"

"It was all over school today," Jeremiah said, callously unconcerned as only a teenager could be. "I felt pretty bad for Eugene. People kept whispering whenever he walked by."

"Yes, I'm sure his peers whispering about him was the hardest thing he had to cope with today," Hazel said sarcastically.

"Yeah, I heard his brother got shot in the head, and he was there." Jeremiah took another bite of his sandwich, the tragedy unable to deter his appetite.

"I don't think he was there," Hazel said quietly.

"But they got the guy that did it."

"Yes, they think so," Hazel said.

"So, Dad's going to put him away?" Jeremiah asked, pride tinging his voice.

"Maybe," Hazel said. Tears pricked her eyes. Jeremiah's innocent faith in the system and his father touched her. "It's his job to build a case against whomever is being charged with a crime in this county. But this case is a big deal, and because the man they arrested is a Trudgeon and there's the feud, it will probably end up being tried somewhere else, so the jury can be unbiased. But your dad is involved."

"Cool," he said around his sandwich. "Is that why you invited Eugene to come over for dinner?"

"Partially," she said. "I met Cash, the man who died, last week in the store, and so I got to know him a little bit. I feel bad for Eugene that he doesn't have a Momma and Daddy at home to take care of him and now one of the brothers who raised him is gone too. I thought he might like to have a nice family meal."

"That doesn't explain why your hair is blue."

Hazel rolled her eyes. Just when she thought they had been having a nice conversation.

"Do you want some help finding that guy?" Jeremiah asked, nodding towards the computer.

Hazel thought for a minute. Jeremiah would know exactly how to find out what she wanted to know. "Alright," she said, wondering what Jason would say about her pulling their son into a murder investigation. She could pretend it was a city council project. "Let's see what you can do."

Jeremiah snorted. "I can do things you don't even know are things." He polished off the sandwich and wiped his hands on his pants. "Who are you looking for?"

"A man named Chris Mills. He is building a boutique hotel close by. It's not about the murder. I just wanted to know a little bit more about him. The city council is going to have to approve some of his plans, roads and whatnot... I want to know if he's a good kind of guy or not. I know it's inevitable that more hotels and things go up, and I know a lot of people here rely on the tourism industry. My shop does better during tourist season but I just can't help but be a little sad when more and more developing is going on-" Hazel had slipped into a monologue that was familiar to her son, and he had stopped listening to her, intent on the computer.

"Found him," he declared.

"What? How?" Hazel was gobsmacked.

"LinkedIn," Jeremiah said in his 'my parents are senile' voice. "It's a social networking site for professional people, you know, grown-ups."

"I know what LinkedIn is," Hazel assured him.

"And look, now we know his middle name. Agapath. That's

kind of a weird middle name. Maybe it was his mom's maiden name. If it is, it would be really easy for us to steal his identity."

"Jeremiah!"

"What? I'm just saying it's a dumb practice for your middle name and your mom's maiden name to be the same thing." Jeremiah shrugged. "Now we can go to Facebook and type in Chris Agapath Mills and see what comes up."

Chris Agapath Mills didn't have an exact match, but there were four Chris A Millses on Facebook. Jeremiah clicked on each one and looked at their stats. Hazel was overwhelmed by how fast he clicked on everything. It hurt her eyes. She pulled a chair up next to him and slumped into it. She had never felt so old.

"But how do you know that wasn't him?" Hazel exclaimed when he rejected one of them.

"He hasn't ever been anywhere near here," Jeremiah said.

"How do you know he doesn't actually live in New York City or somewhere?"

Jeremiah tabbed back over to Chris Mills' LinkedIn page. He scrolled through the page. "Look, here's his resume, Mom. He's spent his whole life in the Atlanta area. He graduated from Kell High School in Marietta. The guy's a local. Probably went hiking and camping up here on long weekends and stuff."

Hazel nodded. "Well, that's promising, I guess."

Jeremiah was reading more closely through the resume now. "Weird. I wonder how he got into hotel development."

"He doesn't have a history in the hospitality industry?"

"No, all his experience is in pharma sales."

"Huh," Hazel said.

"He probably just always had a dream of opening a place up here and finally got the cash together to do it."

"Maybe," Hazel said. "Is there any way you can tell if he has a record?"

"What?" Jeremiah exclaimed. "You mean like a police record?"

"Yeah."

"What makes you think he has a police record?"

"I just heard a rumor is all," Hazel said vaguely.

"Alright," Jeremiah shrugged. "There are a few websites like that." His fingers tapped away at the keys for a few minutes, then a big circle chasing its tail took up the screen. "It's thinking... gathering information from lots of different places to do like an informal background check on the guy."

"Yes, that's exactly what I'm after."

The page finally loaded.

"Wow," Jeremiah said, his eyebrows raised. "This guy's a dirtbag."

There were six charges and no convictions. Two for embezzlement, three for illegal pharmaceutical sales, and one for drug trafficking.

"I wonder how he avoided convictions for all those charges," Hazel wondered out loud. Something to ask Jason about later.

"Maybe he was innocent," Jeremiah suggested.

Hazel snorted. "Sure he was."

Jeremiah blew on his fingers and rubbed them on his shirt. "Well, there you go. Now I have to go bless my social studies group with my genius."

Hazel rolled her eyes. "Right, you do that," she said, chuckling as he sauntered out of the office. She got up from her chair to take the seat in front of the computer again, tripping on Jeremiah's backpack. "Jeremiah!" she yelled after him. "Take. Your. Stuff. To. The. Mudroom!"

Intuiting that the effects of his genius were dampened by his slovenly habits, he sheepishly crept back into the room, gathered his things and disappeared again without a word.

Drugs, it had to be something to do with drugs. Maybe the

hotel was a front for trafficking, or maybe they were making meth or something. Maybe opioids. They had become a huge problem in the community in recent years. Maybe that sleaze ball, Chris Mills, was looking to make money off the opioid epidemic.

NINE

Jason came home early that day, bursting in the door in a flash of yellow and orange sherbet and scooping her into his arms. "I found you something!" he said, excitedly.

"What?" Hazel asked, a rush of adrenaline flooding her head. "What did you find out?" She couldn't imagine what it might be.

"That guy, Chris Mills, that Cash was working for. He's a drug dealer."

"Really?" Hazel said, disappointment replacing the adrenaline. Jason was one step behind her.

"Yes, slippery guy. He's never been convicted, but he's been involved in a half a dozen drug cases. The guy's smart, he knows how not to get caught, but maybe he finally slipped up this time. Maybe he killed Cash."

"Do you think so? What about the eyewitness accounts? And the gun?"

"It's easy enough to take a gun from someone's car and then put it back afterward. And the McCleary boys aren't exactly known for sobriety. It would be easy to fool them. It's not as though they don't have personal reasons to implicate Trudgeon. If we could find some physical evidence to support Mills' involvement, I think it would be enough to throw out the charges against Wallis Trudgeon, who has maintained that he's innocent the whole time." Jason frowned. "The only problem is that he can't produce an alibi, so they might argue that he was an accomplice or something. His were the only prints on the gun- what have you done to your hair?"

Hazel smiled. "I was wondering if you'd notice."

"Of course, I noticed. It's blue." Jason stared at her head, his eyebrows raised. He turned a little bit lime. Not a good sign.

"Is it awful?" Hazel worried.

"It's... different."

"A lot of people are putting bright colors in their hair now. LaShay told me that I was plenty young enough to pull it off." Hazel could feel her cheeks getting hot.

"LaShay?" Jason asked.

"Ummmm, yes. LaShay Trudgeon. She's Wallis' mom."

Jason's mouth fell open. "Ahhhh," he said. "I understand now. Did you find out anything worth the blue hair?"

"She's such a sweet lady. I really enjoyed talking to her. And yes, I did." She took a deep breath, her hand in her hair again. "Chris Mills is a mentor of Wallis Trudgeon."

Jason tore his eyes from Hazel's hair and looked her in the face again. "What?"

"Yes, I'm sure you already know all about Wallis' history with drug abuse. Chris Mills was his sponsor through rehab and has become a mentor of sorts since. Wallis has some money invested in the hotel."

"He has money in the hotel?"

"That's what his family thinks."

Jason whistled. "That's an interesting development. Definitely worth looking into."

Hazel nodded.

"They are getting a warrant to search the trailer at the hotel construction site right now. Should be able to get in there tomorrow."

"I want to go," Hazel said.

Jason looked at her with an eyebrow raised. "You want to go to a police investigation? How are you going to avoid Uncle John?"

"I'm not sure," Hazel murmured, tapping her finger on her chin.

Jason shrugged. "I really don't think that John would skip this one, Hazel. You know how he is about 'outsiders' to begin with. Taking out a hotel developer for opioid trafficking would make his year. His only regret would be not taking me out with him."

Hazel laughed, but Jason just grimaced. "Oh, Jason," she cajoled. "Uncle John doesn't hate you."

"Yeah, he does," Jason said, shrugging again. "I might be the exact opposite of what he hoped you'd marry. Look, I think that if you want to go to a police investigation, I'm not the one you need to be talking to."

Hazel nodded. "I know." She imagined how the conversation would go.

'Hi, Uncle John, I'd like to attend the search of the trailer connected to a murder and possibly a drug bust.'

'Why would you want to do that, darlin'?'

'Because my friend that died, that I told you about? Remember? Yeah, he's actually Cash McCleary, and I'm pretty sure you arrested the wrong guy. I've started my own investigation, actually. So it would really help me out if I could come with you...'

That's as far as she got because she really couldn't imagine what Uncle John would say at that point. Would he sputter and not actually use words like the time she had stayed out all night when she was sixteen? Or would he laugh at her like when she told him she was getting a master's in English Lit? Or, worst of all, he might become completely silent and not talk to her for a week like he did when she told him she was marrying a democrat lawyer from Los Angeles, California.

They heard the back door open. "Hello, Elias," called Jason. "We're in the office."

"Hey, Dad," Elias called from the door. "Um, I have a problem."

Hazel's blood ran cold. A deep, dark blue hung around Elias, he fidgeted and kept glancing back towards the door. She could see Jason panic as well. Elias rarely asked them for anything. Hazel suspected just stringing the sentence together was difficult for her son.

"What happened?" Jason barked, his face turned red. Hazel worried about his blood pressure.

"Come look," Elias mumbled, avoiding eye contact with his father. He turned around and headed back out the door. Hazel and Jason followed him.

Elias' car was sitting in the driveway looking perfectly normal: no bashes, bumps or scratches. Hazel felt air returning to her lungs. It couldn't be that bad if the car was okay.

In the front seat sat Eugene McCleary. He lifted a hand and winced. "It was my fault," he called without getting out of the car. "I wasn't following any good bicycle etiquette. I've been having a hard time focusing lately."

"What happened?" Hazel said.

Elias opened his trunk and pulled out a bike. The front wheel had been crushed.

"Oh, my word," Hazel murmured.

"Are you alright, son?" Jason said, striding quickly to Eugene. He opened the car door wide and checked Eugene over for injuries.

"I'll be okay," Eugene said. "Just a sprain. I'm lucky. I was in the middle of the road. I don't know how I got there. I just zoned out."

"I hit his bike," Elias said.

"Right," Hazel said. "I can see that."

"I told him just to drop me at home," Eugene said. "But he brought me here."

"I'm glad he did," Hazel said. "I told you to come around for dinner, anyways. Jason and Elias, get him into the house. We can ice his ankle and take a better look at it."

Over Eugene's continued protests, Elias and Jason lifted him up and carried him into the house. They settled him onto the couch in the family room. Hazel knelt down to examine the afflicted ankle.

"The swelling isn't too bad," Hazel said. She looked at Eugene suspiciously. "You didn't hear a snap, did you?"

"No, ma'am," Eugene said.

She glared at him.

"I promise," he said, hands raised like she was about to rob him.

She nodded after a few seconds. "We'll just wrap it up and ice it a bit. I don't think that your football coach is going to be very happy about this, though. Sprains can take months to heal. Did you get hurt anywhere else?"

Eugene hesitated, then pulled his sleeve up above his elbow, revealing a large scrape down his forearm. "My ankle got stuck in the bike when it went down. It mostly broke my fall, but I think I landed on my arm too."

Hazel shuddered a bit when she looked at it. "Well, at least your shirt prevented crushed asphalt from getting embedded in your skin."

Hazel found her first aid kit in the garage. When she came back, she found Jason and Elias had gotten some ice and stuck Eugene's foot on top of a pile of pillows. She spent some time treating Eugene's arm before she wrapped his ankle up with an elastic bandage and set it back on top of the pillows and underneath an ice pack.

"Looks like you'll be our prisoner for the evening. Did you let Billy know you won't be home for a while?"

Eugene shrugged. "He won't care."

Jeremiah appeared from the back stairs into the family room. "Eugene!" he exclaimed.

"Hi, Jeremiah," Eugene's face turned red, growing to become three dimensional in Hazel's perception.

"What happened?" concern blossomed on Jeremiah's face.

"I wrecked my bike," Eugene said.

"Elias hit him with the car," Hazel corrected.

Jeremiah looked for Elias, but he had disappeared. "Oh! I bet he's in so much trouble..." Hazel gave him a look and he fell silent.

"You two know each other?" Jason asked, gesturing between Eugene and Jeremiah.

"Oh, yes sir," Jeremiah said. "Eugene is in my graduating class. I have calculus with him."

"Calculus!" Jason couldn't hide his delight. "I see we have another nerd in our midst. So you're a math genius and a football player? The whole package, eh?"

"Yes sir," Eugene said, his crimson coloring extending even further to encompass his whole body. Hazel could feel herself turning red in sympathy.

"Stop it Jason, you're embarrassing the poor boy," Hazel said.

"I was just about to play something. You wanna join?" Jeremiah asked, turning on the television.

Eugene looked from Jason to Hazel. She smiled in encouragement. "I guess so," he said.

The boys started up the game, and Hazel pulled Jason into the kitchen. "I haven't actually thought about dinner yet. Hope

I have some ground beef for spaghetti and meat sauce." Hazel started digging through the freezer.

"It'll be fine," Jason said.

"Can you make a salad really fast?" Hazel asked. "Or wait, go to the store, quick, and pick up some French bread so I can make garlic bread."

"Are you serious?" Jason asked.

"Yes! Go, we're going to feed three teenage boys! We'll need all the food we can get." She dug out two pounds of ground beef. "Besides, who knows when the last time Eugene had a legitimate meal was?"

"I thought you took them dinner yesterday," Jason deadpanned.

"You know what I mean!" Hazel spluttered "Now go! And get a couple of brownie mixes too... And some ice cream."

"Alright, alright. I'm going," Jason laughed. "Before you think of anything else."

Hazel could throw together spaghetti sauce in her sleep. By the time Jason came back, the meat sauce was simmering, the noodles were almost done cooking, and the salad was already made.

"Wow, you do fast work," he said, setting the grocery bags down on the counter.

"Thanks, now go ahead and butter the bread and put garlic and Parmesan all over it. I'll put the brownies together and they can cook while we eat dinner."

Jason made the garlic bread and put it under the broiler before calling the boys.

Eugene appeared in the doorway behind Jeremiah.

"What on earth are you doing?" Hazel squeaked. "You shouldn't be up! Go lie back down, we'll bring you a plate."

"Oh, Miss Hazel, I've been enough trouble as it is." Something in his voice made Hazel pause. The boys didn't notice, but

Hazel could tell that Eugene was holding back tears. She put out an arm to support him and guided him back to the couch.

"It's the least we can do after our son mutilated you like this," she assured him.

"It wasn't really his fault," Eugene pleaded, looking up at her from the couch with big sad eyes. That bruised color she noticed surrounding him when she ran into him at his house returned.

"I know," Hazel said. Someone else might not have noticed, but Hazel could tell that Elias was stricken by what happened. Expressing emotions wasn't his strong point. Hazel often wondered how mothers coped when they couldn't read what their kids were feeling all the time. She patted Eugene's good foot. "But you shouldn't blame yourself either. It was just an accident."

The unshed tears in Eugene's eyes spilled over. Hazel pretended not to notice. "I'll bring you a plate in a minute."

She left him and headed back into the dining room.

"Hey, can we all eat in the family room?" Jeremiah asked, watching Hazel put a plate together for Eugene. "We don't want to leave Eugene in there all alone."

Hazel pressed her lips together. "I think Eugene could use some alone time actually, Jeremiah. We'll just let him eat in peace for a few minutes."

Returning with the plate, Hazel noticed that Eugene's eyes were still glistening, but he smiled at her when she handed him the food. "Thank you, ma'am. It looks delicious. That thing you brought over the other night was good too."

"Of course," Hazel smiled. She opened her mouth to say something else but couldn't think of a thing that would ease the burden that Eugene was carrying. She nodded once and returned to the table.

"Where is Elias?" she asked.

Jason and Jeremiah shrugged. Hazel sighed. "Just a minute," she said. "Don't start without us." She pointed a finger at them.

Hazel headed upstairs. "Elias?" she called. "It's dinner time."

She got to the closed door of his room and knocked. "Elias?"

There was no answer. Hazel frowned and opened the door without much hesitation. Her giant son was sitting on the bed, wiping tears from his eyes. A splotchy midnight blue pigmented his skin. He tried to sit up straight and stop the tears when she came in, but his face crumpled after only a second.

"Oh Elias," she breathed. "It was just an accident."

He nodded. "I thought he was dead."

"Oh, sweet boy." Hazel sat next to him on the bed and attempted to wrap her arms around him. They didn't quite fit. "You did the right thing," she soothed as he cried into her shoulder. "It's okay, everything is fine."

"Dad is gonna take away the car."

Hazel pressed her lips together. It was probably true, but it wasn't the time to talk about it. "Have I ever told you about my first car accident?" she asked.

Elias shook his head, wiping his nose on his sleeve.

"I met my friend's family at a campsite over spring break. It wasn't far, so Gran and Uncle John let me go by myself. It was really hard for all of us, you know, because of what happened to my parents. But I was so proud of myself. I drove on those windy roads and everything was fine. My friend, her name was Jolene, was waiting in the parking lot and she waved me over to a parking spot just on the other side of their RV. I had to make a left turn, and I misjudged the distance and clipped the corner of my car on the RV while I was parking."

Elias smiled. He had stopped crying. Hazel rested her palm on her forehead. She could feel herself blushing, telling a thirty-year-old story.

"Wait, it gets worse. I didn't know what to do when I made contact, so instead of backing up, I kept going and continued to scrape along the RV until I was clear of it."

Elias chuckled. Hazel laughed too. "I'll never forget the look on my friend's face. The RV was fine, but my headlight was shattered. I was sure that Uncle John was going to kill me, but when I got back home and told them the story, he just laughed. 'Everyone gets into a first accident at some point, I'm glad yours was at low speeds.' He made me pay for the repairs, of course, but he wasn't mad." Hazel stood and grabbed her son's hand. She attempted to pull him up. "Let's go eat."

Elias nodded. He got up and followed her downstairs to dinner.

Hazel's family enjoyed their usual dinner conversation, mostly carried by Jeremiah. They talked about the Titans and the Predators, about something interesting Jeremiah had learned in Physics and about movies that were coming out soon.

Hazel glanced at Elias. A grayish blue haze obscured his face. Hazel reached out to him and squeezed his hand under the table. He startled and his head snapped up to look at her. She gave him a big smile, and he shook himself a bit, the haze clearing slightly. He smiled back at her and returned to eating.

"Do I smell brownies?" Jeremiah asked.

"Yes," Hazel said, jumping up. "I have to get them out of the oven."

"Wow, Eugene," Jeremiah called loud enough for him to hear in the other room. "You should come over more often. We never get dessert on weekdays."

"They'll have to cool a few minutes," she said, coming back into the dining room. "Are ya'll up for *Jeopardy* before we have dessert?"

"Sure, I'm not going to disappear when there's brownies around," Jeremiah said.

Hazel sighed as she watched her boys, including Jason, abandon all their dinner dishes on the table and head to the family room. Hazel cleared the table and started the dishwasher. They had already turned on the show when she joined them. She sat down on the floor in front of her husband's easy chair, hoping he might absently rub her neck. Jeremiah sprawled on the floor with his phone out. "No cheating," Jason said.

"Like I need to cheat," Jeremiah said, rolling his eyes.

The contestants cleared out the entire category of "Compound Words" and "His'tory" fairly quickly. Hazel's whole family yelled the answers over each other.

"'His'tory is a trick, you chauvinists!" Hazel cried. "The answers are all about women."

"We know that, Mom," Jeremiah said. "But that doesn't narrow it down much, does it?"

"Sherlock Holmes..." Jason couldn't stop laughing about a Jeff Foxworthy reference. "a secure housing area..." He gasped for breath.

"It's not that funny, Dad," Jeremiah said. But he and Elias were chuckling as well.

Hazel was about to get up and cut brownies when the players cracked open a new category.

"Illegal Legal Drugs for $200, Alex."

"This common kitchen spice could give you a buzz, even causing hallucinations in some cases."

"Nutmeg," Eugene muttered under his breath.

"What is nutmeg," one of the older contestants said.

"Correct," said Alex Trebek.

"Whoa, I didn't know that," Jeremiah said.

"No need to remember it either," Jason said.

"Illegal Legal Drugs for $400."

"This now illegal drug was once legally required by the

British to be grown by American colonists, and many of our founding fathers complied."

"Hemp, of course," Eugene said.

Hazel glanced at him.

"What is Cannabis hemp," a contestant said.

"Right," said Trebek.

"Let's do Drugs for $600."

"This illegal drug's leaves are still used as an herbal remedy to treat altitude sickness."

"Cocaine," Eugene said.

"What is marijuana?" guessed one contestant.

"No," said Alex Trebek.

"What is coca leaves," said another.

"Yes," said Alex. "The coca leaves are of course also used to make cocaine."

"Wow, you're really good at this category," Jeremiah said to Eugene.

Hazel shot a look at Jason. He shrugged.

"Drugs for $800."

"Daily Double," Alex declared as the music played and the audience clapped.

"This drug was initially marketed as a cough suppressant and non-addictive substitute for morphine. It was wildly popular."

"That's an easy one. It's heroin," Eugene said.

"Wow, Eugene," Hazel said. "How do you know so much about drugs?"

Eugene shrugged.

"LSD," guessed the contestant.

"No, that would be heroin," said Alex.

"How did he miss that one?" Eugene said.

Hazel looked at Jason again. He shook his head. He hadn't known the answer either.

"Let's finish the category, Alex," the contestant said.

"Alright for $1000, this legal drug category's recreational use is growing so fast it is considered an epidemic in many parts of the world."

"Opioids," Eugene muttered.

They all knew that one was right before the contestant and Alex Trebek confirmed it. Hazel felt a strange feeling in the pit of her stomach.

Eugene did just as well in a category about SEC football, and Hazel felt a little better. She left to make brownie sundaes. Once the sundaes had been devoured and Jeopardy was over, Jeremiah wanted to turn on Fortnite again, but Eugene declined.

"I'd better be going," he said when they turned off the TV. "My brothers will be wondering where I am."

"I'll drive you home," Hazel volunteered. Jason looked at her quizzically. She nodded at him. "Do we have an old crutch anywhere?"

Elias dug through the garage until he found a set of crutches while Jason helped Eugene into Hazel's car. "Better leave your bike here. We'll have it fixed up for you," Jason said.

"Oh, Mr. Dean, you really don't have to do that," Eugene said.

Jason scoffed. "Nonsense."

It wasn't until Hazel was out of her neighborhood and on the highway that she thought perhaps Billy wouldn't take kindly to her bringing Eugene home. "Um you better not mention that you were at our house tonight," she said to Eugene. "Billy didn't exactly appreciate the dinner I brought over the other day."

Eugene barked a humorless laugh. "Seemed to like it fine while he was eatin' it. But yeah, I won't mention it."

"How are they doing, by the way? Your brothers?"

Eugene sighed, his countenance darkening to a deep blue. "Okay, I guess," he mumbled. "All my brothers talk about is making Wallis Trudgeon pay." Eugene winced and adjusted his foot.

"You don't feel that way?" Hazel asked.

Eugene didn't respond right away. When he did, it was reluctantly, like he was confessing something. "I can't," he said. "Maybe it would be easier if I could."

Hazel didn't say anything.

"We're still looking for Cash's truck too."

"Cash's truck is missing?"

Eugene nodded.

"But wouldn't it just have been at the construction site where he was shot?"

Eugene's eyes widened, and his color changed to a pale yellow. "Um, no. He got a ride to the site that day. With Billy and us."

"I didn't know you were involved in their business." Hazel tried not to sound judgmental. "Does that get to be a lot with school and everything else?"

Eugene shrugged. "They don't mind if I skip out on them for football practice. And I do my homework after it gets dark and we're done for the day."

"Does Billy's truck seat all five of you?"

"Uh, we just all ride in the back."

"Of course," Hazel said. Eugene was clearly not being completely truthful, but Hazel wanted him to come back and visit them again, so she stopped pushing him. "Well, here we are," she said, turning onto the dirt road that led to Eugene's house. She turned off her headlights, hoping that no one would notice her car approaching and confront her.

"Don't worry," Eugene told her. "They're probably passed out drunk right now."

That didn't make Hazel feel very much better, but she was able to pull up to the house without any angry men with guns stepping onto the porch. She got out of the car and helped Eugene out, handing him the crutches.

"Good luck, Eugene," she said. "Don't be a stranger now. You're welcome in our home anytime."

Eugene made a grim face. "Thank you, ma'am," he replied. "But I don't deserve all this kind attention."

"But..." Hazel started. Eugene turned his back on her and hobbled up the stairs into his brother's house.

TEN

"That's it," Jason called from the bathroom the next morning. They had blearily woken up to see the boys off to school, then stumbled around. "I'm going on a diet."

"Again?" Hazel asked. She got on her hands and knees to look for her second shoe under the bed.

"Yep," his voice echoed from the bathroom. "I'm going to take back control of my body."

"Good for you, sweetheart." She found her shoe and sat down on the bed to put them on.

"I'm going to start working out too," he said.

"Good idea," Hazel called.

Jason appeared in the doorway. "What's up?" he said. "You seem a little distracted. Usually when I have a sudden renewed interest in my health, you offer all kinds of unsolicited advice."

"I'm sorry," she said. "Of course, I'll help. I just... What do you know about Cash's missing car?" Hazel asked.

"There's a missing car?" Jason raised his eyebrows. "That's news to me."

"Maybe you should ask John about it? Without telling him that we had Eugene here because Elias ran him over."

"I can figure out a good way to do that, I think," he said, following Hazel into the bathroom where she tried to fix up her hairstyle for a bit. LaShay had made her promise not to wash it for twenty-four hours. "I'm supposed to have coffee with him again this morning to discuss those semi-truck robberies."

"Is that what you two were arguing about the other day?" Hazel asked, looking at Jason in the mirror.

"Yeah, I can't really talk about the specifics. We disagree on how likely certain evidence is to convict."

"I haven't read anything about the robberies in the news. I've just heard you talk about them."

Jason leaned against the door frame. "Some hooligans in our general area are stealing Apple products out of trucks sitting at truck stops or gas stations. Pretty slick operation actually."

"Huh," Hazel said, sliding a mascara wand over her eyelashes.

"Maybe you can wash some of that blue out of your hair," Jason suggested after studying her for a moment.

Hazel spun around to face him. "I thought you said it wasn't that bad!"

"Did I say that?" Jason asked.

"Alright, alright. I'll make an appointment with Tressie to fix it. But I still want to be friends with LaShay Trudgeon." She wound the blue edges of her hair around her finger.

Jason grinned at her.

* * *

THE COUNTY BUILDING was an old-fashioned affair. It had been built from local marble back in the 1800s. It housed the court-house, the county government (although they were only around seasonally), the DMV, the jailhouse and the assessor's office. Pretty much any kind of governmental function in the county had offices here. Even so, it wasn't ever a bustling hive of activity. As a member of the city council, Hazel technically had a shared office in the building. She didn't need to sneak around, but she knew that if Jason or Uncle John knew what she planned to do today, they would be upset. They would want to spare her a potentially unpleasant interaction. But she wasn't afraid of Wallis Trudgeon.

Hazel was gambling that she would even have enough time to talk to Wallis Trudgeon and still make it to the police investigation of the trailer whenever Jason called her.

"Hello Mrs. Dean," Danny chirped, appearing in the lobby. He glowed his usual peppy turquoise. She had never seen him anything but peppy. It put Hazel off a little. She had never met anyone else who had so little variation in emotion. Not that she didn't like him, she just thought he was a little strange.

"Hi Danny," she said.

"Jason isn't here right now," Danny said, sitting down at his desk. "He's out for a cup of coffee with Captain Tate."

"Is he? Oh, what a shame," Hazel said. "I was hoping he'd be able to come out for a cup of coffee with me. I'm still so distraught about the terrible murder that took place in our nice little town."

"It is rather shocking, isn't it?" Danny said, grinning like a little boy.

"I just can't fathom what would possess an otherwise good man to do such a thing. I thought I might talk to Wallis Trudgeon."

"Why would you want to do that?" Danny's brow furrowed, but his turquoise didn't waver.

"Well, you see," Hazel said, clearing her throat. "I took dinner over to his wife and little kids the other day, just out of a neighborly spirit, you know."

Danny lightened, nodding as if she took dinner to the families of everyone who had ever been arrested.

"And his sweet wife, Trudy, is so worried about him being locked up in here," Hazel went on. "She's worried that he might be losing his health, you know, and wondered if I might come in and check on him."

"Why doesn't she come in herself?" Danny wondered.

"Oh, she has those little kids, you know," Hazel said, thinking quickly and hoping that Trudy really hadn't been in to visit. "She doesn't really want the little ones to see their daddy in jail and she doesn't have much help with them, you know." Hazel had said 'you know' one too many times, surely Danny would be on to her.

"I see," Danny shrugged, the turquoise unwavering. "I'll write you up a pass and you can go on down there and give it to Brandon."

"Thanks, Danny," Hazel said as he wrote something on a clipboard and handed her a lanyard with some kind of card attached to it. Hazel eyed the list of visitors, trying to see if anyone else had been in to visit Wallis. She couldn't make anything out though and made a mental note to ask Jason about it later.

She headed through the needlessly wide and grand corridors of the courthouse, passing the offices of a half a dozen government officials but no other actual people.

Finally, she made it through to the very back corner where the police station was. Hazel had never meddled in police business before, and she knew Uncle John wouldn't like it. He was extremely proprietary about the police department. Thirty-five years of service did that to a person.

"Hi there, Mrs. Dean," Brandon said, his eyebrows raised. "We've never seen you down here before."

Hazel handed him her pass. Brandon had only been working for the police department for about five years, but

Hazel got to know him well because he had married Nora's little sister. Between her and Uncle John, their paths frequently crossed at social events. Jason was always floored by the connections everyone had to everyone else in Red Gap. "How are you and Bailey doing?" she asked.

"Just fine," Brandon said. "She just got a promotion at the hospital."

"Of course, she did," Hazel said. "She's brilliant."

Brandon smiled broadly, his pride casting a rusty gold smudge around him. "I came in to see Wallis Trudgeon... On behalf of his wife," she added.

Brandon nodded. Her lie must have seemed plausible to him because he led her past the swinging partition to the holding area. A spacious kind of hallway led to four secure rooms. Two were large ones for holding multiple people, maybe for overnight dry outs, one for men and one for women. As Hazel had learned from her research on the McClearys, drunk and disorderly conduct was the main reason people were arrested in Red Gap. The two smaller cells had cots and crude toilets in them, designed for longer stays and more serious infractions. Wallis was in one of these cells.

The man clearly hadn't been allowed a razor since he was locked up a few days previously, or he had refused to groom himself. His beard had grown unevenly, thick in some spots and patchy in others. His hair had been longish when he was arrested, and now it was greasy and sticking to his head and face. He sat on the cot, throwing a ball against the wall repeatedly, just like Steve McQueen in *The Great Escape*.

"Wish he'd stop doing that," Brandon muttered. "I offered him a book to read, but he said no thanks."

Hazel nodded. There was a definite eggplant smoke hanging in the air around Wallis.

"I'd like to talk to him privately," she told Brandon.

He raised an eyebrow at her. "Are you sure?" he asked. "He hasn't been the most docile inmate I've ever seen."

"Yes, I'm quite sure," she said.

"Alright," Brandon said. "But I don't want Captain Tate to skewer me if things don't go the way you plan."

"I don't want him to skewer me either," Hazel smiled.

"You can chat in this room," Brandon showed her a sound-proof room next to the cells she hadn't noticed previously. "It's where people talk to their lawyers."

"That's fine," she said.

"I'm keeping him cuffed to the chair, and it's got that two-way mirror thing going on so I'll be right here watching in case things get dicey. You should be perfectly safe, but sometimes these guys can surprise you with their creativity."

Hazel furrowed her eyebrows at him and stepped into the small room, taking a seat in the chair opposite the mirror so Brandon wouldn't be able to see Wallis' face or read his lips. Just in case.

A second later, Brandon came in, pushing Wallis into the room in front of him. He guided Wallis towards the chair opposite Hazel and sat him down, then cuffed him to the chair he was sitting in.

"Alright then," he said. "Just wave if you need me. I'll be watching." The last words he said in a menacing voice clearly meant for Wallis. He backed out of the room and the door closed softly.

"Miss Randolph." Wallis growled. "What are you doing here?" It was gravelly and hostile. His eggplant color had turned into a darker raisin. Almost black, but not quite.

"It's Mrs. Dean," Hazel corrected him. "I'm here because I was a friend of Cash McCleary and I believe you are innocent of his murder."

Wallis blinked at her. "You what?"

"I don't think you killed Cash," she said.

"Well, that's interesting," he said, the raisin color lightening to almost lavender. "Because I did."

Hazel's mouth dropped open. "No, you didn't," she said. "I know that you didn't."

"You don't know that," he said, leaning back in his chair as much as he could.

"But I do," she said.

"Okay, crazy lady," he shrugged.

"But you've been maintaining your innocence this whole time."

He shrugged. "I got sick of lying."

She narrowed her eyes at him. "I don't believe you," she said.

"Believe what you want."

"But your sweet wife, your babies..."

His casual demeanor disappeared, his aura darkening again. He leaned towards her over the table and pointed a finger at her. "What do you know about my family?" he hissed. "Just stay away from them. You're the last thing they need right now."

Hazel's mouth opened and closed while she tried to think of another question, one that would give her more information.

"But..."

He leaned back in his chair again, back to lavender. "Listen, crazy lady, if that's all you have to say I'd just as soon get back to throwing my ball against the wall."

"Why?" she finally blurted. "Why would you kill him?"

He shrugged again. It was driving her crazy how casual he was. "The feud. I hate all those McClearys."

She looked at him, rolling her eyes. "Do you?"

"Yes, I've hated them my whole life," he said.

"Of course you have," she said, completely exasperated. "Tell me what happened," she demanded.

He smiled like he had been dying for her to ask him that.

"The scumbags were talking about raping a girl. I wouldn't want to reveal too much about what they were saying in your delicate company, but it was shocking and I don't think any kind of gentleman would have been able to stand there and take it without doing something. So I just shot one of them at random."

"I don't believe you," Hazel shook her head. "It's too extreme. Even if you had shot them in a fit of rage, why wouldn't you have gone to the police instead? Told them it was an accident?"

"My blood was boiling in my veins, ma'am," he said. "I didn't mean to kill anyone. Scare them, yes, maybe maim them a bit. It was too bad I hit Cash like that. He was the best one of the bunch, not that that's saying too much."

Hazel shook her head. She wouldn't let him sidetrack her. "Why were you in the woods that night? Your wife told me that you disappear sometimes, that she doesn't know where you go."

Wallis' face turned hard again, his color instantly darkening again. Hazel couldn't remember ever conversing with anyone so emotionally volatile. "What were you doing talking to my wife?" he growled through gritted teeth.

"I brought her dinner. I was just trying to help her out since you landed yourself in jail."

"My wife is none of your business!" he yelled.

Hazel flinched but didn't move. "Where do you go?" she pressed. "She said you are supposed to be out with colleagues and then you're not. She said you sometimes don't come home from work until hours after you're supposed to." Hazel stood up and pressed her fingertips into the table between them. "When I came to your house and told her that I thought you were innocent, she burst into tears. Do you understand? She was crying, sobbing."

Wallis' purple was changing rapidly into a vivid azure blue, although his facial expression didn't change.

"She told me she was glad that I thought you were innocent because she wasn't sure." Hazel leaned forward over the table towards him, pointing her finger in his face. "She wasn't sure. She thought there was a distinct possibility that *you* had done it. I looked at her and I thought this poor, poor woman. What kind of man is she married to that even she, his wife, can't convince herself from a place of blind love that her husband isn't a murderer? I knew I had to come down here and look at the face of that man."

Wallis still had the audacity to be looking straight at her. The blue sizzled around him with an emotion that Hazel was at a loss to identify.

"And it turns out your wife was right? You are a murderer?"

He finally broke eye contact with her and looked down at his hands. Hazel stared down at his head for a full minute, letting him feel whatever that blue was.

"I don't believe it," Hazel said finally. "You didn't kill Cash McCleary. And I'm going to prove it."

His eyes snapped back up to hers. "Good luck," he snapped, his color changing again, back to the eggplant.

"Thanks," she said, getting up. Brandon met her at the door and let her out.

"Thank you Brandon," she said, then quickly walked down the hallway back towards her car, pulling out her cell phone as she went.

"Hello Hazel," Jason answered.

"Jason," Hazel said, unable to keep a little breathlessness out of her voice. "Jason, when are they going down to the construction site?"

"Hazel..." Jason said gently. "Can I meet you somewhere? I'm out at this ridiculous diner. Can you come here? Do you want me to come down to the shop?"

Hazel blinked. Jason hadn't been down to the shop in over a year. "What's going on?" she said.

"I'd just like to tell you in person."

Hazel knew what he was going to say, but she couldn't admit that she knew what he was going to say. So she agreed to meet him at the shop. She needed a triple chocolate chunk cookie. And some of her escapist hot chocolate. "Did you find out anything about Cash's car?" she asked.

"No, not really. I'll tell you everything when I see you."

"Alright then." She rushed through the courthouse and back to her car. Sometimes Main Street was blocked by big trucks unloading stuff or by tourists driving at two miles an hour and ogling over how adorable the town was. Today she was lucky and made it to the shop in less than ten minutes. She opened the shop back up, inhaling the scent of old books and chocolate. It calmed her. Her heart stopped racing and her fists unclenched. She wandered into the verdant green/cobalt blue section of her store. The section of comfort and contentment. She ran her fingers along the titles. *The Hobbit, Little Women, The Night Circus, Harry Potter*, all of Jane Austen. She felt better just looking at the covers. She pulled out *The Princess Bride* and started reading at a random page in the middle.

Fifteen minutes later, Jason found her sitting in the middle of the aisle, completely engrossed in the book.

"Inventory huh?" he said, taking her hand to pull her up off the floor.

"I was just feeling a little anxious," she said, holding up the book. "Fezzik helps."

"Of course," Jason said. "Come on. You promised me a cookie."

They headed to the back of the shop. Hazel still loved the magical feeling of the dark, cluttered book shop opening up into a light-flooded room full of greenery and coziness.

"You did a really good job with this place," Jason said, admiring the view.

"Thank you," she said. Jason didn't usually like talking about the bookshop.

The two ladies that came in the mornings to bake were already gone. Hazel grabbed the most chocolate-y thing on her menu for herself. Then she made herself the escapism hot chocolate and poured Jason a cup of coffee, black. She didn't even mention to him that the chocolate peanut butter explosion bars were available, trying to support his new diet. Jason had lit a fire in the hearth, and they settled into her favorite chairs. Cash had sat in one of them when he first came into her shop three weeks prior. It didn't seem like that long ago to her.

Jason took a sip of his coffee, then leaned into the high-backed overstuffed chair. He was his typical work-mode beige, but the edges were a bit green, his worried color. Hazel was always amused by Jason's obsession with being professional. It made it so obvious that he was an outsider in this town. He wanted to prove to everyone that he deserved the position that Hazel's family name had procured for him. She loved his earnest face.

"Hazel, I have to tell you something that will upset you," he began.

She nodded. She knew what he was going to say.

"Wallis Trudgeon confessed to killing Cash McCleary." Jason spoke carefully and slowly, trying not to imbue any emotions into his words. He watched her reaction, like she might lash out or pitch a fit.

She pushed her hair out of her face and nodded again.

"He said that he was out hunting and overheard them saying some inappropriate things," Jason went on. "It made him so mad that he shot at them without specifically aiming at anything. Cash's death was an accident."

Hazel blinked at him. "An accident?"

"Yes, Wallis made a very dumb choice and he will probably

be convicted of manslaughter. I heard he brought in a defense attorney. They're working out a plea bargain as we speak."

Jason droned on, spouting different legal scenarios. Hazel's mind wandered to the chubby face of the toddler she read to at the Trudgeon's house. She had never asked his name.

"Okay," Hazel said. "What about the investigation at the trailer? What about Cash's car?"

"Hazel? Did you hear me? Wallis confessed, he's guilty. It's over. The arraignment's like a week away."

"Yes, but Chris Mills. Who knows what he's doing! Probably not just an innocent hikers hotel! It has to have something to do with drugs."

"Hazel," Jason was using his patient voice that he used on the kids when they were upset about something trivial. His neutral beige was being overtaken by the dark green. "Maybe that's a whole other investigation. Right now, the focus is on finding out what happened to Cash. In this country, we don't actually go after people for having a shady past."

"That's ridiculous," Hazel said.

"It doesn't matter if you think it's ridiculous or not. It's civil liberty. You know, the founding fathers, life, liberty, the pursuit of happiness?"

"Yes, yes, okay, fine," she said. She didn't want to hear one of Jason's patriotic legal monologues. The wheels in her mind were spinning out of control. Maybe the double dose of super chocolate-y sugar bombs was a bad idea.

"Hazel," Jason said. The green darkened and overtook him, casting a shadow over his face. "Hazel, what are you doing? I know that look. Don't. It's not your prerogative. It's not your job. Just leave it alone. The public defense attorney is going to do a great job with Wallis' case. He'll be fine. Just let it go."

"No," Hazel said. "No, I don't believe it. I still think he's innocent."

Jason didn't say anything. He just shook his head.

"He didn't do it," Hazel said. "I can feel it. I just know when I look at him."

"Why would a man with a wife and two little kids at home confess to manslaughter if he didn't actually do it?" Jason asked, his voice tinged with exasperation.

Hazel flinched. That was the question that had been mulling in her own head since she talked to Wallis.

ELEVEN

"I'd better get back to work," Jason said, setting his half empty coffee cup on the table. "Things are about to get really busy."

"You mean building your case against Wallis?" Hazel spat. She knew that Jason was only doing his job, but she was still upset with him for it.

"Hazel," he said, ignoring her irritation. "You know we'll never be able to try him here. The case will be transferred somewhere else, where no one has connections to the McClearys or Trudgeons. I'll have a bunch of paperwork to do though, and I'll have to hand my notes to the new prosecutor."

Still a bit miffed, Hazel nodded at him curtly.

"I have a few other cases I'm working on too. Captain Tate is still really pushing me to build a case against whoever he arrested the other day in connection with those semi truck robberies. It doesn't seem like he has much to go on, but he's really pressuring me. Technically, it's my call. I know that's how you talked me into running for DA to begin with, the power not to prosecute. I was driving you crazy with my 'the South is so racist' rants. I guess I was naïve. I didn't realize how upset your uncle would get if I disagreed with him. I should have, it's not like I'm allowed to disagree with him about anything else, but I didn't... am I boring you Hazel?"

Hazel had gotten up and started clearing their dishes. "I'm sorry, Jason," she said automatically.

Jason's eyes narrowed. He got out of the chair and followed her into the kitchen. "You're distracted. I hope you're not planning on doing anything rash."

"I won't, don't worry." She set the dishes down in the sink.

"I do worry," he said, resting his hands on her shoulders. "You tend to act first and think after."

"But that's why you love me," she said, snuggling into his chest.

"Sometimes," Jason smiled, wrapping his arms around her. "Remember when we met? You had climbed onto the roof because you wanted to see the stars better."

"The window was so limiting," Hazel complained. "I had everything under control."

"Sure, you did," Jason snorted. "You practically had frostbite when I brought that ladder over."

"I hadn't even tried to come back in yet. Elizabeth over-reacted."

"I'm just glad I happened to be the neighbor with a ladder in his basement." Jason leaned down to kiss her.

Hazel smiled and kissed him back. "Me too," she said, pushing him away playfully. "Well, go get some work done. I don't want you to have to stay late and miss dinner."

Jason kissed her one more time, then headed out the door to get back to work.

Hazel tidied up the cafe before putting on her coat. She was headed up front to close the shop when she heard voices. Customers.

Hazel didn't often get random customers on a weekday. October weekends could get a bit busy with people traveling to various festivals and apple orchards, but the middle of the week was usually dead.

"Hi there," she called, emerging from the aisle into the front of the store. "Can I help you?"

A well-dressed man was looking at the first bookshelf of books. He turned towards her. He looked familiar, but she couldn't quite place him. She squinted as surreptitiously as she could at him, tilting her head to one side, then she muffled a gasp. It was Chris Mills, she recognized him from his LinkedIn profile. He wore his hair slicked back like he had when he had appeared before city council. He tilted his cell phone away from his mouth and whispered. "Sorry, this is rude. Just give me a minute." He smiled at her and she recoiled at the sight of those sharp incisors. His suit was cheap. She could see it clinging to his shin where static had built up. He exuded an oily purple.

She nodded mutely and wandered towards the register desk to pretend to tidy something up, acting like she wasn't listening to the conversation.

"No, I know it's a lot," Mills said quietly into the phone. "I have to go. I have to, uh," he glanced at Hazel, "pick something up."

Hazel's face settled into a frown.

"Just tell them I'll get back to them," he said, ending the call and putting the phone in his pocket. "I'm sorry about that," he said, crossing the room towards her. His predatory smile unnerved Hazel. "Terribly rude to be on the phone when someone is trying to assist you."

"No trouble at all," Hazel said, willing her voice to stay even.

"I'm Chris Mills," he said, sticking his hand out.

"Hazel Dean," she said, putting her hand into his overly strong handshake for a brief second before snatching it back.

"Mrs. Dean, huh?" he asked. "Any relation to the county prosecutor?"

"My husband," she said shortly, the corners of her mouth barely lifting.

"Small town," he smirked. "Nasty business about Cash McCleary, isn't it? He actually worked for me. I heard that you were friendly with him."

"Did you?" she said. "He came into the store a few times."

"Gotcha, so more of a customer than a friend."

Hazel nodded once.

"The other boys told me that he wrote you some kind of note before he died."

Gooseflesh broke out on Hazel's arm, and she rubbed it away. "Yes," she said.

"I hope you don't mind my asking," Chris Mills' smile reminded her of an alligator. He moved in sudden, twitchy jerks. Like an addict. "But I really liked Cash, and I am just devastated by his death."

"Right," Hazel said, drawing the word out in distrust. The slimy purple didn't exactly evoke devastation. More like deception.

"I just wondered why he would write you a note?"

Hazel narrowed her eyes at this man whom she viewed as an enemy. She decided that the truth would scare him the most, but leave him with the least reason to come after her. "I gave him his first book for free: *To Kill A Mockingbird*. He wrote a note to tell me how much it meant to him and how the book helped him make some decisions. He didn't know that he was going to die when he wrote it."

Mills pretended to get choked up with some crocodile tears. Hazel had seen fake crying too many times in her career as a stay-at-home mom to be convinced. He nodded, coughing into a fist. "I see. That is a great book, isn't it?"

Hazel nodded. "I had a feeling it would help him out when I handed it to him. Now if you'll excuse me." She stepped out from behind the register and gestured for him to head towards the door. "If you're not shopping today, I was just about to go meet my boys for lunch when you walked in."

"Of course," he said, giving a smarmy smile. "I am sorry. I wouldn't want to keep you."

"Thank you," she said, herding him out the door and locking it behind her. "Sorry I couldn't be more help to you."

He looked at her sideways for a few moments before replying. "You were very helpful, Mrs. Dean." He had abandoned the overly friendly tone he had in the shop, his voice turned low and cold. He turned on a heel and walked off down Main Street. Hazel shuddered. Unfortunately, he was walking in the direction of her car. Releasing a shaky breath, she decided to walk the other way for five minutes before turning around and going back towards her car. She hopped in and drove straight to Trudy's house.

When she neared Trudy's house, she saw a shiny red convertible sitting in front of it and none other than Chris Mills striding purposefully across the lawn. Hazel ducked in her seat and turned her face away so he wouldn't recognize her if he turned towards her. She passed Trudy's house and drove down the street and around the block, unsure of what to do next. She desperately needed to talk to Trudy, but what was Chris Mills doing there? What did he want with Hazel? He almost seemed to be conducting his own clandestine investigation.

She drove around the block and down the street five times, but the red convertible remained in front of Trudy's house. Hazel found a nearby park and sat in the parking lot, setting her watch timer for fifteen minutes. Mills would have to be done questioning Trudy by then. There was nothing to do but sit in the car and think about the case. The more she thought about it, the more confused she became. All the questions chasing each other around in her head kept bringing her back to one big one. Why would Wallis admit that he killed Cash when he hadn't? She hoped Trudy would help her answer that question.

When the timer went off, she drove to Trudy's house and saw that the convertible was gone. She parked where it had been sitting before and kicked herself for forgetting to bring any treats.

She knocked on the storm door and the front door opened almost immediately. Hazel expected Trudy to smile and invite her in. She thought Trudy would be happy to see her. She did not expect the suspicious and almost hostile expression that darkened Trudy's face as soon as she registered that Hazel was at the door.

"I don't want to talk to you," Trudy declared, closing the door a bit.

"Wait, Trudy," Hazel said. "What happened? Why was Chris Mills here?"

"None of your business," she snapped.

"But we had such a nice chat the other day," Hazel pointed out. The bottom fell out of her stomach. She felt sick. "What happened? I thought you were glad that I was going to find out who really killed Cash and get your husband out of jail."

"My husband *did* kill Cash McCleary, and you were just here to confuse me," Trudy snapped. "I don't want to see or hear from you again. And if you don't leave my property immediately, I will call the police." Then she slammed the door hard, rattling the storm door in its hinges.

Hazel felt a little dizzy. Her interaction with Trudy was so far from what she had anticipated that it left her reeling. What could cause such a bizarre one-eighty in attitude? Hazel got back into her car, wondering what to do next. She tried not to ruminate on Trudy's hateful expression when she slammed the door. She thought about LaShay. How was she going to take all of this when she found out? Hazel was tempted to call her right then if she could just think of a way to explain how she had so much information about Wallis. She sighed. Everything was spiraling out of control.

She started the car and found herself driving towards the construction site. She wouldn't dare turn down the street, not during the day. She didn't want the McClearys or even Chris Mills himself to observe her, but she couldn't shake the feeling that was where she would find the answers she was looking for. She passed the turn in to the construction site and was surprised to see that there was a new gate blocking the road. She took the next turn towards a hiking hub instead. It was a lesser used one that didn't easily connect to the Appalachian Trail. The parking lot was empty, but she didn't park. Instead, Hazel turned around in a wide circle and drove back to the highway, this time heading towards home.

* * *

AS SHE DROVE, Hazel sorted out what she knew in her head. She tried to read between the lines. No one had reported Cash's truck missing. The McClearys were looking for it on their own. Hazel suspected that the truck was at the real scene of Cash's death. It might have some answers if she could find it. The problem was, she had absolutely no idea where to look.

As she was getting out of the car, her phone rang. She didn't recognize the number.

"Hello? This is Hazel."

"Hazel," said a voice that was familiar and yet distantly so. "This is Jolene Lawson."

Hazel spluttered. "Jolene?" she tried to think of the last time she had heard from Jolene.

"I understand you've been talking to my client. You believe he's innocent."

"Your *client*?" Hazel set down her purse in the mudroom and began to pace back and forth in her living room.

"As a courtesy, I thought I'd let you know that Trudy Trudgeon is talking about getting a restraining order against you."

"Against me?" Hazel's surprise at hearing from Jolene was giving way to irritation. Of course she would get herself wrapped up in this. Even in high school, Jolene always managed to get involved in Hazel's business. "Listen, Jolene-"

"I talked her out of it for now," Jolene cut her off. "But you should stay away from the Trudgeons, Hazel. You always did want to help people who were better off without you. I guess it's some kind of deluded Savior fantasy."

"Jolene, let's not make this about us-"

"I hope I won't have to contact you again," Jolene cut her off again and then hung up.

Hazel stared at the phone in her hand for a moment, then threw it into the couch where it bounced harmlessly. "That insufferable..." she grumbled and muttered to herself, her blood boiling. "Who does she think she is?" Hazel knew that her anger at Jolene was, admittedly, misdirected, but it was so easy to fall back into old habits. She stomped around the house looking for a steno notebook and tried to put Jolene's call out of her head.

She settled into Jason's chair in the family room and started drawing. If she was going to figure out what was really going on, she would need to make some connections. The first one was easy. She wrote down Wallis Trudgeon and Chris Mills and drew a line between the two. On the line, she wrote mentor and business partner. Then she wrote down McClearys and drew a line to Chris Mills. On that line she wrote working for.

Hazel frowned. If Chris Mills had been so close with Wallis, and Wallis hated the McClearys so much, why would he hire them to build his hotel? She shook her head. Something just wasn't adding up.

At the bottom of the page, she wrote "Waylon Gibbons." She drew a big question mark next to him. Cash's note in *To Kill*

A Mockingbird kept coming back to her. Cash thought that he was similar to Boo Radley, a kindly but eccentric character that the children in the book thought was a monster.

Waylon Gibbons wasn't a common name like Chris Mills. Hazel tried to remember the steps Jeremiah took when he found Chris Mills on the internet. She got out of her comfy chair and sat down at the computer. This time she opened several tabs. One to Facebook, one to LinkedIn, and in her history, she found the background check site that Jeremiah had used to find Chris Mills' legal entanglements. She typed in Waylon Gibbons on each site, but not a thing came up. Stumped, she made her was back to the overstuffed chair.

She was back to square one. She wrote the word "Lying" on the page and underlined it forcefully. Underneath she wrote Wallis Trudgeon. She was sure he was lying about killing Cash. Next, she wrote Eugene. Hazel didn't believe Eugene when he told her Cash rode to the construction site in the back of Billy's truck that day. Why would Eugene lie? McClearys. They were lying about Wallis killing Cash and potentially about where Cash died. Chris Mills. She wasn't exactly sure what he was lying about, but it had to be something.

Hazel got out Cash's letter to her again and reread it. She wished that she could just ask him a few questions. Why hadn't he been more specific about the illegal jobs Billy wanted them to take? Building a hotel seemed innocuous enough. It must have been something else.

Hazel thought of Wallis' history of drug abuse, Eugene's extensive knowledge of drugs, and Chris Mills' involvement in illegal pharmaceutical sales. It had to be something to do with drugs, and they were all in on it somehow. Without any other leads, Hazel would never find out how.

Hazel gritted her teeth. One way or another, she was going to find some new evidence. At the bottom of her list of liars, she wrote one more person. **Me.**

TWELVE

Hazel wasn't going to tell anyone her plan this time. It was actually dangerous, and both Nora and Jason would try to talk her out of it. There were precautions that she needed to take though, so she called Uncle John.

"Hello there, darlin'" he boomed when he answered her call.

"Hi, John," she said. "How are things?"

"They would be better if you could talk some sense into that husband of yours," John grumbled. "I keep arresting people and he keeps letting them walk. But how are you doing? I was worried about you the other night."

"I'm okay," she said. "I'm feeling a bit better. I thought maybe I'd go shooting."

John chuckled. "That's a wonderful idea! I'm working right now, but I can make myself available later tonight."

Hazel hesitated. "I thought maybe I'd just go by myself this time," she said.

John was silent on the other end of the line for a moment. "Well, okay then. They're your guns, after all. You don't need my permission to use it."

"Thanks again for letting me keep it at your house. I don't think Jason will ever be okay with me having it at our place. Maybe when the boys are grown."

"I still can't figure out what kind of man you married..." John scoffed. "Doesn't want a gun in the house..."

"Hey!" Hazel snapped. "It's no wonder he thinks you hate him. You've got to stop goading him all the time. Jason believes that guns escalate violence. He's entitled to his opinion and to feel comfortable in his own home."

"I guess..." John said sheepishly. "*I'd* feel more comfortable if you and the boys had proper protection."

"Well, it's not your decision right now," Hazel went on. "It's our decision. Now, I need my gun for the day, and I just wanted to let you know that I was letting myself in so you wouldn't think you had been robbed or anything."

"Hazel, I'm sorry," John could tell he had crossed a line. "You're right. You two have a good marriage and some wonderful children. I don't want to cause problems."

"Sure, you don't."

"I don't!" he protested. "I'll back off. Not at work, but with the family, I will. I promise."

Hazel smiled. "Thanks, Uncle John," she said. They'd had this conversation before and she knew they would again. But Hazel knew that everything John did was from a place of love and concern for her, so she could never stay mad at him. "I'll call you later."

"Have fun shooting. Should help relieve some stress." He said before hanging up.

Hazel walked down the street to John's house and let herself in with the key. Uncle John had multiple gun safes in his house and Hazel had guns in several of them. Most of them had been gifts from Uncle John. He had taught her to shoot after her parents died, and it was something that they did together throughout her life.

John's house screamed interminable bachelorhood. It wasn't a disgusting mess, but there was an air of untidiness about it. Hazel knew that John only used three rooms in the house and the rest were filled with things he'd collected over the years.

She opened a built-in cupboard in the den, revealing a gun safe about the size of a desktop computer. She typed in the code and pulled out her .22 pistol and put it in her bag. She didn't expect that she would have to shoot anything on her outing that night, but carrying the gun made her feel safer and more in control.

After she made her way back home, she found one of her son's duffel bags and put the gun in a side pocket carefully. She proceeded to put in all the black clothing that she could find. She had black leggings and a black t-shirt. Her trail shoes weren't black. Hazel didn't know the distance she would need to hike, and she didn't want blisters, so she put them in the bag too. She rummaged through her sons' drawers and found a black beanie and black cotton gloves. She had a black puffy jacket with a fur-trimmed hood that would work. Then she broke into her husband's closet of gadgets and pulled out some night vision goggles. She had bought them for him as a Christmas gift a few years previously when he was really into playing capture the flag in the dark with the boys and their friends. She zipped up the duffel bag and threw it in the trunk of her Toyota Corolla. Too bad the car wasn't black.

There was nothing else to do for at least an hour before her family came home and another couple hours after that before it would get dark. She turned on her podcast feed, just to have some noise in the background to distract her. But she was still anxiously tapping her foot and playing with her hair. Finally, after feeling suffocated by anxiety, she jumped off the couch and decided it was time to clean out the kitchen. She was on

the floor surrounded by pots and pans and Tupperware when
Jeremiah came home.

"Whoa," he said. "Bad day, Mom?"

She glared wordlessly at him.

"So that's a yes," he said, dropping all his school junk on the
floor. "Can I just step... over... here..." He took awkwardly sized
steps to get to the fridge. He grabbed some cheese and salami.
"And then over... here..." he tiptoed over to the pantry to grab
the crackers. "Then I'll be out of your way," he said, headed
towards the dining room.

"Put away your stuff! And don't you *dare* take that upstairs!"
she yelled after him. She knew that Elias and Jason wouldn't be
too far behind him, so she started putting things away. By the
time Jason walked in, the only things left on the floor were
things she was planning to take to Goodwill.

Jason froze in the doorway to the kitchen. "What's all this?"
he said tentatively.

"Stuff I'm donating."

Jason's eyebrows came together. "Feeling a little stressed,
huh?"

Hazel glared at him too.

"Wait a second," he said, pulling a stack of taco plates off
the floor. "You can't get rid of the taco plates!"

"They're a uni-tasker," Hazel shrugged. "We don't use them
enough to make it worth it to keep them."

"Well then, we're not eating enough tacos in this house,"
Jason said, opening an empty cupboard and putting the plates
on a shelf. "It's not like we don't have space for them," he
added.

"Fine," Hazel said, suddenly less interested in cleaning out
the kitchen. More than anything, she wanted to tell him about
the call from Jolene, but she couldn't do that without also
revealing that she had gone to see Wallis. Her insides clenched
uncomfortably, thinking about the lies she had already told

and the lies she would tell. She took a deep breath and spat out the words she had practiced, hoping that Jason wouldn't notice her face turning red. "So, I'm going to go sit for Nora tonight for a couple of hours."

"Oh," Jason said. "You'll be gone?"

"Yeah," Hazel said, avoiding eye contact. "Nora and Sam want to go see that new movie, so I told them I would come sit with the kids late after they were in bed."

"Oh, good idea," Jason said. He thought for a moment and then smiled, his pallor changing to a pink that she recognized. It made her blush. "What if I come with you?"

"Come with me?" Hazel's face flushed even more.

"Yeah, it'll be fun. Kind of like a date." He wiggled his eyebrows. "We can make out on their couch."

"Uhhh..." Hazel fumbled.

"Mom?" Elias came in through the garage, and the tone of his voice made Hazel freeze.

"What's wrong? -You're home early." Hazel asked. She was terrified that he was going to say that he was in a car accident again. She started thinking about how they should punish him, because this was getting to be a problem.

"What's the matter, son?" Jason asked.

"I came home to tell you... It's Eugene," Elias said.

"Oh no, is he hurt again?" Hazel said.

"Not exactly," Elias was pale and the air surrounding him had a vivid orange hue. Hazel recognized it as anxiety. Elias was not a particularly emotional kid. He almost always had a faint and extremely neutral blue-ish gray tinge to him. "He's still at school," Elias went on. "He had kind of a breakdown today. I don't think they know what to do with him."

Hazel was already grabbing her keys and rushing to get her shoes on.

"I'm coming with you," Jason said, heading to the car right behind Hazel. They left their sons at home and drove as fast as legally possible to the high school. Hazel would have sped if Jason hadn't been in the car.

"What will they do with him, Jason?"

"They'll call CPS, almost assuredly. They'll already have a basic grasp of his precarious family situation. Then with Cash's death on top of that..."

Hazel parked haphazardly and ran towards the office. The door was locked.

"Curse these new safety protocols," Hazel grumbled, jabbing at the button to alert someone she was there.

"How can I help you?" said a cheery voice from the intercom. Jason had caught up to her now, breathing hard.

"This is Hazel Randolph Dean. I'm here to pick up Eugene McCleary."

Silence was on the other end. "Just a minute," she said at last.

Hazel glanced at her watch. School ended an hour previously. The staff would be looking to go home soon. She was hoping that would work to her advantage, not against her.

"Hazel?" the intercom spoke again. "I don't think we can legally release him to you, you're not on any of his emergency forms."

"Is that you, Tonya?" Hazel asked.

"Yes," she said.

"Tonya, you let me into that school this minute. I am not a security risk, and talking over the intercom is ridiculous. I've known you since fourth grade."

"Oh alright," Tonya relented. A buzzing sound came from the door and Hazel ran to grab it before it closed again. Jason followed her into the office.

"Tonya, I'm taking Eugene McCleary home with me. I'll sign anything I need to sign or do whatever I have to do."

Tonya twisted her lips to the side, deliberating for a moment before making a decision. "I'll get Mr. Robertson."

Hazel fidgeted while Tonya disappeared.

"He was a friend of your grandmother's, right?" Jason asked. "It's hard for me to keep all these small-town connections straight."

Hazel nodded as Mr. Robertson, the principal of the high school, appeared. "Hello, Hazel," Mr. Robertson said. "And I recognize your husband." Mr. Robertson put out his hand to shake with Jason. "I understand you are looking for custody of Eugene McCleary?"

"Well, custody is a strong word," Jason stammered.

"We don't want him to go into the system at all," Hazel said.

"I'm afraid it might be a little late for that," Mr. Robertson said. "The school psychologist has been meeting with him since his brother's death, and we've learned a lot about his current situation. With his outburst today, we've gathered enough evidence to call CPS. He'll be placed into temporary foster care while his home situation is evaluated."

Tears came to Hazel's eyes. "Hasn't that poor boy been through enough?" she cried, her voice heavy with emotion.

Jason put an arm around Hazel to steady her and looked directly into the principal's eye. "What does temporary foster care entail?" Jason asked.

"It is a soft place for the child to land until the safety issues at home have been resolved. Ideally, he will go back home soon."

"We can do that," Jason said.

"Oh, Jason," Hazel bit her lip to keep from crying. "Thank you."

"Usually, the approval to become emergency foster care providers takes several months, but I think, under the circumstances and considering Eugene's age, going to stay at a friend's house for a little while would be appropriate. I'll get a form for you to sign in the short term and a social worker will probably contact you tomorrow."

"So we can take Eugene home right now?"

"I don't see why not," Mr. Robertson said.

"Where is he?" Hazel asked, releasing a sigh of relief.

"He is in the psychologist's office. He's not coping with the loss of his brother very well, I'm afraid."

They followed Mr. Robertson through the deserted school hallway. The psychologist's office bizarrely had windows facing the hallway, and they could see Eugene through them, fidgeting on a large beanbag chair. He jumped up when he noticed them coming towards him out the window and began to pace nervously. The psychologist left her office and met them in the hallway.

"He's calmed down a lot," she said.

Mr. Robertson nodded. "This is Hazel and Jason Dean. They are going to be taking over temporary custody of Eugene."

The psychologist's aura tinged blue with relief. "Oh good. Thank you. He is experiencing a range of emotions, but I think he's mostly just exhausted. He'll be able to cope so much better if he can just get some rest. He is exhibiting an unusual amount of sensitivity to the way his brothers are grieving for a child his age."

Hazel nodded. "We'll take care of him. Not to worry."

"I think you should keep him home from school tomorrow as well," the psychologist continued. "I think he's kept coming because he doesn't want to be at home, but maybe he'll be more comfortable in a neutral location." She turned around to glance at Eugene through the window. "If you'll wait here, I'll let him know what's going on. I don't know how he'll react. It might be a minute."

Hazel watched her walk back through the door and begin talking to Eugene. He glanced up at them for an instant, so she smiled and waved at him. He didn't smile back. Hazel noticed that he had begun to emit a red glow, similar to the one he had the other night when Jason teased him about his brains and athletic abilities. Something in Hazel's heart cracked a bit. The boy was embarrassed. She fidgeted with her keys until Jason reached out and grabbed her hand.

"Everything is going to work out fine," he murmured to her. She gave him a grateful smile.

After another minute of conversation with the psychologist, Eugene picked up his backpack and slung it over his shoulder. Then he walked out of the office towards them. He wasn't using the crutches, but he walked with a distinct limp.

"I guess I'm in your debt again," he mumbled, looking at his toes. "Thank you kindly." He was so red that Hazel thought that perhaps it might hurt to touch him. But that was silly. She reached for him and pulled him into a hug.

"We don't mind at all," Hazel said when she released him. "Our boys love having you around. And they could learn a thing or two from you about manners."

"It's just for a little while anyways," Jason said, clapping a large hand on Eugene's shoulder. "Why don't you let me take that backpack for you? You're still limping."

"I'm fine," Eugene said.

Jason looked like he would push the issue, but then shrugged. "Alright, this way to the car. We don't want to be late for dinner. Elias might start eating the furniture."

* * *

ELIAS WAS PACING in the kitchen when they got home. Hazel recognized relief wash over him when they came in with Eugene.

"Eugene is going to be staying with us for a few days," Jason said. "Elias, can you make sure that the guest room is ready for him?"

Without a word, Elias took the backpack out of Eugene's hands and disappeared.

"He was worried about you," Hazel said. But then Eugene turned red again, and Hazel wished she hadn't said anything.

Jeremiah appeared from another room. "Hey Eugene! Back again? You needed some video game lessons? Hey Mom, now that Eugene's back, are you going to make dessert again? How's your ankle, Eugene? Well, come on. I'll queue up the game."

Hazel smiled. Her younger son's casual acceptance of Eugene's presence was exactly what he needed. Eugene's redness faded. He looked over at her, and she nodded, so he hobbled after Jeremiah into the family room.

Hazel glanced at Jason. "We're having tacos for dinner."

Jason grinned. "Nice," he said and started grabbing toppings out of the fridge. "So, this'll be fine. I'm already off Wallis' case at work, so that shouldn't present a problem with conflict of interest or anything. I'll just let the Judge Proust know anyways, just in case. Eugene will just hang out with the boys. Like Jeremiah suddenly has a twin."

Hazel frowned. She got a pan out to brown some ground beef. "Maybe," she murmured. "Hopefully, that's all it is."

"What do you mean?" Jason asked, cutting into an avocado.

"Eugene might need a little more maintenance than that," Hazel said. "You heard the psychologist. He's not well."

"She said he needed some rest," Jason said. "Like emotional rest, it sounded like to me. What would be better than hanging out and playing video games with a couple of carefree boys your own age?"

Hazel nodded. "You're right. It seems like it should help." She stirred the ground beef, wondering what would happen once Eugene's time with them had ended and he had to go back home to his brothers. She shook her head. It would be better to just focus on one day at a time.

Jason interpreted her dazed expression differently. "You should still go to Nora's tonight," he said, crushing avocados with some lime juice and salt.

Hazel grew very still, concentrating on the pan of ground beef in front of her. She couldn't look at Jason. "Are you sure?" she said in a small voice. She considered it. The best help she could give Eugene, really, was to solve Cash's murder. She still needed to look for evidence. Her reasons had not changed, but now it had become even more urgent. Hazel realized that deep down, she believed that Billy was responsible for Cash's death. She hadn't wanted to think it, before. But now, the thought of sending poor Eugene back to that house with that horrible man filled her with desperation. "Okay," she said, finally. "I'll go after dinner."

"Good." Jason walked back and forth from the kitchen to the dining room several times, putting things on the table, and then called out the door to the family room. "Boys! Time for dinner!"

Hazel looked down, realizing she had overcooked the meat. She hurriedly put it into a serving bowl and took it to the table.

"Yay, tacos!" Jeremiah said when he came in and saw the taco plates on the table. "We need tacos for dinner more often."

Jason caught her eye and winked in a nonverbal "I told you so." Elias gave her a kiss on the cheek. She caught his hand and squeezed it. "Thank you for telling us," she whispered to him. "You're a good boy."

Elias blushed and looked away, sitting down in his usual spot.

Eugene silently followed her boys in and sat down at the table. He sat mute, his eyes wide while they said grace, then waited until everyone else had begun eating before he assembled a taco. His face turned red in mild embarrassment and discomfort.

Jason cleared his throat. "So, Jeremiah, I don't know if you heard, but Eugene is going to be staying with us for a week or two."

"Really?" Jeremiah said with his mouth full. "That's

awesome!" He put up his hand for a high five, and Eugene couldn't help but let a small smile escape when he high-fived him. "So that means dessert every night, right mom?"

Hazel was grateful that Jeremiah didn't ask why Eugene was staying.

"So, when's the next football game?" Jason asked. Hazel smiled at him. She could tell he was trying to put Eugene at ease. "Is it this Friday?"

"Yeah," Elias said.

"We're playing against Apple Valley," Eugene said, relaxing at the mention of football. "They're not supposed to be that good. We think that we'll do pretty well against them. At least, that's if I can play on my ankle."

Jason chuckled. It was more information than Elias had ever offered them about football throughout the entire season.

"Great, I'm looking forward to it," Jason said. "You'd better make sure that you keep ice on that ankle until then. And keep it wrapped.

* * *

ONCE THEY HAD EATEN and the boys had helped clean up, Hazel was back to waiting around until it was time for her to go on her little outing. She busied herself getting out extra blankets and pillows, finding an unopened toothbrush and generally making sure that Eugene had everything he needed for the night. She also told the boys in her best no-nonsense voice that Eugene staying with them was not an excuse for them to stay up all hours and that it was a school night, so she expected them to all be asleep by ten thirty. Unfortunately, she wouldn't be around to enforce her ruling, and she didn't trust that Jason would be as strict as her. It would be horrible dragging them out of bed the next morning.

"Mrs. Dean?" The other boys were upstairs in their rooms

working on their homework. Hazel turned to look at Eugene. He was pale, and his bruised-looking cloud was back.

"Yes, Eugene?"

"Do you believe in ghosts?"

Hazel's mind flew to her parents. "In a way, I suppose." She sat down in a reading chair that was positioned in the guest room. "My parents died when I was ten. I sometimes feel like my mother is there, watching over me."

Eugene shook his head. "That's not what I mean." He reached for his backpack and took out Cash's copy of *To Kill A Mockingbird*. He held it out to her. "Please, take it. I think it's haunted."

"Haunted?" Hazel reached out and took the book without looking at it. "What do you mean?"

"Nothing," Eugene backpedaled, shaking his head fervently, "Never mind. It's just too painful for me to keep it."

Hazel nodded. "I'll keep it for you until you're ready to take it back," she said.

"Did you read his notes?" Eugene said, eying the book in her hands.

Hazel opened the book and began to flip through the pages. "Yes, I saw them."

"What do you think he meant with the circled words?"

"Circled words?" Hazel looked up at Eugene and then back at the book, squinting.

"Here, I'll show you," Eugene said. He took the book from her and flipped it to the third page, pointing. "Right here, the word 'it' is circled."

"How strange," Hazel said, taking the book from him and flipping through it. "I didn't notice that when I was looking through it before."

"No, it's circled really lightly. I thought it was a smudge in the book at first but when I tried to brush it off it didn't go anywhere."

"Did you find any more?"

"Yeah, here I wrote them down." He showed her a post-it note he had stuck inside the front cover. He had written each word separately from each other, but they clearly formed a sentence.

"It is east of the work and north of home?" Hazel said. "What does that mean?"

"I don't know," Eugene said. "Maybe Cash wanted to travel? Maybe he was going to move away."

"No," Hazel put her hand on Eugene's shoulder, trying to offer some comfort. "He would never have left you. Hold on a second, there's something I want you to read." Hazel went to the mudroom and pulled Cash's letter out of her purse. "Cash left me a letter inside the book. I think you should read it. It might explain some things."

Eugene took the letter from her and sat down on the couch to read it. He was silent, but Hazel saw a cloud of silvery ash appear around him as he read, clinging to his skin and hair. When he was finished reading, he handed it back to her.

"Thank you," he said.

Hazel opened her mouth to say something comforting, but she couldn't think of anything that could really help.

"I've got some homework to do," he said, looking down at his shoes.

Hazel took the hint and got up. Eugene needed some space. A safe place to process what happened. She paused at the door. "Your brother Cash was a good man. You can be proud of him."

"Yeah," Eugene said, turning away from her so she could barely hear the last words he mumbled. "But now he's dead."

THIRTEEN

The time had arrived for Hazel to leave. Her heart fluttered around in her stomach like a caged bird. She found Jason sitting in his easy chair, browsing through Reddit. "I guess I'll go now," she said. "Make sure these boys don't stay up too late." When her boys played video games, it was like they went into some kind of bizarre alternate dimension where time moved a lot slower. No matter how long they played, they acted like it had only been five minutes when it was time to get off.

"I will," Jason assured her, without looking up from his phone. "Not too late."

"Uh huh," Hazel grunted skeptically.

"Let me know if you get lonely and bored over there," he said.

"I will," she said. She turned towards the garage, and the bottom fell out of her stomach. She couldn't do it. She couldn't lie to Jason like this. She turned back around. "Jason?"

"Yeah," he said. He set his phone down and got out of his chair. "What's wrong?"

"I..." She almost told him the truth, but then Eugene's tired voice echoed in her head. *"Do you believe in ghosts?"* She had to help that sad, sweet boy, whatever it took. "I just love you," she said finally.

Jason chuckled and pulled her into his arms. "I love you too, Hazel. You're a good, compassionate woman. We're doing a good thing for that boy."

Hazel nodded and turned quickly away before he could see the tears that had welled up in her eyes. Would he still think that she was good if he knew what she was about to do?

He stood in the garage doorway and waved a hand while she backed out of the driveway and drove away. Her heart went from fluttering to pounding. She could feel her pulse in her ears. She couldn't remember the last time she had done anything that made her so nervous. She pulled onto the road and began to drive in the opposite direction from Nora's house, towards the hotel construction site.

Hazel assumed that at ten o'clock at night any construction site would be pretty deserted. But if, like Hazel thought, the construction site was actually a front for some drug related operation, ten o'clock at night might be its busiest time. She wouldn't know until she got there. She wanted to see if she could find anything to prove illicit activities, anything to get the investigation opened up again. It was also the only place she could think of to start searching for Cash's truck.

Hazel drove past the gate blocking the road to the construction site and turned down the hiking hub she had noticed earlier that day. The parking lot was at the end of a bumpy dirt road, and she felt a little nauseous from the drive. Or maybe it was from lying to Jason. She was hoping that the road ran parallel to the highway in the opposite direction. Otherwise, she could be looking at a three or four-mile hike before she got where she wanted to be. She felt a flicker of doubt. At the least, she should have looked more closely at the map on her phone before she lost service. Perhaps doing this without telling anyone was a bad idea after all.

She realized that the movie couldn't be more than three hours long, so Jason would start to get anxious if she was gone for more than three and a half hours. Maybe she could get another hour out of having a chat with Nora. She set a vibrating alarm on her watch for four hours. She had to be done by then.

Hazel got out of the car and opened the trunk. She donned her all-black outfit, pulling the hat down over her ears. Before she put on her coat, she donned her strong side hip carry and holstered her gun. Then she put on her coat. She turned her phone on silent and shoved it in the pocket of her coat, then switched on the night vision goggles. The world immediately became varying shades of clouded neon green. She felt a little disoriented and began moving slowly, consulting her compass and ignoring the trail. It was something that she had never done before, but she knew from painful experience that if she strayed from the path, she could encounter a sudden drop off or varying sizes of creeks and streams. She avoided steep inclines, heading down the gap between two ridges.

She made her way slowly through the trees, jumping at every rustling or sound of movement in the underbrush. She stumbled and tripped over rocks despite the night vision goggles. The further she got from her car, the more it felt like a bad idea, but she wasn't sure what else to do. Everyone else seemed satisfied with the way the case was going, and Jason had said there was no way to investigate Chris Mills without some kind of evidence that he was doing something wrong. Well, she was going to get some evidence, and then they could investigate him.

"Hey!" a voice echoed through the dark forest.

Hazel froze, her heart climbing into her throat. She grabbed her gun out of its holster but didn't know where to point it. The voice echoed through the stillness of the forest.

"How-" another voice called, but it was cut off in a strangled, choking sound. Hazel felt her insides turn to jelly with fear. She paused a moment, straining her ears to catch the sound of footsteps. Then an airy sound beat past her through the air, and she realized with a rush of relief that the voices she had heard were just owls. She sat down for a few minutes to catch her breath and wait for her heartbeat to stop rushing through her ears. Then she had to chuckle at herself. It wasn't the first time she had ever heard an owl's call. She couldn't remember having ever been so scared before. She re-holstered her pistol.

Her fitness watch told her that she had hiked a little less than a mile when she almost ran into a dilapidated structure. She pulled off the night vision goggles, trying to make out what she could in the moonlight. She would have dismissed it during the day as an old, abandoned barn or some other such building. It was so close to the protected lands of the national forest that it must have predated its establishment. Part of the roof was caved in, and the boards on the porch were rotted through. Hazel would never have expected it to be inhabited, but she could see light coming from deeper inside the building.

Hazel's imagination started spinning in overdrive. The building would be perfect as a base of operations for an opioid ring. It was close enough to the hotel that they could come and go without raising suspicion.

Trying to move as silently as it was possible for a woman slightly over forty to move, she crept up to a window on the side of the house to peek in. She avoided the front porch, thinking it might collapse underneath her or creak loud enough for someone inside to hear.

She looked through the window and blinked in surprise. There was a kitchen table with a tablecloth over it and a vase with something inside it. There was an old wood-burning stove glowing with orange heat. A kettle sat on top of it. An old-fashioned water pump sink was in another corner. She noticed curtains on the windows and cans of food on open shelves. It didn't look like Hazel imagined an opioid den would. Then again, Chris Mills had come across as fastidious.

Hazel backed away from the window and slowly circled around the house. When she turned the first corner, she saw a large clearing with a vegetable garden and some flowers. Hazel frowned. It was another thing that didn't fit in with the use of the barn as the center of a drug ring.

One of the windows on the back side of the house was brightly lit, and Hazel ducked to crawl beneath it so she wouldn't be seen.

Turning the next corner, she saw a large shed the size of a garage. She crept towards it. It didn't have any windows, just a door with a lock on it. She tried the door to see if it would open, but it held fast, jiggling the chain in a merry sound.

"Hello," said a voice behind her.

Hazel turned, stifling a scream. A brightness blinded her, and she put one hand up to take off the night vision goggles. Her other hand hovered above her gun, ready to pull it out, but the tenor of the voice made her hesitate.

"Are you alright?" he asked.

"Can you put down your light?" she pleaded.

"I'm not holding a light," he said.

Hazel squinted, her eyes adjusting slowly. Indeed, he wasn't holding a light. It was just that he was glowing with whiteness. The sudden exposure to the color in the middle of the dark forest had tricked her eyes into seeing light. She should have been terrified. The man was well over six feet tall and quite bulky. He could have killed her easily, or worse. But somehow, she didn't feel afraid at all. The white surrounding him signaled peace, she was sure.

"Who are you?" the man asked.

"I... I... I am sorry," she stuttered. "Clearly, I'm intruding on private property. I didn't mean to cause you any inconvenience. I thought I was somewhere else."

The man nodded, smiling broadly. "That's okay. I like visitors. Come inside. I'll make you cocoa."

Hazel smiled at him and followed him into his home. There was something odd and halting about his speech, almost childlike. She wondered at her judgement, but again, the pure white color and his friendly demeanor comforted her.

They climbed the steps of the front porch, Hazel careful to step only where her host had for fear her foot might go right through the wood. Hazel gawked at the interior of the dilapidated structure. The wood-burning stove radiated with heat, and despite the state of the walls and windows, it was quite warm and comfortable. A moment of terror seized her when she saw a large, wood-handled knife lying casually on the kitchen table. The man settled her in a kitchen chair and took down some mugs from a shelf. The terror ebbed away, although she kept one eye on the knife.

"Do you live here all alone?" she wondered out loud, trying to peer down the hallway.

The man nodded. "Yes, all alone."

He didn't offer any more information. Hazel tried her trick of waiting in silence, but the man wasn't forthcoming with any more information.

"Why are you here?" he asked her finally.

"Oh, I uh..." Hazel hesitated. "I'm looking for a friend of mine."

The man lit up even more. "Oh, I have lots of friends," he smiled. "What is your friend's name?"

"Cash McCleary," she said.

The man's whiteness dimmed to the glow of a candle. "Oh. Cash was my friend too. But he is dead now."

"I know," Hazel said. Her feeling that this man had some kind of mental handicap intensified. "I miss him. Do you know what happened to him?"

The man shook his head. "He was here. Then he left. Now he is dead."

"He was here?" Hazel asked.

"Yes, Cash visited me here a lot. We were friends."

"Did he ever talk to you about a moral dilemma he was having?"

The man brought her a mug of cocoa, his brow furrowed and his light tinted brown. "Moral dilemma?" he pronounced the words carefully.

"Like a super big problem?"

His brow cleared, and he lightened again. "Yes. Cash had a big problem. His brother wanted him to break the rules. Cash didn't want to."

Hazel nodded. She couldn't help but smile. What was this sweet man doing, living all alone in the woods? "That's right. Do you know what rule it was?"

The man shook his head. "No, Cash didn't tell me that. He just wanted to keep his truck here. To hide it from his brother."

Hazel spilled her cocoa on her lap, almost dropping the mug.

"Oh no," the man said. "You spilled. I can help." He opened a drawer and handed her a perfectly clean and pressed napkin. Hazel was too excited to wonder about this man's strange lifestyle.

"Cash's truck is here?" Hazel tried to sound only mildly interested, but the suppressed excitement made her voice come out in a squeak.

"Yes, but Cash's brothers can't know that."

"Listen..." Hazel realized she never caught the man's name. "I'm Hazel Dean," she said, putting out her hand.

"Pleased to meet you," the man said. "I am Waylon Gibbons."

Hazel's mouth fell open. "Cash mentioned you," she murmured.

"He did?" Mr. Gibbons asked happily.

Hazel nodded. "Mr. Gibbons, I'm trying to figure out exactly how Cash died. I feel that we owe it to his memory to find out the truth. I need your help."

Mr. Gibbons nodded. "I will help you, Miss Dean. What should I do?"

A few minutes later, Hazel was digging around in Cash's truck. Of course, there would be some important evidence inside. Why else would he want to hide it from Billy? A story was coming together in Hazel's head. Cash was planning on reporting his brother's nefarious activities. Billy found out about it and shot him, then blamed it on Wallis Trudgeon. It was perfect. Except it didn't explain why Wallis confessed.

Cash's truck wasn't exactly organized. She looked through the glove box, but all she could find was the car's registration, a couple parking tickets and a few maps. She looked under the seats and in each door pocket, but all she found was old food wrappers and fountain drink cups. Finally, she turned to the stack of papers on the passenger's seat and started flipping through them. Maybe Cash thought to hide things in plain sight.

It was an interesting stack of papers. The first several pages were copies of building permits for the hotel. But just underneath those were all of Cash's identification documents, including his birth certificate and social security card, as well as Eugene's. Behind those was an old address book. Hazel opened it up. Girlish cursive filled the inside. The cover was signed Aubrey Reeves.

At the bottom of a stack, she found an envelope with a letter inside. It was postmarked in Sevier County, Tennessee. Hazel felt a little strange about reading someone else's mail, but under the circumstances she figured Cash wouldn't mind. She unfolded the letter and read the elegant script inside.

DEAR CASH,

I can't express how thrilled I was to receive your letter. I wish I could say how much I've missed your mother all these years. The news you shared, of her death long ago, was a bitter shock. When she ran away with your dad all those years ago, we looked for her for a while, but we didn't know his name or where he was from, so there was nothing to go off of. We never stopped hoping that someday she might come home. It's devastating to know that she never will. To see you and your brother would be the next best thing. Please come and see us. Your grandparents are still living in the house where your mom grew up, and I'm just down the street. I have three kids of my own now - your cousins! Though they're quite a bit younger than you.

It would be nice to have a faster way to communicate, but I understand you don't have the internet at your house. But it's nice to have something coming in the mail to look forward to. I anxiously await your next letter. Please tell me more about your mother and her life there and about you and your brother.

Your aunt,

Anne

HAZEL TUCKED the letter back into its envelope and set it carefully with the rest of the papers. She knew where to look next. She reached up slowly and pulled down the sun visor. A thick envelope full of cash landed in her lap.

"Mr. Gibbons?" she called.

Waylon Gibbons had been standing just outside the truck watching her rifle through Cash's things. His light had muddied to a brackish murk. "Yes?" he was by her side in an instant. She put the money back where she found it.

"Was Cash planning on going anywhere?"

The murk grew a little darker.

"It's okay, Waylon," she said gently. "You can tell me. Cash is gone and I want to make sure that we help his brother Eugene."

He lit up again. "Eugene is a good boy. A very nice boy. Cash didn't want him to stay here."

Hazel nodded. She didn't want to press Waylon to break confidences any further. Hazel could piece together what Cash was planning on her own. Unfortunately, although it was interesting information, it wasn't exactly useful.

"I have to go, Mr. Gibbons," she said.

"So soon?" he asked, pouting a bit.

"I'm running out of time tonight, and there's still one more thing I need to do. But I will come back and visit you again."

Waylon nodded emphatically. "I like visitors," he said.

Hazel smiled at him. "Can you point me in the direction of the hotel Cash was building?"

Waylon nodded again. "I can take you there. It's not far."

Hazel gathered her things, and on impulse took the few building permits that were on top of the stack of important papers and stuffed them in her bag. "You won't let anyone else see Cash's truck, will you? It's important for Eugene that no one else find this. Well, except the police, I suppose."

Waylon nodded his head. "I will keep Cash's truck safe."

FOURTEEN

Hazel followed Waylon Gibbons through the woods. She carried her night vision goggles in her bag. She was amazed at Waylon's ability to pick his way through the forest with the limited visibility available to him. It must have been like trudging through his own backyard.

The minutes ticked by and Hazel felt impatient. She didn't have very much time to find the incriminating papers she knew were in the trailer. Although Cash's truck gave her some valuable information, it didn't cast any new light on Cash's death. For that, she would need to find out what Chris Mills was hiding in the trailer. Something that would explain the connections between him and the McClearys and Wallis Trudgeon.

If only Waylon knew more about what was going on. Hazel's mind tumbled with questions about the strange man. How long had he been living out in the woods on his own? He took very good care of himself. Hazel couldn't imagine living alone in the woods. She would die of loneliness. She felt a wave of pity for the poor man and promised herself she would continue to visit him, but perhaps not in the middle of the night from now on. Maybe she would be able to find out more about him. She felt like if her tiny community had a hermit living in the woods for the last who knows how long, it wouldn't be the best kept secret in town. How had she not heard about him before? She remembered Trudy's stubborn insistence that she didn't know who Waylon Gibbons was and Billy's defensiveness about the carved fox. She started to ask Waylon about the carvings when she caught a glow of light through the trees.

Light wasn't a good sign for her. If there was light, that would mean that there were people.

"I see it, Waylon," she whispered. "I think you should go on home now. I don't want to get you into trouble."

He turned and peered at her through the darkness. "Will you be safe?" he asked.

"I think so," she said. "Here, take my pack. I have some important stuff in there. I don't want it to fall into the wrong hands." Before she handed him the backpack, she grabbed a piece of paper and a pen from inside, making sure that it wasn't one of Cash's important legal documents. She found a receipt and flipped it over. She scrawled out her phone number and Jason's phone number. "If anything happens to me, give one of us a call. That's me," she said, pointing. "That's my husband, Jason."

Waylon crossed his arms over his chest. "I'm staying here until you come back," he promised.

"Okay," Hazel nodded. "I shouldn't be too long." Having Waylon Gibbons waiting just beyond the tree line was a comfort to her. Emboldened, she crept closer and closer to the light, crouching low towards the ground. She got to the edge of the tree line and lay on her belly, taking in the landscape that lay in front of her.

She had come out a little north and west of the road that came into the site. Large spotlights, like the ones nighttime construction crews used to work on interstates, lit up the area, but she didn't actually see anyone. Unfortunately, her view of the trailer was mostly obscured by the framework of the hotel. She lay on her stomach without moving and strained her ears to hear any conversation or construction noises, but she heard nothing. It was completely quiet except for the buzzing of the huge spotlights.

Hazel sat and listened for a few full minutes. Aware that she was running out of time, she decided she couldn't wait anymore. Trying to memorize where she had started from, she rose to her hands and knees and then sprinted as crouched as she could to the nearest framework of the hotel. She tried to use the shadows to her advantage, making sure that her whole body was opposite the frame from either of the spotlights.

The view of the trailer was a little better from this vantage point, and Hazel still didn't see or hear a soul. Gaining confidence, Hazel darted from room to skeletal room of the hotel towards the trailer.

Finally, she was in one of the small rooms at the front of the hotel that she had investigated on her last visit. The trailer and the tracks were within her view now, and she saw no cars. Hazel felt a well of panic bubble up from her gut. She couldn't believe what she was doing. Why had she gotten herself into this? She was just a mom, a middle-aged woman. She had absolutely no business running around in the middle of the night in potentially mortal peril. She sank to the ground, trying to breathe and finding that she couldn't. This would not end well, she could feel it in her bones. But what else could she do at this point? Tears filled her eyes. She tried to remember the reason why she started this outing in the first place. It was for Cash and for Eugene, forgotten children who had never been properly taken care of. It was for her town—to prove that they weren't held hostage by an ancient feud. To make sure that the devastating and cliche plague of opioid addiction would stay the hell out of her home.

She found her breathing return to its normal pace. Her

vision cleared and focused. This had to be done, and no one else was going to do it. She checked her watch. She had about a half an hour before it was time to head back to the car.

Hazel continued to crouch, just in case, and headed towards the trailer. The foundation was shorter on the north side, making the windows closer to the ground. She pushed her fingers against one of them and attempted to slide it open. It budged a little, enough to tell her it wasn't locked and she would be able to get in that way if she needed to. She preferred to use the front door.

She crept along the front of the trailer and up the stairs. She grasped the doorknob and almost cried out in satisfaction when it turned and opened. She stepped into the room and closed the door behind her. The spotlights outside illuminated just enough for her to see her way around inside. She didn't need to turn on any lights.

The first thing she did was check out the desk by the broken window she had noticed on her last visit. The window was still broken, but now a piece of cardboard had been taped over it to keep out the cold. The top of the desk was bare, so she started opening drawers.

The top drawer of the desk looked like the top drawer of her desk at home, just Post-It notes, paper clips, pens, and a stapler. Nothing incriminating there.

She opened the second drawer and found that it was full of blank printer paper, ready for use. She looked around the trailer, but she didn't see a printer anywhere, or a computer. She frowned and looked in the next drawer. This was more like it. It was a stack of invoices, bills, and other official-looking documents. She took out the stack and sat down at the desk's swivel chair.

Most of the papers were just delivery confirmation slips for various construction supplies. Hazel didn't know anything about construction and certainly didn't know if any of the deliveries were items that would be suspicious. There were a few bills for disposal of construction materials and rental agreements for various trucks and construction vehicles. Hazel got through the stack of papers and sighed. She wasn't exactly sure what she was looking for, but she knew she didn't find it in that stack. She put it back inside the drawer and tried the bottom drawer in the desk. It was locked. Clearly, that's where all the good stuff was. She had to get into that drawer. She wished she had brought Elias' pocket knife with her. She scanned the room, looking for a tool that would help her unlock it.

There was a couch along one wall and a kitchenette down the far end of the room. There was a door leading to what must have been a bathroom next to the kitchenette. A filing cabinet stood on the other side of the room from the couch. Hazel walked towards the filing cabinet and ran her hands down the back and sides of it to see if a key was hanging from a hook but wasn't surprised when she didn't find anything. All of the drawers in that cabinet were locked as well.

She crossed the room and started opening and closing drawers and cupboards in the kitchenette. Most of them were empty. One cupboard was full of coffee mugs. One of the drawers had a few spoons in it, but no knives. She opened the fridge but didn't see anything except some expired creamer. In the freezer were some popsicles that had melted at some point and then been refrozen.

Tentatively she opened the door to the bathroom, worried about what she might find in there. It was shockingly sterile, like it had never even been used. There was no cabinet space inside, nothing but a commode and the tiniest sink she had ever seen. She tried to take apart the toilet and looked all around the sink, but there wasn't the slightest hint of hidden anything or secret compartments. Hazel checked her watch again. She only had ten minutes left. Having ruled out all other options, she went back to the desk and opened the top drawer. She got out a paper clip and twisted it into a straight line with a small hook on the end and set about trying to pick the lock on the bottom drawer of the desk.

Hazel knew she was about out of time. She had to start heading back to her car. But she was so close. Any second she would hear a click and the drawer would pop open. She kept telling herself just one more minute until another five minutes had gone by.

Finally, she had to admit defeat. She was just about to give up and stuff the paper clip into her pocket and head out when she heard it. There was a click, and the drawer popped open. She squealed with excitement and had her hand on the drawer to pull it open when a siren blared outside.

"This is the police. We have you surrounded," a voice called over a loudspeaker. "Come out with your hands up." Blue and red lights flashed through the windows. Hazel froze, unsure of what to do. Were they talking to her or did they finally figure out that they needed to arrest Chris Mills and they thought that she was him?

"We know you're in there," the voice said. "If you don't come out, we'll come in and we are armed."

Hazel didn't want a squad of armed policemen busting in around her. Her eyes wide, she opened the door and put her hands up, stepping out into the blinding spotlights that were trained on the door of the trailer. "It's just me," she called. "Hazel Dean. Chris Mills isn't here after all. You can turn off all the lights and put your guns down."

"Hazel Esther Randolph." another voice called over the loudspeaker, now. The blood drained out of Hazel's face. "You ridiculous girl. Get down here now."

Hazel sheepishly descended the steps, knowing that Uncle John's fury now was far worse than what she would have experienced if she had told about her interest in Cash's case earlier.

In a daze, she watched Brandon and another officer approach her and put her in handcuffs.

"Excuse me," she blustered, trying to turn around and get a good look at their faces. "Is that really necessary?"

The policemen didn't answer her. They pushed her gently towards the stairs and walked her towards a squad car. There were two sitting in the space in front of the hotel's framework. The red and blue lights continued to rotate, flashing manically in her face, turning the dim landscape into a circus.

"I'm so sorry about this, Mrs. Dean," Brandon murmured while the other policemen pushed her against the car and frisked her, taking her phone, gun, and the paper clip. "You have the right to remain silent..." he began.

"This is ridiculous," she sputtered, finally realizing that she was being arrested. "I'm not the bad guy here."

"I'm afraid that's what they all say," the unknown officer said. She caught a glimpse of Brandon rolling his eyes.

"Don't worry, Mrs. Dean," he said. "I'm sure this is just a misunderstanding. Captain Tate will work everything out."

Hazel cringed. A million lectures from when she was a teenager flashed through her head. Uncle John had always made it exceedingly clear that if she ever found herself on the wrong side of the law, he would be harder on her, rather than easier. He wouldn't be bailing her out of this mess. That would be up to Jason. Jason, who was about to get a call from Uncle John about finding her here. Hazel prayed he would under-stand why she did it, why she lied to him.

Deflated, she let Brandon help her into the back of a squad car. She flinched when he slammed the door shut and looked dejectedly out the window. The car backed up a little, making a several-point turn so it could drive away down the road towards the highway. When they pulled around the other squad car, she saw Uncle John. She instinctively crouched lower in her seat, trying to hide, but he wasn't looking at her at all. She craned her neck to get a glimpse of who he was talking to so intently. It wasn't until the car pulled forward even more, she saw that it was Chris Mills.

He turned around and saw her staring at him through the window, then raised a hand to smile and wave.

* * *

RED GAP LOOKED different from the back seat of a squad car, her hands bound together with handcuffs. An eerie pallor settled over it. She almost felt that it was embarrassed of her. It was turning her back on her, its once-favorite daughter. Hazel turned away from the window. She went over her choices in her head, wondering if she should have done anything differently. Maybe she should have gone to Uncle John. She shook her head. That wouldn't have changed anything. He wouldn't have listened to her. She was the only one who wasn't satisfied with Wallis' confession. It had to be her. She tightened her jaw and sat up straighter. They got back to the courthouse and pulled her out of the car and into the police station.

Wallis Trudgeon had come up to the window of his cell to see what was going on. When he saw Hazel in handcuffs, he started laughing. He cackled wildly while she glared at him. Waves of squiggly highlighter purple came off him.

"I'm glad I could provide you with some amusement," Hazel said, especially aware of her posture.

Uncle John came in, and Wallis was still laughing.

"Shut up, you maniac," he growled at Wallis in a low voice. Wallis stopped laughing abruptly and disappeared to the back of his cell. "Those aren't necessary," Uncle John said, pointing to the handcuffs. Brandon immediately took them off of her, giving her a quick "see" kind of smile. She shook out her arms. Uncle John took her elbow and led her into the interrogation room where she had met with Wallis earlier that day.

"Uncle John, I can explain," she said. She briefly considered lying some more. Saying she had gotten lost in the woods while she was hiking and that her phone had run out of batteries and she was looking for someone to help her. But it was useless, John would see right through it. Besides, she was done with lying. It was too exhausting.

"Save it," John said, his expression blank. He flashed s myriad of colors in quick succession. Hazel couldn't tell which of his emotions was winning his internal battle. "Chris Mills called us a little while back and reported a break in at his construction site, still in progress. Imagine my surprise when I found it was you that was our little break and enter-er."

"What? No, this is a big mistake," Hazel said, at the same time that a gnawing sense of dread settled in her stomach. "I didn't break and enter. The door was open."

"So, this is why you wanted your gun? Why are you wearing all black?" Uncle John asked her. "And where exactly is your car?"

Hazel blinked at him.

Hazel buried her face in her hands to hide her reddening face. She was glad that they hadn't found Waylon Gibbons. He must have withdrawn into the woods before they got around to searching that far away from the trailer. "Are you asking as a concerned relative or as the police captain?"

"Hazel, you know how I have to answer that." The tone of Uncle John's voice made her lift her head. She realized that ever since she had heard John's voice over the bullhorn, she had been acting like a teenager caught in her parent's liquor cabi- net. She squared her shoulders and sat up straight again, staring John down.

"I think I'd better talk to my lawyer then," she said with an attempt at haughtiness.

Uncle John's countenance flashed yellow and purple. She remembered seeing the same combination on him when they watched sitcoms together or when Jeremiah had said hilarious, precocious things as a toddler. Hazel tried not to be insulted. It was probably a good sign if he wasn't taking it seriously.

"That's probably a good idea," he said. "I'll call him and have him come down here. You'll be good if we leave you in here, right? Or should I put you in a cell?" His voice cracked into a guffaw.

"I think you're enjoying this just a little too much," she grumbled. She knew she should be relieved, but she wasn't. Uncle John smiled.

"Say cheese," he said, snapping a picture of her with his phone.

"That's professional," she said.

"Maybe you should put your mug shot on your Christmas card this year," John said, still laughing.

"Alright, alright," she said.

John sobered. "Seriously though, you and I will be having a talk off the record. Soon. And I don't envy the conversation you're about to have with Jason. Chris Mills says he wants to press charges. This is really serious, Hazel."

"I can tell by the way you keep cracking up."

Uncle John sobered. "Sometimes laughing prevents other emotions from overwhelming us." He left her alone in the room.

Hazel groaned and buried her face in her hands again. She tried to look at her situation objectively. The night vision goggles and all-black outfit did not make her look good. Not to mention her pistol. She really didn't want them to find out where the car was. That would make it look worse. She also realized that the specially bent paper clip in her pocket wasn't helping her cause either. She had not broken and entered; the door had been unlocked, so the worse that she could be charged with was trespassing. The problem was that it would be her word versus Chris Mills on that point. If he swore the door was locked, the police would probably believe him, the landowner, over her, the person caught sneaking around on his property with clandestine intentions.

It took Jason forever to get to the station. She wondered if he was punishing her for lying to him by letting her sit in that room and stew. Maybe he was even watching her from the other side of the large mirror on the wall. She kept reaching for her phone to check various points of the law, but it wasn't in her pocket. All she could do was sit and try to convince herself that she had done the right thing.

"Hello, Hazel," Jason said when he finally stepped into the room. He looked at her in a serious, businesslike way and crossed the room to sit down in the chair opposite her.

Hazel imagined all the policemen in the station crowded behind the two-way mirror watching her interaction with her husband.

"Jason, it was like you said," she started.

"Don't you dare blame this on me!" he snapped, jumping up out of the chair. His voice louder than she thought it would be.

Hazel flinched and tears stung her eyes. "But you said the police probably wouldn't search the trailer anymore, since Wallis confessed. I couldn't let it go like that. Don't you see? It was the only way. I thought it through this time, I swear I did. I couldn't think of another way around it."

"Damn it, Hazel," Jason started to raise his voice again.

"Jason, please," she said. She was dangerously close to sobs. "They're all watching."

Jason pulsed with red, a deep crimson that she had never seen on him before. Suddenly he reached out and threw the chair in front of him across the small room. Hazel jumped and began to sob quietly.

Jason paced back and forth across the room, taking deep breaths. Hazel brought her legs up onto the chair and tucked her knees under her chin. Curling into a ball helped her stop sobbing. She watched Jason's color lighten as he paced and breathed.

When he finally spoke again, his voice was much calmer, albeit maddeningly patronizing. Darker streaks of red flickered out from him at intervals. "Hazel, you've really made a mess of things. Chris Mills wants to prosecute you as aggressively as possible. If he can get you on a burglary charge, that's a felony. You're looking at some real jail time. Even if it's just breaking and entering, that could be a few months in prison."

Hazel bit her lip and blinked. "I'm so sorry, Jason. You're right. I just didn't know what else to do. I didn't think that it mattered... what happens to me. I just... Eugene... What are we going to do?"

"Right now, I'm going to bail you out of jail." Her husband continued to flicker with angry streaks of dark red. She couldn't bear to look at him. She looked down at her knees. "Then I'm going to come up with a way to get you off on a trespassing charge instead of breaking and entering. Did you really break a window or pick the lock to get into that trailer?"

"No!" Hazel wailed, her head snapped up. "No, Jason, I swear, the door was open, and I just walked in."

"What was with the paper clip then?"

Hazel looked down into her lap. "I may have broken into a drawer in the desk."

Jason rubbed his face with the palm of his hand. "Of course. Did you find anything incriminating Hazel? Was this all worth it?" He had started to yell again.

Hazel bit her lip again, but it didn't stop a few tears from spilling over onto her cheek. "No, I didn't find anything suspicious," she said. "I didn't have time to look through the locked drawer before the police came and I was... I was..."

"Arrested!" he shouted. "You were arrested, Hazel, because you were *trespassing*. This is freaking po-dunk-ville Georgia, you could have been shot! People shoot trespassers here!"

Hazel had broken down into sobs again. She couldn't even answer. Jason was breathing hard, the red had retaken him. He stared at her for a full minute.

"Oh, Hazel." Jason shook his head. "Sometimes I think you read too much."

"I'm so sorry I lied to you, Jason," Hazel choked. "I knew you'd talk me out of it, and I didn't want you to. I need to know what really happened to Cash."

"Why?" Jason asked, leaning over the table towards her. His voice pained, his aura suddenly saturated in a sickly green. "Why is that guy so important to you?"

Hazel blinked at him. "Jason, it's not like that. I didn't have a crush on him or whatever you're thinking. I just felt so sad for him. He was so lonely and lost. He needed me, and all I did was hand him a book and send him on his merry way. I sent him off to die!" Hazel couldn't stop her sob on the last word and all the tears she had been fighting off the whole week caught up to her. "I could have done something," she choked out. "I could have helped him. It might have been different. It was my fault he died."

"No, no," Jason said. He was no longer sickly green, just that green color of worry. Like his anxiety was as deep and dark as the forest. She still saw the flickers of red anger. Like a forest on fire. He walked around the table and crouched down. "It wasn't your fault he died." She knew he meant it in a nice way, but he was still so angry that the words came out clipped and impatient.

Hazel tried to get her tears and sobs under control and after a few minutes she managed, although she began hiccuping instead.

"Hazel, let's go. We can talk about this at home," Jason muttered once she was in control of herself.

FIFTEEN

Their argument continued in the car. "Are the boys asleep?" she asked.

"No," he said, flatly. "I stayed up and played video games with them."

Usually Hazel would have been irritated, but not this time. "I'm so sorry, Jason."

"Hazel, did you ever think about how this would affect my work?"

Hazel's eyebrows furrowed. She couldn't think of what he meant. "But you're not on the case," she said, her confusion overwhelming her feeling of dread.

"It doesn't matter. You're being charged with a serious crime. This doesn't look good. It's bad for my career. This is exactly what your Uncle John wanted all along. Why do you think he was so tickled about the whole thing?"

Hazel snorted. She had been certain, when Jason won the election for district attorney, that his connection to the Randolphs was a big piece of his victory. And, despite Jason's insistence to the contrary, John was not out to kill Jason's career.

Jason's insecurities were getting the better of him. "Don't be ridiculous."

"This is serious, Hazel. This is my job. If I'm incriminated in this somehow, that's it. I'm not practicing law anymore."

Hazel didn't want to talk about Jason's job. She wanted to explain why her actions were justified. She responded without thinking. "We don't need your job, anyway. I have plenty of money."

The atmosphere in the car immediately changed. It was as though, with that one comment, all the oxygen had disappeared. She clamped her hand over her mouth, her blood turned cold in her veins. She tried to take it back right away. "Jason, I-"

"Stop. Hazel." Jason's voice had grown quiet with hurt and rage. It was dark in the car, but Hazel could see the deep crimson flare up around him. "We agreed... You said..." He had become inarticulate with anger. "I thought we decided we weren't going to take your trust fund into consideration when making family decisions," he said finally.

"We did," she said, backpedaling wildly. "You're right. That was a stupid, thoughtless thing for me to say. I'm so sorry. Of course, your job is important. I just-" she hesitated, wondering if more apologizing was necessary before she got back to what they were really talking about. "It's just that... I mean, I can't believe that your job would actually be in danger over this."

"Hazel, I don't think you understand the severity of the situation. There are all kinds of ramifications of your actions. If you had just listened to me yesterday when I told you to leave it alone-"

Hazel's temper flared. She regretted her thoughtless words, but she wasn't going to let Jason use them to control her. "I'm a grown woman. I get to make my own choices. I don't have to do what you say just because you're my husband. What is this,

1860?" They made it home and Hazel got out of the car and slammed the door.

* * *

"MOM!" Jeremiah attacked her when she walked in the door. Eugene and Elias had been smart enough to make themselves scarce. "You were arrested? How did that happen? What did you do? Did Dad bust you out? Are you on the run?"

"I'm not going to discuss it with you right now," she said through clenched teeth. "You shouldn't be up this late. Get to bed."

"But—" Jeremiah protested.

"To bed, young man!" Jason shouted from behind her.

"Jeez, I'm going," Jeremiah grumbled. Hazel ignored him and fled to her room. Jason was right on her heels. He slammed the door behind them and then began to whisper-yell. The crimson around him was darker than ever.

"So, my opinions and concerns mean nothing to you?" he asked.

"Of course, they do," Hazel said, snapped. Her body was pulsing with irritation. She was just as angry at herself for bringing up her money as she was at him for trying to control her. "I will take them into consideration. But you don't get to tell me no. If our roles were reversed and you were the one seeking justice for Cash, you would be viewed as a hero. And you're telling me I'm being selfish?! I will do what I think is right, regardless of the consequences. If that bothers you, then you should have married someone else."

Jason groaned a little too loudly. After her thoughtless comment about not needing his money, Jason didn't even try to censor himself like he usually would. He angrily brought up things he usually only spoke about with compassion. "I think you'd be much easier to deal with if your parents hadn't died in that accident and you never got that settlement. Your grand-mother and beloved 'Uncle John' spoiled you."

Hazel's eye pricked with tears. He was right; she knew she was spoiled.

"I would much rather have had my parents and no money," she wailed, missing her mother so much that she couldn't breathe.

They were both too angry now to turn to each other for comfort. Too many hurtful things had been said between them for a reconciliation tonight. Hazel didn't even brush her teeth, just pulled on some pajamas and got into bed, glaring the whole time. They lay in a stony silence until Jason rolled over in bed and eventually began snoring. But Hazel couldn't sleep. She sobbed as quietly as she could. After crying for a long time she began to hope that he would notice her crying, that it would soften his anger and he would roll over and tell her not to cry. That everything would be alright and that he still loved her. She wished she could roll over and bury herself in Jason's embrace. But she knew that what she had said about his job was unforgivable, so she faced the wall and cried until the exhaustion of the day overwhelmed her.

* * *

HAZEL AND JASON moved around each other like zombies in the morning. They got the kids off to school. Eugene came out to eat breakfast but went right back to the guest room afterward. Hazel hoped he was going back to sleep. The boy had dark circles under his eyes. After the boys left, Jason got ready and left for work without saying goodbye. Hazel went into her room and shut the door. She sat on her bed, wrapped in several blan-kets, and began to cry again, trying to be quiet enough not to bother Eugene. She jumped guiltily when she heard her bedroom door open. But it wasn't Eugene, it was Jason.

"I thought you went to work," she sniffled, looking at him with red, puffy eyes.

"I did. I got all the way there and then turned around. I can't function with things left like this between us." He sat down hesitantly next to Hazel on the bed and took her hands in his.

"Me neither, Jason." In relief, she buried her face in his chest. "I'm so sorry."

"Look, Hazel." He took her by the shoulders and gently pushed her away from him so he could look into her face. "This is really hard for me. I understand you can make your own choices. I would never ask you to just do what I say because I'm your husband. I just ask that you be more aware of how your behavior affects other people."

"I know, Jason," Hazel said in a rush. "And you're right. I only thought about it from one angle. I thought I could do it by myself."

Jason nodded. "I know. I also realize that your fierce sense of care for everyone you meet is one of the things I love most about you. I want you to act on the things that move you."

Hazel's eyes lit up. She dropped his hands and opened her arms to hug him. "Oh, Jason..."

"Wait, Hazel. I'm still concerned about your safety and my job." He closed his eyes for a second and took a deep breath. Hazel noticed suddenly that he was surrounded by glowing shiny yellow. "I would like you to bring me in on this."

Hazel hesitated. "What do you mean?"

"I want you to tell me about everything. Let me know what you're going to do. I'll try to help you the best I can. If you believe Wallis didn't do it... Well, I can't say that I agree completely, but it casts enough doubt for me that I'm willing to help you. Whatever it takes."

Hazel sighed, thinking seriously about his request. He studied her.

"Can I also point out, that one of the things you love about me is that I also feel a responsibility to make the world better. I get it, Hazel. I do."

Hazel twisted her lips, thinking. She liked to be independent. Talking to Jason about everything she did beforehand would mean that she had to think through things. Deep down, Hazel was worried that if she did that, she would lose her nerve. "That's an extremely reasonable request, and obviously there are lots of ways in which you could be quite helpful. Thanks Jason, I think that's a great idea."

Jason beamed at her and enfolded her in a hug that consumed her. "It feels so good to be on the same team again."

Hazel smiled into his chest. It did feel good. "Oh, Jason, I was so worried you'd never forgive me." She could feel tears pricking her eyes at the thought of it. "I love you so much."

Jason grimaced. "Can I make one more suggestion?" he asked tentatively.

"Sure."

"I think you might want to let John know what's going on."

"No way," she said. "That's a terrible idea. You, of all people, should realize that. Plus, you know how he feels about my gifts."

"Alright, alright." Jason put his hands up. "He could be helpful, but you would know better than I would. I was just a thought. Maybe you should think about it."

"Okay, I'll think about it," she said.

"Good." Jason got up and started pacing around the room. "So I think we should palaver."

"Pa-what?" Hazel wasn't sure what Jason meant.

"Palaver, it means put our heads together and share our knowledge."

"In what language?" she grumbled, pulling herself into a sitting position but maintaining her cocoon of blankets. "Lawyer-ese?"

"No, it's from Stephen King."

"Ah, of course." Jason didn't read a ton, but when he did, it was Stephen King. "Where's your car?"

"I left it at the parking lot where all the hikes start."

"You hiked in? Wow, this was a well-planned burglary."

Hazel rolled her eyes. She knew he was making an attempt at humor to ease the tension between them, but Hazel was too tired for a courtesy laugh.

Jason reached over and patted her on the hand. "You're lucky you didn't get lost out there in the woods, alone, at night."

"I had a guide," Hazel said. "Have you heard of a man named Waylon Gibbons?"

Jason frowned and shook his head.

"I hadn't either until I saw a note Cash had written in *To Kill A Mockingbird*. I ran into him last night."

Jason immediately turned back to forest green. He looked like the floor had disappeared from underneath him.

"Don't worry. He's completely harmless. A little slow, I think. He lives completely off the grid in the woods. I thought his house was an old ruin at first, but it's quite comfortable inside. It turns out, he's hiding Cash's truck in his garage."

Jason raised an eyebrow. "Really?"

"Yes, he said Cash asked him to keep it hidden from Billy, but he let me in to look around. Jason," Hazel lowered her voice just in case Eugene was up and could hear them. "I think that Cash was planning on taking off and taking Eugene with him... curses! My backpack."

"Your backpack?"

"Yes, I found all their identification documents in the truck along with a fat wad of cash and a letter from their mother's sister, reestablishing a connection. There were some permits from the hotel construction site too. I took them all, but I left my pack with Waylon Gibbons. We'll need to get it back. I'm pretty sure those permits are incriminating somehow."

"Hazel, that's all very interesting," Jason said slowly. "But it doesn't actually do anything for your case."

"It casts more suspicion on Billy and the others, doesn't it?" Hazel protested.

"I suppose so, but it doesn't negate Wallis' confession. Unless you can prove he's lying, nothing else really matters."

"I know," Hazel sighed.

"Okay," he said, nodding. "Let's go get your car. I'll tell you my stuff on the way."

Hazel felt a bizarre sense of relief having Jason in on things. He was a strategic thinker. His insights would help her, would help Cash and Eugene. "Do you think it's okay to leave Eugene here alone?"

"We'll check on him first," Jason said.

They stepped softly down the stairs. Hazel tapped on the guest room door. "Eugene? Are you alright?" she called quietly.

"Come in," came a reply.

Hazel opened the door. "I have an errand to run. Will you be okay for a little while by yourself?"

Eugene didn't look any better. In the bright morning light of the bedroom, the circles under his eyes looked even more pronounced. He was easily startled, jumping a bit when she opened the door even though he had told her to come in. "Are you alright?" she asked. She walked towards his bed and put her hand on his forehead. He leaned away from her.

"I'm okay," he said. "You go ahead. I'll be fine here."

"Do you want some advil or a melatonin?" she asked, looking for some way she could help. She walked over to the blinds to lower them, but Eugene jumped up.

"No," he cried.

Hazel looked at him, her eyes wide in surprise. Eugene took a deep breath. "No thank you," he said, taking a deep breath. "The light is nice."

"Okay," she said. "Try to get some rest. I'll come back and check on you when I get back."

He nodded, getting back into bed. Hazel left the room, shutting the door softly behind her. "I'm really worried about him, Jason," she said as they headed to the car. "Last night he asked me if I believe in ghosts."

Jason furrowed his eyebrows. "Ghosts, huh?"

"Just now he wouldn't let me close the window. He was scared of the dark like a little boy."

"His brother just died," Jason shrugged. "He'll feel better, eventually."

Hazel didn't know how to tell him that Eugene would never feel better again. She knew from personal experience.

They got into the car and started driving towards the hiking hub.

"I already told you about the gunshot wound that killed Cash," Jason picked up their earlier conversation. "I didn't want to tell you too many details back then, I didn't want to upset you more, and I didn't realize that you would get so worked up and obsessive about the case..." he gave her a meaningful look.

"Yeah, yeah, okay," she said, stung a bit. "Keep going."

"So, the gunshot to the head wasn't the only injury that Cash sustained."

"What?"

"The other wounds were found to be unrelated to Cash's demise and therefore irrelevant in the murder case, but a few of the cops found it suspicious."

"What was wrong with him?" she asked.

"He had multiple lacerations on his hands and forearms, like he was trying to reach through something that cut him up."

Hazel's blood turned to ice. "Like a broken window?" she asked.

"Yes, that was one of the suggestions," Jason nodded.

"Did they ask the McClearys about it?"

"Yes, they told the police that those kinds of injuries were common in the construction business and that they didn't really notice them or think to ask Cash about them. Couldn't tell the police when he got them either, although the coroner thought they couldn't be more than 48 hours old. Poor kid really sliced himself up. It must have hurt."

"I wonder what he was reaching for," Hazel said.

"I don't follow," Jason said, squinting.

"While I was at the construction site the first time, I noticed a broken pane in one of the windows of the trailer. It's like the project management office or something. Yesterday when I was snooping around, someone had taped a scrap of cardboard over it."

"But you didn't find anything suspicious in the trailer?"

"I told you, I was just about to when the police carried me away in handcuffs."

"Anything else?" Jason asked.

"Actually, last night, Eugene showed me what he thinks might be another message from Cash. Cash circled certain words in the book. If you string them together, they say something. I'll show you.". She grabbed it and pulled the book out, opening to the third page where Eugene had found the first circled word. "It's faintly circled. Eugene found a bunch of them in there and when he strung them together, they formed a sentence." She flipped to the front cover where Eugene had put the Post -It. "It is east of the work and north of home."

"It is east of the work and north of home," Jason repeated. "What's that supposed to mean?"

"That's what I said too."

"Well, did you go through the book?" Jason asked. "Maybe Eugene missed a couple and it'll make more sense when we find them."

"Oh, that's a good idea," Hazel said. "I haven't had time to think much about it. He just showed it to me last night."

Jason shrugged. "It's worth a shot anyways. Interesting. I should also tell you that Wallis wasn't the only suspect before he confessed. There were some hunters that said they were hunting in the woods in around the same area and they worried that they might have accidentally shot Cash."

"What on earth were they doing hunting in that area?!" Hazel remembered hunting trips she went on with Uncle John as a child. They were always in designated hunting areas or on private land far, far away from any hiking trails or roads.

"My thoughts exactly," Jason said. "But it says a lot that they just heard about what happened on the news and then came into the police station themselves."

"I suppose," Hazel grumbled. "They can't be from Red Gap. No one who lives here would be so irresponsible."

Jason rolled his eyes but ignored her comment. "They're from Apple Valley. They weren't really serious suspects, but the police were looking into it. Honestly, the police didn't have anything besides the McCleary's eyewitness accounts. It would probably have been enough to convict Wallis, but no one puts much stock in the McCleary's telling a straight story. It didn't sit right with a lot of people, your Uncle John included. It was Wallis' word against the McClearys. Of the two of them, we were more inclined to believe Wallis."

"Okay, I get it," she said. "So they would have released Wallis?"

"Possibly, but then he confessed and made the whole thing moot," Jason said. "He probably didn't realize."

"Interesting," Hazel said.

"One more thing," Jason said, leaning away from her as if preparing for another outburst. "Chris Mills visited Wallis Trudgeon in prison right before he confessed."

"What?!" Hazel shrieked. "Can't they arrest him just based on that?! Clearly, he's manipulating Wallis somehow into taking the fall for Cash's murder. The only reason he would do that is if he was guilty! This is ridiculous. What are the police even doing?"

"They're doing their jobs, Hazel," Jason spoke in a calm, soothing voice. "You can't arrest someone based on a hunch, and I can't prosecute them without evidence. Remember how we talked about how we live in America yesterday? We have due process. We're protected from all the stuff you're talking about."

"But he's a bad guy! Why should he get due process?"

"Hazel, you don't really believe what you're saying," Jason said. "You're just upset right now. I know you understand why due process is necessary, and the USA is such a great place to live."

"Yeah, it's great if you're a criminal," she grumbled, crossing her arms over her chest.

"Don't worry, sweetheart," Jason said, turning off the highway onto the bumpy road that led to the hiking hub. "We'll figure it out. If you let me help you instead of vigilante-ing around town by yourself. We'll pick up your car, then I can go to the courthouse and spy for you some more, okay?"

"Alright," Hazel said. "I want to talk to those hunters. If they were in the area that night, they might know more than they realize."

Jason sighed. "Fine. I'll take you and we can meet with them together."

SIXTEEN

Hazel and Jason drove through the early morning fog to the parking lot where she had stashed her car the night before. It was hard to see more than a dozen feet ahead of them. It was as though the land itself was feeling gray, anxious, or vaguely depressed. But it was always foggy in the mornings, and Hazel didn't think of it as ominous. Until her car materialized out of the gloom ahead of them.

Hazel gasped.

Jason reached over and took her hand as he came to a stop. Without a word, they climbed out of Jason's SUV.

The tires of Hazel's car had all been slashed and were completely flat. Someone had taken a baseball bat to her windows and the windshields. Dents and scratches covered the paint job. Hazel's stomach clenched. She took a deep breath to avoid throwing up.

"We know who did this," she rasped.

Jason shrugged. "I assume you're referring to Chris Mills."

"Who else would it be?" Hazel shrieked.

"The murderer," Jason used a small voice she hadn't heard

since college. His face turned ashen, the color drained from it. A stiff breeze blew across the parking lot. Jason shivered.

"He's going to get away with it." Hazel reeled.

Jason tore his eyes away from the car to look at her. "Unless you had a dashcam running or something."

"Let's go." Her voice came out hoarse with emotion.

Jason tentatively circled the car, taking in the damage and shaking his head. He hadn't heard her. Panic welled up inside her and her next words came out too forcefully.

"Jason, let's go!"

"What?" He jumped and ran back to her side. "Do you see something?"

She grabbed his hand and pulled him back towards the car. "No, I don't see anything. Let's just go. I'm scared."

Jason nodded. He looked around the deserted parking lot again. The fog was dissipating a bit. He opened the door for her, and she didn't let go of his hand until she was in the passenger seat. She felt shaky.

"Are you okay?" he asked, rubbing his hand where she had gripped it.

"No, I'm not okay," she said. "Jason, this isn't like Red Gap. I don't recognize my home anymore."

Jason pressed his lips together. He didn't say anything, but Hazel knew what he was thinking. In the past, he had always shaken his head at her affectionate belief in the exceptionality of her hometown. After her parents' accident, she had been on the receiving end of a million kindness. The town had rallied around her grandmother and helped raise her. Her faith in Red Gap was rooted in experience.

But Chris Mills wasn't from Red Gap. He was an outsider. He was the one who had destroyed her car. He had to be the one that killed Cash. Everything bad that happened was because he came to town. And she allowed him to be there by voting to approve his hotel.

Hazel didn't feel like she could breathe until they had driven all the way back down the bumpy road and back out onto the main highway. Jason jabbered to her the whole time, but she didn't hear anything he said. She scanned the woods looking for vandals, people who may want to hurt her. She worried about Waylon Gibbons. Had Chris Mills tried to hurt him too? She hoped he would call soon. Maybe they should go out to his house and check on him.

"Stop," she said.

"What? Why?"

"We need to find Waylon Gibbons. I want to make sure he's okay and we need that backpack back. If Chris Mills knew that was my car somehow, he might have harassed Waylon."

"Okay," Jason nodded. "That makes sense. He waited for a break in traffic, then flipped a U-turn and headed back towards the parking lot they had just left.

"Do you think you can find his place again?" he asked.

"I don't know," Hazel fretted. She kneaded her hand with the opposite thumb. She was so tired. She hadn't slept at all the night before. Less than an hour, easily.

"Hazel?" he reached out and put a hand on her knee. "Hazel!"

"Oh," she said, turning away from the window. "What did you say?"

"I asked if you want to file a police report. I doubt they'll be able to pin it on anyone, but you never know."

"Maybe not," she frowned. "Mills might be more likely to drop the trespassing charges against me if I don't."

Jason's shoulders slumped. "What about your car? I can get it towed right away, but the repairs will take some time, I think. You'll need a new paint job and all that."

"Sell it," she said, waving a trembling hand. "I'll buy a new one." Her voice was shaking.

"I'm worried about you." He patted her knee, trying to bring her out of her daze. Hazel glanced at him and noticed that the dark green had overtaken him again.

"I'm just a little spooked," she said, trying to smile at him. "It's hard for me to believe that someone would want to wish me harm."

Hazel's phone began to buzz. The number wasn't one that was saved in her phone. She picked it up. "Hello?"

"Miss Hazel?"

"Waylon!" she cried with relief. "Are you alright?"

"Someone attacked your car, Miss Hazel," Waylon said, his voice tinged with concern.

"I know, I saw. Are you there now?" She and Jason were bumping down the road to the parking lot now.

"Yes, I thought I'd bring your backpack here for you."

"That was a wonderful idea, Waylon, thank you," she said. "We're very close. We'll be right there."

She hung up the phone. "Waylon is at the car now," she told Jason.

"Huh, smart guy," Jason said. "You said he's handicapped somehow?"

"Yes, I think so," she said.

"Interesting." They made it to the parking lot and saw Waylon standing by Hazel's car. He stepped backwards into the lingering fog when he saw Jason at the wheel. Hazel could barely wait for Jason to stop the car before she got out.

"Waylon, are you okay? Did you see anyone last night?" she asked. He still had a bright white impression about him.

Waylon held out the backpack to her and glanced at Jason.

"This is my husband, Jason." Hazel took the backpack and took a step back towards Jason.

"Thanks for helping my wife out last night," Jason said, putting out a hand to shake Waylon's.

Waylon grinned. "I like to help," he said, shaking Jason's hand. "It is nice to meet you, but I need to go now."

"Wait, Waylon," Hazel said. "What about last night?"

"After you left with the police, I went home," he said. "You didn't come back for your pack, so I brought it here today. I'm glad you have it now."

"But did you—"

"Oh, I almost forgot," he said, pulling something out of his pocket. "I made this for you this morning."

He handed Hazel a beautifully carved rabbit. Its ears pricked up and listening, curled up but ready to hop. Hazel gasped. "This is beautiful. You did it just this morning?"

Waylon grinned again. "Yes," he said. "Come visit me again. I like visitors."

Hazel was about to ask him again if he saw anything the night before, but Jason broke in before she could speak.

"We would love that," he said. "Take care, Waylon."

Waylon waved at them and disappeared into the trees.

"But I had more questions for him," Hazel said.

"He told you everything he knew Hazel. Whoever bashed in your car didn't bother Waylon. Either they didn't know he existed, or they already knew that he wasn't a threat."

Hazel's mind leapt to the carved fox at the McCleary's house and the wolf that Wallis had. She looked down at the rabbit in her hands. Could Waylon had carved those as well? "This is extraordinary, isn't it?"

Jason took it from her and turned it over in his hands. "It really is," he said. "It's got so much life to it. Waylon has quite a talent for that. He could set up a stall at the farmer's market or even have a little stand on main street during tourist season and do quite well."

They got back in the car and made their way back towards town.

"I've got to get back to Eugene," Hazel said.

"I'll drop you off at home and call those hunters. I can come get you before they come in."

* * *

THE HOUSE WAS quiet when Hazel came in through the garage. She padded towards the guest room, putting her ear to the door. Behind her a clattering came from the kitchen and she jumped, letting out a startled yelp. She put a hand to her chest and laughed at herself as her heartbeat returned to a reasonable cadence. She headed towards the kitchen. "Eugene? Need help?"

He froze when he saw her standing in the doorway. "I'm sorry," he said. "I hope it's okay..." he gestured towards the dishes in front of him. He had found a frying pan and some butter and eggs. Hazel could smell bread in the toaster.

"Of course, it's okay," she smiled. "It's not like we're going to let you stay with us and refuse to feed you." She sat down on one of the bar stools at the kitchen island. "Make yourself at home."

He smiled at her nervously before turning on the range and setting the frying pan over the flame. She watched him melt butter in the pan and expertly crack the eggs into it.

"You should teach my boys how to cook for themselves," she said, intrigued by his self-sufficiency.

Eugene snorted. "If I didn't cook for myself, I wouldn't eat," he said, covering the pan with a lid. He studied the eggs rather than look at her.

"So healthy too," she commented.

Eugene shrugged. "Coach says to eat eggs."

"Would you like some cheese or avocado on it or anything?" she asked. "Ketchup?"

"Just salt," he said.

"Oh, I know what you need," Hazel got out of her seat to rummage through her cupboards. Eugene took the lid off the pan and flipped the eggs perfectly. No broken yolks. Hazel handed him a shaker.

"Everything Bagel Seasoning?" Eugene asked.

"It will change your egg-consuming life," she said.

"Ok, I'll try it," he said.

Hazel began to unload the dishwasher. "Eugene, I wanted to ask you a little more about what you said last night, about being haunted."

Eugene shook his head. "Forget it. I was just tired."

Hazel shook her head. "Have you seen Cash?"

Eugene didn't answer. He picked up the frying pan and flipped the eggs onto the waiting buttered toast. He sprinkled a bit of the seasoning on top.

"Eugene," Hazel went on. "You've been through a lot of trauma. It wouldn't be surprising if you saw things in your state. You need some help, just to get you through these first few months."

Eugene still didn't respond. He took big bites of the eggs, standing across from her with his plate on the island. "You're right," he said. "This bagel stuff is great."

"Last night, I told you my parents died when I was ten." Hazel looked down at her hands. She kneaded her right thumb into the fleshy place between her thumb and pointer finger on her left hand. "I wasn't in the car when it happened. My dad was a trucker. My mom went with him on a trip up to Nashville because it was their anniversary. They left me with my grandmother."

Hazel took a deep breath and let it out slowly. She didn't talk a lot about her parent's death with anyone, not even Uncle John. It got too heavy. She used to talk to her grandmother, but she was gone now. Jason listened with sympathy, but he had strained relationships with his parents, so his perspective was a little different.

"The thing is- I wasn't there, but I can hear it. I can see it. I'm not sure why or how, but I witnessed my parents' death. It's almost worse than being there because my perspective isn't fragmented. I never blacked out. I just watched my parents die, in pain. My mother was calling out for me." Hazel felt a tear fall on to her cheek and wiped it away, blinking quickly to clear the other tears away. Her vision cleared, and she looked back up at Eugene. He had set his fork down and was looking intently at her. "I don't know if it's actually real," Hazel went on, waving her hand dismissively. "It might all just be a figment of my over-active ten-year-old imagination. But it stuck with me like a memory and haunts me even now."

She reached across the island and patted his hand. "You're a good boy, Eugene. You're going to be okay, but it's not bad to get some extra help when you need it. And I am always here for you, in case you need anything." Hazel hesitated. She thought about telling Eugene about what she found in Cash's truck, but decided against it. She didn't think that he was in a good enough mental state to be able to process something like that. As soon as he was a little better, she would tell him about his aunt and grandparents in Tennessee.

✳ ✳ ✳

Hazel left Eugene playing video games and rushed to where Jason was waiting for her in the car. He leaned over to kiss her when she got in. "How are you feeling?"

She shrugged. "Not the best. I'm worried about Eugene. I'm worried about my new friend Waylon Gibbons. I'm a little scared, but mostly I'm angry with Chris Mills. I'd like to run him out of town."

Jason frowned. "Me too," he said.

Hazel blinked. Jason was usually all about peace, justice, liberty, and fairness. Especially at work. "I made a map," she said. "I thought it would help when we're talking to the hunters."

"That's a good idea," Jason said, nodding.

"Hi, Mr. Dean," Danny greeted them when they walked into the courthouse. "And Mrs. Dean, what a wonderful surprise, it's lovely to see you."

"You too, Danny," Hazel said, but without her usual warmth.

"Are you alright, Mrs. Dean? You seem upset." Hazel was struck again by how constant Danny's turquoise emotion was. She couldn't decide what emotion it actually depicted. The tenor of his voice changed, his facial expression changed, but it was like he was just going through the motions. In this instance, his voice sounded concerned, but his color still didn't waver.

"She'll be okay, Danny," Jason said. "But maybe you could get her a cup of tea? She had a little scare this morning. Chamomile tea would be a great help."

"Right away Mr. Dean," Danny said saluting, he disappeared into another room for a minute.

"Come on down to the office when you get your tea," Jason said, hurrying off to get back to work.

Hazel waited for Danny less than five minutes, but she noticed something on his desk she had never noticed before. Gooseflesh broke out on her arms.

"Danny, what's that?" she asked when he came back, handing her a cup of tea.

"Oh, that?" he said cheerily. "That's a gift from a friend. Isn't it beautiful?" He held up a carved raccoon, about the size of her hand, clearly made by the same person that carved the fox and the wolf she saw at the McClearys and the Trudgeons.

"It's gorgeous," Hazel settled the raccoon back down onto the desk carefully. "It has a very distinct style, doesn't it?"

"It's hand-carved," he explained.

"Do you mind if I ask who the artist is?"

"It's this man I met. He's a bit of a recluse. His name is

Waylon Gibbons." Danny smiled. The turquoise around him didn't flicker.

Hazel's heart began to race. It couldn't have been a coincidence. Waylon Gibbons must have carved the fox and the wolf too. Perhaps the fox was a gift to Cash, but how did Waylon connect to Wallis? Or Danny, for that matter? "Oh, does he have a stall at the farmer's market or anything?" she asked, pretending she had an interest in buying one.

"Oh, no. He doesn't come into town, doesn't like crowds."

"Oh?" Hazel asked. "How did you meet him?"

"I was out hiking in the woods a while back and ran into him," Danny explained. "He's a very nice man."

Hazel stopped herself from continuing to interrogate Danny. She didn't want to make him suspicious.

"It's beautiful," she said again, heading back towards Jason's office.

"Danny knows Waylon Gibbons," she whispered to Jason.

"Huh," Jason said. He was reading through a document printed in tiny font single spaced on legal-sized paper.

"Why do legal documents come on bizarrely large paper instead of the regular eight and a half by eleven stuff?" Hazel wondered out loud. "It's not easily filed anywhere in your house. It's so pretentious. *These documents are so important that they need extra-large paper that you will never know where to put.*"

"Mr. Dean?" Danny's voice spoke up over the phone's intercom system. "There are a couple of people here that say they have an appointment with you."

"Yes, yes," Jason said. "Send them back, Danny."

A minute later, a man and a woman in head-to-toe camo outfits came into Jason's office. Their emotions rolled off of them in waves, a frenetic lime green from the woman and a grumpy muddy brown on the man. The colors mixed together around their arms and hands where they were almost touching, mixing into a darker, grumpier brown. Jason got up and shook their hands and introduced Hazel as "his assistant." Hazel snorted but reached out to shake hands with the hunters.

"I'm Mallory, and this is my husband, Ike. Are we in trouble?" Mallory asked, sitting down in a chair across from Jason.

"No, no," Jason said. "Like I explained over the phone, we were just hoping that since you were in the area at the time of the incident, you might be able to give us a little bit more information."

Mallory nodded her head but didn't look appeased. Ike sat back in his chair with his arms folded across his chest, looking at them through narrowed eyes and not saying a word.

"Can I just ask," Hazel said, pulling out her hand-drawn map. "Where you might have been hunting in relation to this map?"

They both stared at it blankly.

"It's mostly of the hotel construction site as you can see," Hazel said, trying to excuse her drawing skills, "but this over here is the hiking hub and the highway runs across the bottom of the page."

"I think we were right about here," said Mallory, pointing to a space between the hiking hub and the construction site, very close to Waylon Gibbon's house. "I don't think there's a house there or anythin' though. I swear that we didn't know nothing about a building goin' up there. We'd been huntin' there lots of times and we always stay well away from the hiking trails and everything."

"You're worried that we're going to have you arrested for hunting illegally," Jason said, discerning the reason for their nervousness. "That's not what we're after today. But I would recommend that in the future you only hunt in designated areas so you avoid a scare like this going forward."

"We will, sir, I swear," Mallory said. "We was right spooked when we heard that a boy was shot right in the same time and place that we was huntin'. I was so worried we done it. I was so relieved to hear that it was someone else after all."

"But you were in the area at that time?" Hazel pressed.

"Yes, ma'am"

"Did you hear anything? Maybe shouting or gunshots?"

A fresh wave of colors rolled off of them. The man still a muddy brown, the woman's lime green turning pale. "No, no, ma'am we didn't hear a thing. You know it's hard to hear much of anything when you're shooting off your own gun, not to mention that most of time we're wearin' earmuff headphones so we don' blow out our own ear drums. And it was mighty cold that day so we was wearin' hats too."

"I see," said Hazel, although she didn't at all. Although it was unseasonably cool, it wasn't cold enough that they would need hats. It seemed crazy, but she could have sworn that the woman was getting more nervous despite their reassurances. "What about your guns? What kind of guns were you using?"

Mallory glanced quickly at her husband who didn't say anything, just continued to sit there as a great big arm-folded glaring statue. "It was a Ruger 10/22 rifle," she said.

Hazel nodded. "Thank you. Listen, are you sure you can't remember anything from that day? I just... We're just trying to make sure that the boy's death wasn't senseless. I mean it was, but we don't want him to just be another violent crime. We want to find out the truth of what really happened. He has this little brother, you see, and I have a hunch that the boy died heroically. It would sure mean a lot to the brother if we could share that with him. He's just a high school sophomore."

"I'm so sorry," Mallory began. "I wish we could tell you more but-"

"We can't because we weren't actually there," Ike said, speaking for the first time.

"Ike!" Mallory whisper-yelled at him. "We took the money. We can't go back on our word..."

"I don't trust that man, Mallory," Ike said. The muddy brown that was clinging to him during the whole meeting began to dissipate, but Mallory's lime was getting paler and paler.

"But... but..."

"Look, this nice lady is trying to do something good, and I don't want to get in the way of that." He leaned over the desk towards the Deans. "Will you swear that you won't tell anyone what we say? It's just that my wife is scared that the man would come back and hurt us if we tell you anything."

"I can keep a secret," Jason said. "It's kind of a professional skill. This is all off the record. I won't use it unless you say to."

"Thank you, sir," Ike nodded at him. "We were hunting in the woods that day, but we were down south on the other side of the highway in the designated hunting area there. We were far from the road all day and didn't see or hear anything from the other side of the highway. When we were packing up our stuff at the end of the day, someone approached us and said that in a few days we would read in the paper that a boy died of a gunshot wound nearby. And that he would pay us one hundred thousand dollars if we went down to the police station and said that we might have accidentally shot him while we were hunting. He promised us we wouldn't get in trouble because it was just an accident and the police would be able to tell. Then they would just send us home."

"So we did, and one hundred thousand dollars in cash showed up in our mailbox when we got home. Everything went right as the guy said, but the more I think about it the more I think this guy, the one who gave us all the money, is the murderer."

"Did you catch his name?" Hazel asked.

"No, he never did say," Ike said, scratching his head. "He was a medium-built guy, about your height, sir, with dark hair."

"Was he wearing nice clothes?"

"I can't say I noticed what he was wearing," Ike said. "So it couldn't have been nice. That would have been memorable out in the forest like that."

"What about you, Mallory?" Hazel asked. "Do you remember anything about the man?"

"No," Mallory said, her lip quivering. "Do you swear you won't tell anyone? I'm afraid that— If that man killed once, he could come back and kill us if he knew we squealed on him."

"We won't tell anyone, but are you sure that you won't consider going to the police and testifying in the case against him?"

Mallory's eyes widened. "No, ma'am. I don't think it's a good idea."

"I would," said Ike, "if it wouldn't kill my wife, but look at her. She's been afraid of her own shadow since we got that money."

Jason put Wallis Trudgeon's mugshot on the desk in front of them. "Was this the man that offered you the money?"

"Nope, that's not him," said Ike. "This guy is a lot wider and more muscley than the one who gave us the money. He was a little bit scrawny."

"Thank you," Jason said, pulling a card out of his desk and handing it to Ike. "Here is my card. Please give me a call if you think of anything else or if you change your mind about talking to the police. Thank you very much for coming down here on such short notice."

Ike stood up and shook both their hands again. "Thanks for the invitation. I gotta tell you. It's quite a relief. I feel two feet taller after talking to y'all."

"I'm glad," Hazel said. "Don't worry, Mallory, everything will be fine. We won't tell anyone."

Mallory smiled weakly and hung on her husband's arm as they left Jason's office.

Hazel turned to Jason. "It was-"

"Hazel, don't jump to conclusions."

"Who else would it be? Who else would have that kind of money to just put in someone's mailbox?"

"I don't know, Hazel," Jason put up his hands, like he was trying to soothe a skittish horse. "This doesn't make any sense. I think we'll have to bring Captain Tate in on this."

"We shouldn't have let them leave yet," Hazel said. "We should get a picture of Chris Mills and show it to them. The man's been arrested a half a dozen times, there has to be a mugshot of him in the system somewhere, right? Go find it."

"Hazel, slow down."

"No, there's no time," she said. "Wallis ruined everything with his confession. We have to hurry before he goes to trial. You find a mug shot, I'll stop them before they leave."

Jason hesitated, looking between her and the door before he sat down at the computer. "I'll get the picture," Jason said.

"Good," Hazel ran out the door to stop Mallory and Ike. She threw open the front door, ignoring Danny's cries of alarm, and saw them headed towards an old beater truck on the far side of the parking lot. "Ike! Mallory!" she yelled across the parking lot. "Wait!"

They turned towards her, and she ran down the steps and out to meet them. They walked back towards her. "What is it?" Ike called.

She caught up to them, breathing heavily, putting her hands on her knees. "There's... one more... mugshot... we wanted to... show you," she gasped.

"Alright," Ike said.

A loud popping sound made them all jump. They whirled around and saw that the truck had begun smoking from underneath the hood.

"What's going on?" Mallory said, her gaze darted around her like a frightened rabbit. Hazel took tentative steps towards the truck, and her eyes widened. The smoke started billowing even more from under the hood. Hazel heard a rushing sound in her ears. Things seemed to be moving slowly, underwater-like, as she tried to make sense of what happened to the car. Mallory's panicked voice brought her back to herself instantly.

"Get back in the courthouse," she ordered, ushering Ike and Mallory back up the stairs. Another loud sound came from the truck. Hazel instinctively crouched to the ground. Mallory screamed, and Ike pushed her through the door to the court-house. Hazel pulled herself up and ran in after them. "Danny, call the fire department and Captain Tate."

"What's going-" Danny began.

"Now, Danny!" Hazel snapped.

"Yes ma'am," he said, eyes wide.

"Come back this way," Hazel told Ike and Mallory. She worried how Mallory might react if the truck went up in flames. She led them back to Jason's office. Mallory was already crying softly.

"There's just a little problem with Ike and Mallory's car," Hazel said to Jason. "I'm going to have a chat with Captain Tate."

She strode out of the office and back up to the lobby, looking out the window at the car that was now billowing smoke. Danny was watching it too.

"I called Captain Tate. He should be here in a minute. The fire department too," he said. He looked out the window like a child watching a favorite TV show but his turquoise hue didn't waver. "Do you think it will light?"

"I don't know," Hazel said, crossing her arms over her chest. His youthful enthusiasm for destruction made her uncomfort-able. "I don't know much about cars."

"What happened?" he asked eagerly.

"I'm not sure. There was a popping sound, and it started smoking." She didn't mention that she suspected it was some kind of bomb.

"What the devil is going on down here?" Uncle John stormed in from down the hall. "Hazel, I thought it could wait until this afternoon to have our little chat, but here you are again where the trouble is. Explain yourself."

"We don't have time right now, Uncle John!" Hazel declared, pointing out the window at the smoking car. A small crowd had formed on the sidewalk outside the parking lot, watching the smoke rising into the sky. Probably wondering, like her, if it would catch on fire. Hazel hoped they thought it was some kind of engine malfunction, that they wouldn't be able to tell that it had been sabotaged. That kind of thing would put the whole town on edge and get them in the news. Not good for tourism.

John looked out the window and gritted his teeth. He strode outside, down the stairs and across the parking lot. He made a wide circle of the truck, Hazel knew that he would be noting all the damage, looking for clues as to the motivation behind the crime and who might have done it. He didn't know who the truck belonged to. He would have some unbiased opinions.

The fire truck pulled up and began their work. The truck never truly burst into flames. John walked back towards the courthouse after speaking briefly with one of the firefighters. Hazel sucked in her breath, bracing herself. She reminded herself that she was a grown woman, not a little girl.

John opened the door. "Well?" he asked, his hands on his hips.

Hazel glanced at Danny. "We can talk in my city council office," she said and took off down the hall without looking backwards to see if John was following her. It wasn't exactly her office, it was a shared office, but no one else would be around until the beginning of next month.

She flipped on the light and held the door open for John.

"Should I start from the beginning or the end?" she asked.

"I think you'd better start from the beginning, don't you?" It wasn't really a question.

Hazel took a deep breath and spilled the basic story. Her relationship with Cash and Eugene, her visit to the McClearys, both visits to the construction site, her visit to Trudy Trudgeon, and even her talk with Wallis Trudgeon in his cell. The only things she left out were meeting Waylon Gibbons and getting her hair done at LaShay's salon.

John didn't interrupt or rage or yell. He just sat very quietly and listened. His emotions were apparent in a kaleidoscope of color and Hazel couldn't tell which ones were winning. She did see the unmistakable copper that he had when she had earned her scholarships to GSU and when he had held Elias and Jeremiah for the first time. It was pride. He was proud of her. She tried to cling to that thought as she saw all the other colors as well.

Hazel told him about her fight with Jason and their new resolve to work together. She told him about visiting with Mallory and Ike that afternoon and finally about what happened outside with the truck.

John pressed his mouth into a thin line. He shook his head, slowly. "So many things," he said. "Oh, Hazel, you have no idea what you're doing, do you?"

Hazel cringed. "I wouldn't say *that.*"

"I think you're in more trouble than you realize," he said, standing up. "I'm glad you are safe for now, but Hazel, you have mixed yourself up in some dangerous business. This will not end well. Take my advice," he put his hands on her shoulders. "Stop. Don't go poking a sleeping bear. Take care of that poor child. Let that be the service you do for Cash."

"But John, Wallis didn't kill Cash. This isn't about the feud. If a Trudgeon goes to prison for killing a McCleary, all of those hard feelings will blow up again. People will start taking sides. I will not let that feud do any more damage to Red Gap than it already has. I have to clear him. I have to."

John nodded. "I understand your sentiment, but I can't help

you with this. I won't. Why should *you* be the one to clear him? Why does it have to be you? I can't protect you if you go down this path."

Hazel looked up at John and the tears sparkling in his eyes caused hers to spill over onto her cheeks. "If not me, then who?" she asked quietly. John let his hands fall from her shoulders. He didn't say anything.

John reached around behind him and unhooked her holster and gun from his belt. He pressed it into her hands. "I was worried you would say that," his voice was strained. "Please be safe darlin'. You're all I have in the world. I love you."

Hazel gave him a sad smile. Then she left him in the room and went back to find Jason.

SEVENTEEN

"I can't believe that after all that, they didn't recognize Chris Mills," Hazel said. The Deans were back in bed at the end of the day. Jeremiah had called saying he was going to a friend's house to practice for their academic decathlon. Elias told them he had to catch up on the homework he had been neglecting the last few days since Eugene moved in, but Hazel suspected he needed a nap because they stayed up so late the night before. Eugene had gone out with a couple friends to get fries and milkshakes. Hazel was glad that he was doing something so normal, she hoped it would help him feel better.

"That's because Chris Mills is smart and didn't offer them the money himself," Jason told her.

Hazel pounced on his language. "So, you believe it was him now?"

"I didn't say that." Jason shook his head, his face impassive. The air around him turned a dull tan. Hazel had seen that color on him often before when he was working. It meant he was trying to maintain balance, to remain unbiased and not to feel much of anything. Hazel wished she had honed a similar skill.

"What will happen to Ike and Mallory?" she asked. Hazel

reached over and began to scratch Jason's back, her agitated fingers moving erratically.

"I'm not sure," Jason winced. "It's unclear whether the bomb was meant as a warning or to hurt them. Mallory was very upset and convinced that there was some kind of spy in the courthouse. They've been taken into protective custody. I think that means that they'll be house guests at Captain Tate's."

"Well, that's something he's doing, anyways." Hazel had spent the evening feeling betrayed by Uncle John. A small part of her had hoped that when she told him everything, he would take her investigation up himself. That she could hand it off to him and focus, like he himself had suggested, on helping Eugene. She sighed and let her hand fall away from Jason's back. "So, it was a bomb?"

"Oh yes, they found an incendiary device in the engine. It was on a timer."

"I'm sorry I had you call them in," Hazel said in a quiet voice.

"Hazel, you shouldn't feel responsible for this." Jason took Hazel's hands in his. "Taking money for going to the police and telling them that you might have killed somebody when you didn't was a stupid thing to do. They should have thought through it."

"I guess," Hazel reached for the tea on her bedside table.

"The good news," Jason chuckled, "is that Ike is madder than a hornet, and he's more than happy to testify if we can ever figure out who to arrest."

"So what happens to them in the meantime?" Hazel let the warmth of her mug warm her hands.

"They'll stay at Captain Tate's indefinitely."

"Seriously?"

"At least until we can get this all sorted out."

"Argh," Hazel moaned. "We've ruined their lives."

"No, Hazel, they ruined their own lives. Or maybe they were

just in the wrong place at the wrong time. Either way, it wasn't your fault." Jason reached for his phone and checked his emails. "With the truck blowing up, Ike's testimony, and that conversation you had with the captain, he's agreed to reopen the case and Judge Pruitt has issued a warrant to search the trailer at the construction site." He frowned. "Chris Mills still wants to put you in jail, though."

"Argh," Hazel muttered, setting her tea back on the bedside table. "Just pay him off."

"Um, not legal," Jason gave her a wry smile.

"You know what I mean. Settle it outside of court. Give him whatever he wants."

Jason's mouth fell open. He put his phone down. "You want to dip into your trust fund? That won't make the criminal charges go away."

"Yes, can I just do community service or something? I can explain everything to the judge." Hazel covered her face with her hands and groaned, scrunching her eyes shut.

"You haven't delved into your trust fund since you opened the bookshop." he pointed out.

"That's not strictly true," she said, dropping her hands and turning red. "The shop isn't exactly profitable on its own."

"Are you sure you want to—"

"Just make it go away, Jason," Hazel blurted, burying her head in his chest. "I don't want to deal with this guy anymore. I just want to put him in jail."

Jason chuckled, and she could feel the vibrations against her cheek. He kissed her head. "Okay, my little diva. I'll do the best I can. We'll settle the civil suit, and I'll ask Stephens about some kind of community service plea deal for the criminal charges. Everyone's had a good laugh down there about you being arrested, but I don't think that anyone really wants to punish you for it."

Hazel looked up at him and forced a smile. "Thanks, Jason. I think I just need some rest. I'm going to go to sleep."

"I'm going to get a shower. I still smell smoky," Jason disappeared into the bathroom. Hazel chuckled. Jason's car did have a distinct smoky smell when they got in it to come home. It was parked upwind from the truck. Jason had some fastidiousness about his car lingering from his Los Angeles upbringing. He had already made an appointment with a detailer in Atlanta for the following week.

She lay down, trying to quiet her mind, but then she sat up in bed. "Jason," she called. "I forgot to mention something."

But Jason was already in the bathroom with the shower on and couldn't hear her.

Hazel ran downstairs and grabbed her backpack. She opened it up and pulled out the papers she had grabbed from Cash's truck the night before.

There were several construction permits and as she suspected, they were for the hotel. Why had Cash made copies of them and put them in his hidden car? They appeared unremarkable to her. She flipped through them until another few papers jumped out at her. She examined them closely. Something seemed wrong about them. She jumped when her phone rang. She picked it up and was surprised to see that it was LaShay Trudgeon.

"LaShay?" Hazel answered.

"Miss Hazel, is that you?" LaShay's voice sounded ragged.

"Yes, hi LaShay, how are you doing?"

"Hazel, they took my boy. They put him in jail. They're saying he killed someone."

Hazel sat in a chair. "I'm so sorry, LaShay."

"I thought he was doing better," LaShay went on. "I thought he had his life back together."

"Did you try to contact him?" Hazel asked.

"I..." LaShay said. "I went to his house. I saw my daughter-in-law. She wasn't very warm."

"Who knows what Wallis told her about you," Hazel said. "Give it some time, keep trying."

"Do you think I should go see Wallis in prison?" LaShay asked.

Hazel hesitated. Did she think it was a good idea? "As long as you are prepared for a less-than exuberant reaction," she said. "I think if ever there was a time that a man needs his mother, it's when he's in prison. It might be a way to show him that you are less judgmental now, that you want a relationship with him regardless of his choices."

"I don't know if my heart can take it."

"It's a hard decision," Hazel said. "Find some place quiet to sit and breathe for ten minutes and then do what your heart tells you to do."

There was silence at the end of the line for a moment. "Alright. Okay, I'll do that."

"You can call me if you need to psyche yourself up," Hazel said.

LaShay gave a halting laugh. "Thank you, Hazel. I'll let you know what happens."

"You should come into the bookshop sometime, LaShay. Do you read?"

"Not much," LaShay laughed. "I never had much time for it when I had all those kids at home."

"You should join our book club. You would be a great addition."

"I'll think about it," she said. Hazel could hear the smile in her voice. "Thank you again."

"Bye," Hazel hung up. It filled her with warmth that LaShay would call in distress.

She had forgotten what she was working on but remembered in a flood of excitement when she saw the paper in her hand.

"Jason!" she yelled. "Jason, look at this." She ran up the stairs waving the paper in front of her.

"What?" Jason asked. He was out of the shower and already half dressed.

She thrust the paper into his hands. "Look, this is a copy of a correspondence between Cash and Chris Mills. Cash points out some code violations and shortcuts they are taking on the hotel and Mills just dismisses him. Look."

Jason stared at the paper. "Where did you get this?" he asked, "I thought you didn't grab anything from that trailer."

"I didn't, Jason! I got this out of Cash's car. It has copies of the construction permits too. I'm not sure why."

"Let me see them," Jason said. He followed Hazel back downstairs and studied the documents Hazel handed him. Hazel held her breath.

"I don't want to get your hopes up," he said. "But I think these might be forged."

Hazel sucked in her breath. "The construction permits are forged? But why?"

"I don't know, but I think you just found the evidence we need to open a case against Chris Mills. I'll work on it tomorrow."

Hazel lay down with a smile on her face. Finally, she had done something right. She fell asleep quickly but vaguely woke up when Jeremiah came into their room. She heard him and Jason speaking in low, murmuring voices.

"Yeah, I know," Jeremiah's voice said. "It doesn't sound good."

"Shush," Jason said. "I don't want you to wake your mother. She would be broken up about this. She's been so worried about Eugene."

Hazel's ears perked up even more.

Jason got out of bed. "I'll go down to the hospital," he told Jeremiah. "You stay here and go to sleep."

At the word *hospital,* Hazel was immediately wide awake. Hazel felt the mattress shift beneath her as Jason climbed out of bed.

Hazel sat up. "Eugene?" she murmured, squinting through the darkness to see his face.

Jason ran a hand over her hair, soothingly. "It's okay, honey," he whispered. "I'm taking care of it. You go back to sleep. You need some rest."

"What happened to Eugene?"

"He fell," Jeremiah said. "He was out hiking in the woods nearby that construction site where his brothers work, and he didn't see a drop off and fell. His leg is broken, I'm not sure what else is wrong with him. He texted me from the hospital that we shouldn't worry when he doesn't make it home tonight."

"Why would he be out hiking on a sprained ankle?" Hazel looked at Jason. "I'm coming with you."

"I know you are," he said, giving her a thin smile.

"I've gotta get some sleep," Jeremiah said. "Hey, I heard that a car was on fire at the courthouse today? What was going on there?"

Jason waved a hand. "Don't worry about it. Just go to sleep."

Jeremiah must have been tired because he just nodded and went off to bed without further questions or commentary.

* * *

FIFTEEN MINUTES later they were in the overly bright lobby of the hospital trying to figure out where Eugene was. At first they were told to look for him in the ER, then they said he had been moved into surgery, but they couldn't tell them what for because they weren't family. Hazel paced around the waiting room and generally pestered the nursing staff. Finally, when she explained that she was Eugene's foster parent and had temporary custody of him, the receptionist gave up the top secret intel that Eugene had suffered from a collapsed lung and was in surgery for that.

"It'll be another hour and a half at the least," the nurse told them, with a conspiratorial glance from side to side.

"Thank you, thank you," Hazel said. "We'll wait."

She and Jason sat down in a couple of chairs with a shared wooden armrest.

"You don't think that Chris Mills is responsible for Eugene's injuries as well?" she asked Jason.

"No way," he said. "Eugene is just a reckless teenager. He shouldn't have been out hiking to begin with, not on that ankle."

"It doesn't make any sense," Hazel fretted. "Why would he do that when he was trying to recover enough to play football on Friday night?" She wound her arm around his.

"Kids are dumb," Jason shrugged.

"Maybe," Hazel said. She couldn't sit still. She got some coffee for something to do, but she was already anxious, and it made her twitchy. She paced around the mostly empty waiting room. She sat with each of the other people waiting for a little while, offering them any encouragement she could muster. She was thinking about asking the nurses if they needed help with anything when someone approached them and said they could see Eugene.

Hazel wished the nurse would move a lot faster as she followed behind her at an uncomfortably close distance. Jason held her hand and tried to pull her back towards him, but she pulled him along instead.

The boy was cleaner than she had ever seen him. It looked like a nurse had taken advantage of his unconsciousness to wash his hair and give him a bit of a sponge bath. Hazel was planning to breach the subject of personal hygiene the following day, but it looked like she wouldn't have a chance. He was in a white hospital gown with tiny blue polka dots all over it. One of his legs was a comical size underneath the blankets, presumably enshrouded in a cast. A fire engine red mist settled around him. It looked like an angry color, but Hazel thought from the groggy look on his face, it was probably his color for physical pain.

"Eugene, how are you?" she crooned, sitting down in the chair next to his pillow.

"You had quite an accident, son," Jason said, hovering at the foot of the bed. "Why on earth would you go on a hike when your ankle was hurt?"

"I had to... find it...," Eugene moaned.

"What happened?" Hazel asked. "Can you talk about it? If you're in too much pain, we can let you rest and come back in the morning."

"No... I'm glad you're here," he said. "I have to tell you... I think I found it."

"You found what?"

"I found it, north of home," he said.

Hazel froze. "Did someone hurt you? Was this really an accident?"

Eugene didn't answer her question. "It's not that far to the east," he said. "There's a path... through the woods."

"Slow down, Eugene," Jason said, glancing at his increasing heart rate on the monitor. "Slow down and start from the beginning."

Eugene took a deep breath. "I went out looking for it... that thing Cash mentioned in the book." He stopped. "I think they gave me a lot of painkillers."

Hazel shot a concerned glance at Jason, who patted Eugene's un-casted foot.

"So you went off into the woods in search of... what?" Jason asked.

"Anything odd," Eugene said. The red around him darkened to more of a deep purple. Hazel thought he was getting sleepy.

"We should go," Hazel said, starting to get up.

"Miss Hazel," Eugene looked at her and she could see the tears behind his eyes. "I saw my brothers. They were at some cabin. I tried to get closer to see what was going on, but my ankle wasn't cooperating, and I fell down an embankment. I screamed as best as I could until Roy found me. I think I'm lucky it was him and not Billy. Roy's got a soft streak on account of his kids. And he's not the brightest. He bought my story about just being out hiking. He picked me up and carried me on his back to the highway before he called an ambulance. It hurt like a..." he glanced at Hazel. "A lot. It hurt a lot." He lay back on the pillows, and suddenly the dark circles under his eyes became more pronounced and the bruising on his arms looked a little more black and blue.

"You were so brave," Hazel said, patting his hand. "You rest now, we'll take care of you. How long did they say you have to stay here?"

"They said the recovery in the hospital will be at least two days," he groaned. "So much for playing on Friday."

"Good," Hazel said. "I mean, it's good that you can be somewhere that you can get the care you need. By the time you're ready to leave, we should have that paperwork from CPS, so we'll be able to take you home."

"Thank you ma'am, sir," he said, a couple tears escaping from the corner of his eyes. "Y'all have been so kind."

"It's our pleasure," Hazel said. "I just wish your momma was still around to take care of you."

Eugene squeezed his eyes shut, causing a few more tears to crash onto his cheeks. "I do too, ma'am."

"You rest now," Hazel said. "Go back to sleep. The people

here will take good care of you. I'll be back tomorrow."

He nodded, his eyes already drooping. Hazel got up and grabbed Jason by the arm, pulling him out into the hallway.

"We have to go out there and figure out what's going on," she said. She was practically running through the hospital, as if they would go out into the woods at that exact moment.

"Excuse me?" Jason said. "Haven't you learned your lesson about that?"

"What else can we do?"

"Go to the police. You already told John everything. We could get him involved."

"No," Hazel said flatly. "He already said in no uncertain terms that he wouldn't get involved."

"But with Eugene's story—"

"Look, Jason," Hazel interrupted. "The police are satisfied that Wallis killed Cash, but there's definitely something going on in the woods. We need proof. It's the only way we can get John to help us. An innocent man died. My car was destroyed, and our new friends got their truck blown up. That little boy in there is living in a house full of criminals. We're not going to just sit and wait until something else tragic happens? I don't think so, mister. It's not happening."

Jason stared at her with wide eyes for a minute, then took her face in his hands and kissed her. She tensed for a second because the kiss was so unexpected. Then she melted into him, burying her fingers in his hair. She finally broke away from him, unable to breathe. "What was that for?" she gasped, unable to contain her smile.

"You're hot when you're filled with righteous indignation," he grinned roguishly. "I don't think it's a good idea, but I see that I can't stop you, so I'm coming too. Hopefully, our children will be okay once they're orphaned."

Hazel wished she could laugh, but instead the hairs on her arms stood on end.

EIGHTEEN

"Okay, remind me of the rules again?" Hazel asked, checking to make sure she had all the appropriate contacts saved in her phone.

"If we actually find evidence of illicit activities, we can call the police and they have enough probable cause to come in with guns blazing and all that." Jason explained. "If all we find is pornography and guns, then we're out of business and we'll just have to pack it up, go home and think of another way to expose Chris Mills."

"What counts as evidence of illicit activities?"

"Illicit materials would work. The actual drugs you think they're making or trafficking or whatever you think they're doing."

"What about people walking around with guns or something?"

Jason shrugged, "We could call in suspicious behavior. Guys in the woods with guns may or may not count in North Georgia. Unless they were anti-government somehow or something."

"Ok, so I'm looking for drugs or treason." It sounded like a joke, and she wanted to laugh. But she didn't. It was all too serious.

"Or if they had illegal weapons. You know, like big machine guns or something."

"Drugs, treason, or machine guns. Got it." She gave him a wry smile.

They were driving down the road to the hotel construction site in Elias' twenty-year-old Impala. They had traded him for Jason's beamer.

Jason had convinced Hazel that going in the middle of the day would work better than the middle of the night. They wouldn't need night vision goggles or to wear all black. They would just be out hiking like regular hiking people. Plus, it seemed to him, criminals were nocturnal, and their fortress would theoretically be emptier during the day than at night. These were all good points, and Hazel wished that she had consulted Jason before her own ill-conceived attempt to spy. She could have avoided being arrested.

Jason's phone began to ring. He had taken the day off, but that never seemed to actually mean much.

"This is Jason," he said.

Hazel watched him react to the voice on the other end. He turned to a dark slate. Bad news work mode. "Yes," he said. "I understand... No... Yes... Alright. No, I get it. Okay. Talk to you soon."

"What on earth happened?" Hazel asked.

"It's the construction site. The trailer was lit on fire."

"The trailer was lit on fire?" she repeated, trying to process what that meant.

"Hazel, the trailer is gone, destroyed."

"But how?"

Jason shrugged. "If you're right about Chris Mills, it means that he didn't want it searched," he said. "But they can't find any evidence of arson."

"This is too much, Jason," Hazel said. "Bombs and fires? What is even happening? What does it mean?"

"There'll be an investigation of the fire. They'll probably find code violations in the hotel construction. The penalty for that isn't nearly as serious as forging government documents. But we have those at our house. Mills had to know that they were missing, right? Do you think he knew that Cash took them?"

"You already know what I think." Hazel crossed her arms over her chest.

"Maybe you're right." Jason shook his head. "I'll never get over what some people will do for money."

"Anything that will tie him to drug trafficking probably got burned in the trailer."

Jason shrugged. "Maybe not. Let's see what we find today."

They chose a route down an access road east of the construction site that Jason had noticed in the satellite mode of Google Maps. It didn't have a name, but it looked like someone had used it regularly at some point. Branches and bushes jutted out into the road, scraping against the side of the car in some spots where it was narrow. Luckily, Elias' car was so dinged up already that he wouldn't notice the new scratches. The potholes were a different story.

"We'll have to get it realigned before Elias drives it again," Hazel said, grabbing on to the roof handle as the car lurched for the tenth time.

Jason nodded, turning the wheel sharply to avoid a branch in the road.

"I guess it's safe to assume that our suspects haven't been using this road for their nefarious activities?"

"Not necessarily," Jason said. "If you knew the road and used a small truck, it wouldn't be so bad. It's a great cover."

The road finally got so overgrown that they couldn't continue driving on it and had to stop.

"Alright," Jason said, getting out of the car. "Let's make it easy to find the car again." He pulled out an orange tarp and draped it over the top of the car, rolling down the windows and inch so he could secure it to them with bungee cords.

"Good idea! That will make it easier for the bad guys to find Elias' car and bash it to bits." Hazel said, getting out her phone. "Let's see if we can do this the easy way." The phone had one little bar of service on it, and when she tried to load the maps app, it just put them as a blinking blue dot in the middle of a field of white. She tried to zoom out, but nothing happened. "The easy way isn't going to work."

"That's okay," said Jason, pulling his map out with a boyish grin. He had marked where the hotel construction site was before they left. "We came in on this road," he pointed, "going about ten miles an hour for around thirty minutes."

"That puts us right about here," she pointed to another spot on the map. "If Cash was right and whatever is going on is happening east of the construction site and north of his house, that means we need to hike northwest from here at about ten and a half o'clock for several miles. We'll walk right into it at some point."

"Ten and a half o'clock?" Jason asked.

"Yeah, halfway between ten o'clock and eleven o'clock."

"Right." The corners of his mouth twitched.

"It's a thing! Uncle John always used to say it."

"Well, if we haven't hit it by noon we should come back." Jason folded the map back up and put it into his pack. "We don't want to worry the boys."

"Agreed," Hazel said, shouldering a backpack full of granola bars and water bottles. "Let's go."

"Hold on just a minute," he said, pulling his mostly unused hiking boots from the car and tying them on. "We should really do this more often."

"Investigate a murder?"

"No, not that," he said. "Go hiking together."

"Maybe," Hazel said. "But next time let's use an actual trail."

"Where's the fun in that?" Jason asked, pulling a sheathed machete out of the trunk and strapping it to his chest.

"Where did you get that?!" Hazel pointed and took a step back.

"It's just in case we need to do some bushwhacking," he shrugged. Sometimes it became painfully obvious to Hazel that her husband was really just a permanent tourist in her natural environment. "We don't want to get bogged down because of undergrowth. I'm just being prepared, like in Boy Scouts."

"You did Boy Scouts with Elias for like two seconds. You never got up to bushwhacking." Shaking her head, she turned to move in the direction they had decided upon. "I've been hiking in these hills my whole life, and I've never seen anyone wielding a machete."

"But we're not sticking to trails," Jason pointed out. "I should go in front of you. I'm the one with the machete and the compass."

She turned and squinted at him.

"I'm just saying," he said in a smaller voice.

Heaving a sigh, she rolled her eyes and said, "Fine, go ahead. But, if you're bringing that, I'm bringing this." Hazel got her holster out of the back seat and put it on.

Jason's eyes widened. His mouth opened and closed twice before he spoke. "Just in case, right?" he asked.

"Right," she assured him. He smiled, but his gaze was still focused on the gun.

"Okay," he said and set out ahead of her into the forest, clomping ahead in his big, waterproof boots, checking the compass every minute or so to make sure they were still on track. He got out the machete anytime any foliage crossed their path. Hazel suppressed a laugh when he tried to cut away some green vines that the machete didn't seem sharp enough to hack through.

"Really, where did you get the machete?"

"I borrowed it."

"From who?"

"From Danny."

"Why does *Danny* have a machete?" An image of Danny's excited face when he watched the hunter's truck smoking flashed through Hazel's mind.

"He did some kind of mission trip to South America when he was in high school and came home with it. He mentioned it once before. I grabbed it from him this morning."

"Did you tell him what we were up to?" Hazel asked, her eyes widening.

"No, no. I just told him we were going on a little day trip hiking for our anniversary."

They hiked in silence for a while, and Hazel actually began to enjoy herself a little bit. She let her mind focus on the beauty around her instead of the purpose of their outing. She thought maybe Jason was right, they should hike together more often. The leaves crunched under her feet, releasing the pungent scent of fall. The trees were emblazoned with color and the sky was a deep blue.

"So about the snakes..." Jason said.

Hazel laughed. Apparently Jason's thoughts weren't occupied as pleasantly as hers. "Right now is actually a good time to hike because it's been cold for a while," she explained. "Usually you have to worry about copperheads and rattlesnakes, but they're probably settling down at this time of year. You should watch out for poison ivy or sumac, but that will just make you uncomfortable later. The tricky part is the bugs. There are scorpions and spiders and a thousand different kinds of wasps. Ticks are really the most dangerous though, 'cause of lyme disease and all that. Still, fall isn't the most buggy time of year."

"What about bears?" Jason asked.

"No one has seen a bear in this area for like ten years. Too many humans."

"That's a little sad," Jason remarked.

Hazel laughed again. "You wanted to meet a bear?"

Jason shrugged. "Just indicative of diminishing habitats and all that. Did you know that the bird population in North America has declined twenty-nine percent since the seventies? It's tragic."

"I hadn't heard that." Hazel crushed a mosquito that just bit her on the forehead. They walked on, Hazel thinking about what was actually dangerous about hiking in the Appalachians.

"Your biggest problem is actually going to be your body. Blisters, heat exhaustion, falling like Eugene did. You're much more likely to hurt yourself than have nature hurt you."

"What? Oh!" Jason nodded. Hazel guessed he had still been thinking about conservation. "I guess that makes sense... I also read that two hundred years ago this area was filled with gigantic American Chestnut trees. They got to be like a hundred feet tall, just huge. There were tons of them. Then some kind of virus came along from cross continental trade and wiped most of them out. Which, of course, affected the entire biome." Jason placed his palm against a nearby tree trunk. "It's such a shame."

"You're standing in poison ivy," Hazel pointed out. Jason jumped away from the tree. They hiked in silence for over an hour before Hazel agreed to stop for water and sustenance. They crested a particularly tall hill and Jason collapsed onto the ground.

"How's that exercise program coming along, darling?" she asked him sweetly.

"I think I've lost ten pounds just this morning," he heaved. She handed him a water bottle. He chugged it down. She tried to hide her own shortened breathing. It had been a little while since she had been out hiking. She forgot how unforgiving the hills were. They had just crested the top of one, and it provided a relatively unobstructed view. The swaths of orange and yellow and red leaves blocked a bit of the land below, but a lot of them had already fallen as well. Hazel scanned the gap below her for anything out of the ordinary.

Jason pulled off his shoes.

"Don't do that! You might not get them back on. Your feet will be swollen."

Jason peeled off his socks. "Blisters," he moaned. Hazel suddenly noticed that he had a burnt orange hue to him.

"Oh dear," Hazel pulled a first aid kit out of her bag and sat down next to him. He had matching blisters on each heel. They were the size of nickels and had already popped. "Are you going to be okay?" she asked, applying moleskin.

"Just duct tape them," he winced.

Hazel blinked at him.

"Then they won't rub anymore," Jason explained.

"I've never heard of that," Hazel said.

"Just do it," Jason pleaded.

"Okay." Hazel's voice rose with skepticism. "But it might hurt even more later." She unrolled some duct tape and stuck it on the back of his heel as gently as she could. "Put on some new socks," she suggested. "That might help."

"Thanks." Jason pulled a pair of new socks out of his backpack and stretched the openings as wide as he could before putting them on his feet. Then he put the shoes back on. Hazel searched his face for pain, but it didn't betray any. The only clue was the burnt orange surrounding him. Hazel worried that Jason might not make it back to the car, let alone find the cabin Eugene had mentioned.

"Still want to go hiking more regularly?" she smiled.

"Yes!" Jason exclaimed. "Then my feet wouldn't have this problem anymore."

"Fair point."

Jason pushed himself to his feet and stood on the edge of a precipice, looking out at the landscape around them with binoculars he had pulled from his pack. "I think I can see what we're looking for now."

"What, you can?" Hazel hadn't noticed anything herself. "Where?"

"Do you see that little log cabin down there?" Jason said, pointing.

Hazel squinted but could hardly see anything through the trees. "No," she said.

"Here," Jason stepped back and handed her the binoculars, "stand right where I'm standing."

Hazel scooted over into his spot.

"Now look right where I'm pointing." Jason stood behind her and pointed over her shoulder into the valley they were staring at. Then Hazel saw it, a small log cabin.

"I don't know," Hazel said. "What makes you think that's what we're looking for?"

"Just it's location," he said. "It's on our ten and half o'clock bearing, and it's been a few miles. I think that the construction site is just beyond that little hill there."

Hazel nodded. "Well, it's worth a look, anyways. How do we get down there?"

"Rappel?" Jason guessed.

Hazel laughed again. "You watch way too much Bear Grylls," she said.

"Okay, okay," he said. "I guess we just keep going this way."

"Let's go." Hazel said, slinging her pack across her shoulders.

"Can I have another couple minutes?" Jason asked. He walked back towards his backpack but made no move to pick it up. Hazel agreed, but only because she didn't think that the log cabin was what they were looking for. She checked her watch.

It was getting close to eleven. She tried to push negative thoughts away. They would find something. They had to.

It took another half an hour of hiking along the ridge to find a place to get down from the mountain without breaking their necks. Even so, it was slow going, finding the footing and concentrating on each step. Jason didn't complain about his blisters, but she was sure that they were slowing him down even more.

"We made it!" she called back to her husband when the ground leveled off. He was almost twenty yards behind her. As she waited for him to catch up, Hazel felt a twinge in her back and her knees. She wasn't as young as she used to be. And she had been up really late two nights in a row. Once they figured out what was going on, and drove that Chris Mills out of town, she was going to sleep. Jason finally caught up with her and she turned around to look at him.

"Are you okay?" she asked.

"I'll be fine," he said, through jagged breaths. "Let's keep going, we're running out of time. We have to check out that cabin first."

Hazel nodded, and turned back around to continue, but she was worried about her husband. His jaunty quips about boy scouts and bushwhacking were gone. All she heard from him was gasps for air.

Eventually, they made it to the log cabin they had spotted from the cliff. It wasn't well cared for and had no access to any kind of road. The porch was covered in leaves and webs. One of the steps was caved in. It was completely deserted. Not a soul was around or had been around for a long time.

"I don't think this is it," Hazel said, handing Jason a water bottle and a granola bar.

"Huh," Jason said, rubbing the back of his neck. "I thought for sure this would be it. I'm just going to take a look around."

"Go for it," Hazel said, settling herself onto a porch step that looked pretty stable. "I'll just be here."

Jason went off to the other side of the cabin. Hazel did her best to stretch, trying to get the kink out of her back from where the weight of her pack rested.

"Hazel!" Jason yelled minutes later.

"What?" she walked around to the back of the cabin where Jason's voice was coming from.

"Come look at this," Jason called.

"What did you find?" Hazel asked. He stood above some doors in the ground that he had thrown open.

"It's a storm cellar," he said.

"Like in the Wizard of Oz?"

"Yes, just like that. Come on down. Watch out, it takes a second for your eyes to adjust." He shined a flashlight from his pack and led the way down the stairs. The air of abandonment wasn't thick down here the way it had been above ground. Hazel would expect to walk into cobwebs and experience a strong smell of mildew, but it seemed fresh and clean down there.

Reaching the bottom a step ahead of her, Jason shined the flashlight around a large cellar, possibly even the size of the entire cabin upstairs. It was completely filled from floor to ceiling with boxes. "What's all this," Hazel asked, puzzled.

"Look," Jason said, shining the flashlight beam on a label affixed to the box closest to them.

"Apple?" Hazel said, taking in the easily recognizable apple logo.

"iPads, iPhones, Apple Watches," Jason shined his beam on label after label. "They're all Apple products, and I'm pretty sure they're stolen. There must be millions of dollars of merchandise in this room. I think we're looking at the result of those semi-truck robberies Captain Tate has been going on about." They roamed the stacks of boxes, taking in the massive undertaking it would have been to move them all here.

"So it wasn't drugs like I thought," Hazel mused, her brain racing to readjust all her assumptions to account for the new evidence.

"No, but we can call the cops. They'll be able to get a warrant without any trouble to search the cellar of some old abandoned cabin in the middle of nowhere. I mean, look at all this stuff!"

"But how did they get it here?"

"That is the magic trick, isn't it?" a cold voice spoke from up the stairs behind them. Hazel whirled around to see Billy with a gun trained on them.

NINETEEN

J ason jumped in front of Hazel, but she pushed him aside, reaching for her holster.

"This is the second time you've pulled a gun on me, Billy." Hazel aimed her gun at him. "You didn't shoot me then, and I don't think you're going to shoot me now."

"I wouldn't be so confident about that if I were you," he hissed. Before she could react, Billy jumped closer to Jason and put him directly between them. Hazel looked for the shot. She thought she could take it, but Jason was shooting out jets of inky black fear. "No Hazel, please," he yelled. His eyes were wide. Hazel deflated. She slowly crouched to the ground and dropped the gun, then kicked it over to Billy. He let go of Jason and picked up the gun.

Billy spat on the ground. "The boss is on his way. He'll decide what we should do with you." He waved the muzzle of his gun off to the left. "Find a seat," he said. "It'll be a few minutes." He turned and called up the stairs. "Roy, Virgil, come on down. Pay no attention to our visitors."

Hazel and Jason slowly walked to the wall and sunk to the

floor. The two brothers came down the stairs, squinting into the darkness.

"Start loading up," Billy said. "We've got to clear this whole place out."

Roy and Virgil grabbed an armful of boxes each and hauled them up the stairs. Virgil looked at Hazel, but quickly averted his gaze when he saw her staring back at him. Billy stood at the bottom of the stairs with his gun lazily trained on Hazel and Jason.

"How are we going to get out of this?" Hazel whispered to Jason.

"I'm thinking," he replied.

Hazel was thinking too. She was thinking that any minute Chris Mills was going to walk down the steps and then any chance they had to convince Cash's brothers to let them go would disappear. She could hear a faint roar she recognized as ATV engines.

"Did you kill Cash?" blurted Hazel at Billy, her words like a weapon she flung at him. She was gratified when she saw him flinch, just as though he had been hit by a projectile.

"No," he growled.

"What happened to him?" she demanded.

"I don't have to tell you nothin'" he snapped, "you're nothing but a nosy old gossip."

"Don't you talk to Hazel like that," Jason growled.

Billy laughed.

"Look," Hazel said, her voice softening to try another strategy. "I just want to know what really happened to Cash. He was a good man, and I feel that his memory deserves some truth."

Billy was across the room in three steps and smacked her across the face. She grunted and fell to the side, grabbing her cheek and feeling the sting of tears come to her eyes.

"How dare you!" Jason roared. He shot a leg out, sweeping Billy's feet out from under him. Billy fell to the ground, momentarily loosening his grip on the gun. Hazel grabbed it out of his hand and pointed it at him. Jason kicked him in the gut with his big bulky hiking boots. "How dare you hit my wife!" he yelled, kicking him again.

"Jason," Hazel pulled on his arm. The same crimson red fury Jason exhibited when she was arrested now consumed him. She couldn't even see his face, just a haze of red. "Jason! Jason, stop! You're scaring me. We need to get out of here." She looked around for something else to use as a weapon, but Jason was one step ahead of her. He had drawn his machete from the sheath across his chest and was brandishing it at Billy.

"He needs a lesson in manners," Jason returned with venom.

Hazel reeled. The world spun around her. It felt like she was watching everything that was happening from far away, like in a movie. "Let's go," she urged.

Jason moved in her direction, but he kept his attention trained on Billy.

Hazel's stomach turned, and her chest felt tight. She had to get out into the open air before she had a heart attack. She headed up the stairs, her gun aimed ahead of them where Virgil and Roy would appear any second. She didn't know if they were armed or not. Jason was behind her, keeping Billy at bay with the machete.

She reached the top of the stairs and saw nothing, not Roy or Virgil or any ATVs. The boxes that they had been carrying had also disappeared. "They're gone," she breathed, the pain in her stomach loosening a bit. A stiff breeze blew around them and Hazel shivered. Her face throbbed where Billy had hit her. The feeling of being far away from her own body was suddenly gone, and she missed it.

"They'll be back to reload," Jason said, scanning the area for threats.

"How long?" Hazel asked.

"Who knows?"

"Let's tie Billy up."

"With what?" Jason asked.

"Whatever you were going rappel down that cliff with," she said, making large dramatic gestures towards his backpack.

"What's that going to do?" Jason wondered. "They'll just come back and untie him in a minute."

"It'll give us a head start," Hazel said, pulling the rope out of his pack.

"I guess you're right." Jason's head darted around in every direction.

They descended the stairs and found Billy looking at his phone.

"Don't move," Hazel yelled down at Billy. "Drop the phone." Billy put his hands in the air and let the phone fall to the ground.

"You're going to shoot a man after you brought him dinner and cleaned his kitchen?" Billy said ironically.

"I might shoot you, but I'm not going to kill you," she said.

Billy scoffed. "Your aim ain't that good."

Irritation flared in Hazel, and she found herself pulling the trigger. She had been practicing her aim with Uncle John longer than Billy had been alive. It scared her how easy it was to do. But the noise made her headache and the throbbing spread from her cheekbone up into her head.

"Hazel!" reprimanded Jason. Black fear overtook his crimson anger.

"Yow!" Billy shrieked, falling hard on the wood planked floor. "You shot my foot!"

"That's for hitting me," she said, trying to keep the tremble out of her voice. "Jason, I think you'll find him a little more cooperative now. If he's not, just stomp on that foot."

Jason looked at her with wide eyes but stepped forward and

pushed Billy towards a post at the bottom of the stairs. He pulled the rope from his bag and tied Billy to the post, ignoring his injured food. Hazel stomped on Billy's phone until it crunched.

"Hey!" he whined. "That wasn't necessary. No one gets any reception out here."

Hazel ignored him, grinding the phone under her heel.

"Virgil and Roy will be back any minute with the boss," Billy said. "You won't be able to escape."

"Should we cut out your tongue?" Hazel asked, pointing at the machete in Jason's hand.

"Hazel," Jason whispered out of the side of his mouth. "Aren't you taking this a little too far?"

Hazel didn't answer. She glared at Billy the entire time Jason tied him up. She was surprised that he stared right back at her. Swirls of charcoal and midnight blue surrounded him, but Hazel could see in his eyes that all he felt was grief and anger. Her last suspicions that he might have killed Cash disappeared.

"Let's go," Hazel said once Billy was securely tied. They ascended the stairs and ran back to the front of the house to retrieve her backpack. "What's the plan?"

"I don't know," Jason said, running his hands through his hair. The black and red around him had given way to that familiar forest green. "Billy's right, they'll be back soon and scrambling away on foot isn't going to get us enough distance to avoid them when they come looking for us."

"Then we hide," Hazel shrugged. "Where do you think they're driving in and out from?"

"I saw some tracks by the cellar door. Looked like ATVs with trailers attached to them."

Hazel nodded. "Then we hide on that side. I'm going to leave my pack over here to throw them off."

"Hurry," Jason said, already heading into the forest.

Hazel pulled out her phone and as many granola bars as she could fit into her coat pockets and a water bottle.

Jason took her hand and pulled her back around the cabin and then into the woods. They ran through the forest for several minutes before Hazel had an idea.

"Jason, we have to go back!" she exclaimed. "Their ATVs are our ticket out of here."

Jason stopped short in front of her. "You're right," he said. "Why are we so bad at this? Come on then."

"Don't get too close," she said. They turned and crept back through the forest this time, more aware of the noise they were making and no longer talking at full volume. The leaves were too noisy beneath their feet. Roy and Virgil would be back any time with Mills. Hazel tried to extend her hearing, listening for the sound of ATV engines. They found a spot where they were within view of the cabin, but it was still quite a ways out, midway up a slope. Fallen trees offered some cover and a little warmth. They made themselves comfortable behind a four-foot diameter trunk, covering themselves with leaves as much as possible to camouflage.

"Once they're all downstairs, we'll make a break for it," Jason whispered. "If there's two ATVs, we'll have to grab both so they can't chase us."

"What if they hear us?" Hazel whispered back.

"We didn't hear them when we were in the basement, so maybe they won't hear us either."

"I heard the engines, faintly. But we should be far enough away by the time they rush back upstairs. Maybe." Hazel murmured. Then she pulled her phone out of her jacket. There were still no bars of service. "Do you have any phone service?"

Jason pulled his phone out of his pocket. Every movement either of them made resulted in a cacophony of rustling leaves. "No," he said, glancing at the phone. "We'd better stop moving so we don't make so much noise."

Hazel's stomach churned as they sat in tense silence, waiting for Roy and Virgil to come back. She felt nauseous and the pain in her head was getting worse. Hazel found her eyelids closing without her permission and her brain slipping into unconsciousness. When she woke up again, it was dark.

"Jason," she croaked softly, panic seizing her for a moment because she couldn't see anything.

"I'm here," Jason said quietly. "You fell asleep. I'm worried you might have a concussion."

"How long has it been?"

"Three hours or so," Jason said.

Hazel moaned. "Why haven't they come back yet?" she willed herself not to lose control and start sobbing. Her body ached everywhere. Her face felt like it was on fire. "Jeremiah's already home from school. Elias will be back soon."

"I think they went out looking for us instead of coming straight back here," Jason said.

"But what about Billy?" she asked.

"They don't know he's tied up down there with a hole in his foot. We made him drop the phone before we tied him up. They'll probably be back soon though, they'll want to get on with their operation. They probably have someone to meet and they'll have to risk letting us go in order to make their appointment."

Hazel didn't say anything. It was a nice theory, but Hazel had lost all confidence in theories. "We have to contact John. Can you pull out that compass and figure out where the highway is from here?" she asked. She couldn't see his face at all in the darkness, but she could hear a hint of a smile in his voice.

"I think so," he said.

"Okay, new plan. We'll walk straight to the highway. We'll be careful and avoid open spaces. Hopefully, they've gotten tired of looking for us and aren't being as careful. Or maybe you're right and they'll come back here to finish their job. In any case, we can't just sit around waiting for them. The only way out of this is to get the police involved. All we need is a couple of bars of service. I'm buying a satellite phone when we get home."

"Ok," Jason said, pulling out his compass.

Hazel ate her last granola bar while Jason was calculating which direction they should go. She was thirsty, but she didn't have any more water.

"Wait," Jason said.

"Did you figure it out?"

"Yeah, but I was just thinking... if we're out all night, then our kids would call the police. They'd tell them we were hiking in these woods and got lost or hurt or something. They'd pull out all the stops looking for us. There'd be helicopters and dogs and all kinds of things. They would stumble on the McCleary's operation by accident, and the whole thing would be blown wide open."

Hazel blinked at him. "*If* they don't disappear with the evidence. And *If* they find it before they find us. And *if* the McClearys don't find us first. And *if* the McClearys haven't finished their job and disappeared with all the evidence. And *if* we don't die from exposure and thirst. When's the last time you had some water?"

"It's been a while," Jason admitted.

"We need to get out of here," Hazel said. "It's a good idea, but not the best one. Let's go."

Jason nodded, "You're right. Alright, let's go. I think it's four miles that way."

They started moving slowly through the woods, careful not to make too much noise or movement. It would take a long time to go four miles in the woods at that speed. Once they were out of sight of the cabin, they picked up the pace a little bit, but even if they weren't trying to be quiet, it would have been slow going, anyways, because it was so dark.

"I wish we brought the headlamp," Hazel whispered.

"No, it would light us up from miles away. Look!" Jason said. Hazel tried to see where Jason was pointing in the dark but didn't need to when she noticed a beam of light about a half mile away to their left. "Get down," Jason said.

They crouched down below the underbrush. A list of nocturnal animals ran through Hazel's mind, causing shivers to go down her spine. They waited there, watching the beam get closer and closer to them. They crouched lower and lower, eventually hugging the ground when the beam got close enough that they could hear the voices associated with it.

"We gotta get back, Virgil. They disappeared like magic. It's dark, we're not gonna find 'em out here now."

"The boss ain't gonna be happy if we give up now," a voice presumably belonging to Virgil replied.

"He's not going to be happy if we don't get all those boxes loaded neither."

"Yeah, you're right. Let's go."

The beam and voices turned around and went back the way they came. Neither Hazel nor Jason moved an inch until the light had faded away.

"Looks like we're in the clear," Jason said finally, rising to his feet then reaching down to help Hazel up. Hazel stood, then brushed all the leaves and dirt off herself.

"We can go a little faster now," Jason said, taking off through the trees. "We don't have to be as quiet." Hazel followed him with a feeling of weightlessness. They had dodged the search party, so they should be able to make it home. They slipped through the trees and stumbled over underbrush.

"Hazel?" Jason's voice was barely audible above the crunching of leaves and the night noises of the forest.

"What?"

"I've never told you this before," he began. "But when I was a kid, I watched someone get shot."

Hazel stopped short. "You what?" she tried to keep her voice calm and quiet.

"I had just turned twelve. I used to ride my bike all over town wherever I felt like. You know my mom never really paid attention to where I was or what I was doing if I left her alone. I've told you this part before."

"Yes," Hazel breathed.

"I was at the Seven Eleven. They had Slurpees there for cheap. I used to get them a lot. I guess I was out a little too late that night, but my mom had some guy at the house. I can't remember why I wasn't with any of my friends. There were a couple of people I could usually crash with when my mom was acting that way..."

Jason fell silent for a moment, lost in painful memories. "Anyways, I was coming home on my bike when I heard someone yelling. I don't know what I was thinking, but I followed the noise and saw these men in an alley. One of them was getting harassed by three other guys. He was yelling at them to go away. I wasn't the only who stopped to watch. Someone next to me ran off to call the police. *I'm warning you! Leave me alone!* The one man yelled. Before I knew what was happening, he had pulled out a gun and shot one of them. There was so much blood."

"Oh, Jason." Hazel reached out for him, but he didn't stop hiking through the trees. She couldn't see what color he was through the darkness.

"I was in the way. The shooter ran into me on his way out of the alley. I think I'm what slowed him down. The police picked him up just a block away. It was in the news. He went to prison for life. They said he was a murder. But I knew that it was mostly self-defense. If he hadn't had a gun, he might have gotten beat up, but he wouldn't have gone to jail. All guns do is escalate things. I hate them."

"Why haven't I ever heard this before?" Hazel wondered.

"I've never told anyone about it before. I felt like it was my fault for a long time. Like I should have gone to the police and told them what I saw. That the man wouldn't have gone to jail if I had." Jason's voice changed. It became a little stronger, he sounded more like his normal self. "Maybe not though, there's probably nothing I could have said or done that would have helped anything."

"Probably not." Hazel reached out for him again, and this time she caught his hand. "That must have been a heavy burden for you all these years."

Jason pulled her into his arms and hugged her so hard she gasped. "I don't think I'd make it if anything ever happened to you."

"We're going to be okay," she promised.

"Yeah," he murmured. "We are going to be okay. Let's go home to our boys."

They almost-ran through the forest for another fifteen minutes. Hazel worried about Jason's blisters as they tripped their way through fallen logs and mostly dead foliage. Eventually, they stumbled up an embankment and found themselves on the highway.

"We made it!" Hazel squealed. She grabbed Jason by the collar and kissed him, then broke off abruptly. "The phones!" She and Jason pulled out their cell phones.

"Still no reception," Jason cursed.

"I'm so thirsty," Hazel said.

"Me too."

Hazel tried sending a text to Jeremiah and Elias despite having zero bars, but a red exclamation mark popped up, informing her that it didn't go through.

"We'll have to keep hiking down the road towards town until we get reception," Jason said. "Or someone picks us up." Hazel groaned. "I'm going to flag someone down," she said. The traffic on the highway wasn't exactly heavy, but a couple cars passed. Hazel stepped onto the road and waved her arms, but neither of them slowed for her. One honked and yelled out the window. "Get off the road, lady!"

"I don't know if this is going to work," Jason said.

"It doesn't hurt to try," Hazel said. "We don't have anything else to do."

"I think you're sleep-deprived and delirious," he grabbed her and looked into her eyes. "Do you have a concussion? He hit you pretty hard."

Hazel didn't answer. Another set of headlights came blinking into view, this one driving a little slower than the others. Hazel stepped out into the road and waved her arms above her head. She tried not to let the desperation she felt show on her face. She had been hiking in the woods for twelve hours with nothing but a few paltry granola bars, she'd gotten a cumulative seven hours of sleep in the last forty-six hours, and she was exhausted. Not to mention that she had been held at gunpoint and hit by a lunatic. She could feel her face swelling around her eye and knew that it would look terrible the next day. She was done, and she wanted to go home and sleep for twelve hours while the authorities took care of everything else.

To her surprise, the car slowed and stopped at the shoulder of the road.

"It worked! It worked!" she cheered, clapping her hands together.

"Mrs. Dean? Mr. Dean? Is that you?" Danny's voice called.

"Danny," Jason came forward and shook Danny's hand through the window. The headlights illuminated the road in front of his car and cast a long shadow on his face. "It's so good to see you."

"What happened to your hike?" he asked.

"We got a little lost," Hazel said, attempting to look sheepish.

"I've still got the machete," Jason blushed, holding it up.

"Oh, dear," Danny chuckled. "Do you need a lift back to your car?"

"We'll never be able to find it in the dark," Jason said with a wave of his hand. "Would you mind giving us a ride back to the house? We think our boys are going to be worried."

"Sure," Danny said. "Get in."

Hazel surreptitiously handed Jason the guns she had taken from Billy and her backpack before jumping into the backseat. Jason put her things along with his bag and the machete in the trunk, then hopped in the front seat. "I'm never going to live this down, am I?" he grimaced at Danny. Hazel was distracted when Jason opened the door. The light illuminated Danny's face for a moment, and he was a different color than his usual turquoise—a kind of a fiery gold. Her forehead wrinkled with confusion that turned into a wince.

Danny's laughter faded when he turned to look at Hazel. "Oh no, Mrs. Dean, what happened to your face?" Danny exclaimed.

Hazel's hand flew to her cheek. "I... uh... fell," she stammered. "My face landed on a rock."

"You might have a concussion," Danny said, staring intently at her. "should I take you to the hospital?"

"No, no," Hazel said. Danny's sudden change in color and over attentive behavior was making her nervous. "I just want to get home and see my boys. I don't feel nauseous or anything."

"Are you sure?" Danny asked.

"Yes, I'm sure," she said.

"Okay then." He said, pulling back onto the road.

"Where are you coming back from?" Jason asked conversationally. Hazel was surprised that Jason hadn't noticed Danny's sudden transformation.

"I had a blind date out in Mosswood," Danny made a face.

Jason laughed. "Doesn't sound like it went very well," he said.

"She was quite a bit older than me," he said. "I think the picture on her profile was fifteen years old, I just don't think that it's going to work out."

"That's a shame," he turned around to smile at Hazel. "It's nice to have a partner-in-crime."

Danny laughed a little too loudly. "Nicely put Mr. Dean."

Hazel sat in the back seat, feeling more and more uncomfortable in Danny's presence. Something was off. She didn't believe him when he said he had been on a blind date. Why would he lie?

"Do you guys mind if we make a little detour?" Danny asked. "I promised I would pick something up from a friend for my mom on the way home."

Hazel's pulse quickened. She did mind. Terribly. She pulled her phone out of her pocket to see if she had service yet. No bars.

Jason said, "We're just thankful for the ride Danny, you do whatever you need to do." Of course, Jason's response was the right one. As long as they got somewhere there was phone service, they would be able to reach John and get the cops out to the cabin. Danny was doing them a favor, and they weren't in a position to make demands. Gratitude was the proper emotion. She forced a smile.

"Yes, of course," she said.

"Thanks," Danny turned down a side road and Hazel looked longing back at the highway toward home. "It won't take long," Danny promised.

"Do you have any water in your car?" Hazel asked.

"Oh no, did you run out of water?" Danny crooned. "I'm not

sure if I do, Jason. Do you want to look in the glove compartment there?"

Jason opened the glove compartment and although there was a wide variety of camping and hiking paraphernalia, there were not water bottles.

"I'm so sorry," Danny said. "I should really keep water in my car. It seems dumb not to. Hardly what I was taught in Boy Scouts."

"You were in Boy Scouts?" Jason asked, excited. "Elias did Scouts for a little while, but we couldn't get him to stick with it," Jason sighed with regret. "He wanted to do sports instead."

"I was never very good at sports," Danny said. "Scouting was a good spot for me." He glanced into the rear-view mirror at Hazel. "I can probably grab some water from my mom's friend," he said. "Here we are." He pulled off the road.

Hazel looked around, confused. She didn't see a house or a driveway. All she saw was a big rig truck and a couple of ATVs.

"Wait a second," Hazel said. "Aren't those the same ATVs..."

When she glanced back to the front seat, she saw that Danny had a gun aimed at Jason.

"Get out of the car, Mr. Dean," he said. "You too, Mrs. Dean. I wouldn't want to have to shoot your husband."

TWENTY

All the sounds around Hazel seemed muffled, underwater. All she could really hear was her own heartbeat thudding in her ears. She grasped the door handle with a shaky hand. She heard Jason's voice, argumentative and insistent, but she couldn't make out what he was saying. Her vision tunneled. All she could see was Danny holding a gun aimed at her husband's head.

It took her a couple of tries to find the door handle and pull it. Her hand didn't seem to work exactly the way that she told it to. Jason got out of the car, and he grabbed her hand as soon as he could. At his touch, everything came into focus.

Danny got out of the car and slammed the door. The sound made Hazel jump. He kept the gun pointed in their general vicinity and walked around the car towards the big rig. "Come on, you two. Move your feet."

Hazel's automatic inclination was to reach for the gun, but it was still in Danny's trunk, along with the machete. Jason sputtered, but Hazel grabbed his hand and pulled him along. Her mind was spinning in circles. Danny. Who would ever have suspected Danny? He was a nonentity in her mind, a compliant people-pleasing robot. Now that he had a gun aimed at them, the fiery gold grew deeper and richer. Hazel couldn't fathom if he fit in to all the intrigue with Cash or if he was acting in some other capacity. Maybe Mills had offered him a lot of money, and he had been blinded by greed. Surely he wouldn't really shoot anyone. She scrutinized his posture, his body language.

"Danny," she found herself saying. "You don't really want to hurt anyone, do you?"

Danny smiled at her, aiming the gun a little more intentionally. "I don't know, Mrs. Dean, do I?" he said in a conversational tone.

Chills ran up and down Hazel's spine. She didn't want to ask him any more questions. Jason squeezed her hand. They walked down the length of the truck. Hazel noticed that the cab was empty. Clomping and banging were coming from the inside of the trailer. The back of the truck came into view slowly and Hazel flinched, waiting to see Chris Mills ready to kill her and Jason. But all she saw was two ATVs with trailers parked behind the big rig. The road stretched out behind it, narrowing into a dirt road that Hazel assumed eventually led to the log cabin where they had left Billy.

She tried to peer into the darkness of the big rig's trailer but couldn't see anything; it appeared empty from where she was standing. If they were planning on filling that truck this evening, they had a long way to go. The sound of men lifting and moving things echoed out of the trailer.

"Be careful in there," yelled Danny into the trailer. "Come on out for a sec. We have company."

Virgil, Roy, and Billy appeared from deep within the trailer. "Well, looky here," Billy said in a quiet, menacing voice.

"We was lookin' everywhere for them!" Virgil shouted. "Where'd you find 'em?"

"Well, I was just driving down the road when they magically appeared," Danny said. "I wasn't even trying."

"Great job, boss," Billy said. He carefully sat on the edge of the truck and lowered himself to the ground, not putting any weight on the foot Hazel shot.

"Boss?" Hazel blurted, unable to hold her tongue.

All of their heads snapped towards her. "Surprised?" Danny asked, smiling. "Why is that? Don't I seem smart enough to be the boss?"

"No... I..." Hazel said, looking towards Jason who was shaking his head in an attempt to get her to stop talking. "I just thought that Chris Mills..." she trailed off.

The four men started laughing. "Chris Mills?" Danny choked. "You thought he was the mastermind behind this operation? Nope, he's trying to get on the straight and narrow. Reformed himself a few years back. He can't quite seem to get there though, can he? He had to take shortcuts, poor man. Oh, well. Too bad these morons told the cops Cash died at the construction site and dragged Mills into this mess." Danny explained, waving the gun at them conversationally. "That's okay though. I got him out of it. Made some proverbial lemonade, you know what I mean? Me, on the other hand. I just skim a little off Apple's bottom line. I think they can afford it, don't you? You know what I hate? I hate how after a while your iPhone won't hold a charge anymore. Pretty soon it's only a few hours before you have to charge it again. You end up getting so frustrated that you buy a new one."

The McCleary brothers were nodding in agreement.

Hazel looked at Jason.

"They do it on purpose, you know," Danny went on. "They're con artists over there. Running the biggest scam in the history of the planet. Well, I don't feel at all bad for taking a little piece out of them."

"But what about Cash?" Hazel asked. The conversation they were having was surreal. Her hands twitched. She grabbed Jason's hand to keep them still.

An identical hard look appeared on the faces of the McClearys, the swirling black and blue around them darkened. "Don't you talk about Cash," Billy snarled.

"Cash was going to leave," Hazel spluttered.

"Hazel, don't." Jason murmured to her. "You'll make it worse."

Hazel bit her lip. "He didn't want to do this anymore, he thought ya'll had gone too far."

Billy snarled. "I've had just about enough of this."

"Me too," Danny said. "You see, Miss Hazel Dean, we don't owe you an explanation. Boys, throw them in the back of the truck. Tie them to something. They'll enjoy a nice long road trip together."

"I think you should just shoot them both right now," Billy protested.

"So bloodthirsty, Billy." Danny shook his head. "I think they'll be worth more to us alive than dead. You know the Randolphs have significant funds available to pay ransom demands." He chuckled. "Into the truck they go."

Billy and Virgil walked down the ramp and grabbed Hazel and Jason, pushing their hands behind their back and forcing them up into the truck. Two lamps in yellow plastic cages hung inside, illuminating the half-filled interior. Hazel's eyes darted around the interior of the truck. She couldn't breathe. Her heart was pounding, her head throbbing. "Jason," she said, clutching at his hands. "Jason, I can't be in here. I'm going to die. I can't do this."

"Take their cell phones," Billy told Virgil.

Hazel couldn't catch her breath. She felt like her heart was going to explode in her chest. On top of that, she was dizzy. She leaned over the side of the truck and vomited.

"Woah," Virgil jumped back.

"Please," Jason said, looking at Danny. "I'm pretty sure Hazel has a concussion. And she has a thing about semi-trucks because her parents died in an accident when she was a kid. We've always been kind to you, haven't we? Please, just leave us here and go on your way. You'll be long gone before we'll be able to reach anybody."

Danny stared at Jason for a minute, then looked at Hazel. Then he shook his head. "Tie 'em up, boys," he said, turning back towards the ATVs.

There was a wooden board attached to one side of the trailer, presumably to keep merchandise from crashing into the side of the trailer. Roy tied Hazel's hands together roughly and then looped it around the wooden board, pulling it tight.

"Enjoy your trip," he said.

Hazel realized that she wouldn't be able to sit for who knew how long and suddenly felt light-headed. Her breathing was still ragged. Her knees were weak. She felt sure she would faint.

"Roy," Danny called. "You stay here and watch these two. We'll go back to the cabin and get another load."

Roy nodded, walking to the trailer wall opposite Hazel and Jason and sitting down.

"Too bad they took my gun," Billy said, glaring at them.

"You mean this gun?" Danny asked, flourishing the gun Hazel had shot Billy with. He must have noticed Jason put it in the trunk earlier. He handed it to Roy. "Take it."

Roy wrapped his fingers gently around the grip and tried holding it at varying distances from his body. He looked like he would be more comfortable with a hunting rifle.

"Just make sure you watch 'em," Billy said. "They're tricksy."

"I will," Roy promised.

"Are you going to be okay on that foot?" Danny asked Billy, his expression amused.

"I can drive, can't I?" Billy snapped, limping off with one last murderous glance at Hazel.

They heard the ATVs start up and drive off.

"Hazel," Jason said urgently once they were gone. With both

their hands tied behind their backs, he couldn't reach for her. "Hazel, you're fine. It's okay. The truck isn't moving, it isn't even running. Everything is going to be okay. Take a deep breath." Jason modeled some deep breaths. "Look at me, Hazel. Look at my face. Good, good girl. Now breathe. The ground is beneath you. It is supporting you. The air you breathe in gives you life. You are alive. You are safe."

Hazel did her best to breathe and listen to the sound of Jason's voice. To only see Jason. It worked a little bit. Her heart was still pounding, but she didn't feel like she would suffocate.

"What a bunch of new age mumbo jumbo," she heard Roy mutter.

Hazel tried to scoot her feet over in Jason's direction, but more than a small shuffle in any direction caused the rope around her wrists to cut in painfully. Jason seemed to have a little bit more leeway and scooted towards her enough that his bicep rested against her shoulder. She tried to lean her head against him, but she couldn't quite reach. "Jason, my head hurts," she said.

"I know, I'm going to get you out of here," he said.

Frustration overcame her, and she was afraid that she was going to start crying again. The only other thing she could think of to do was talk.

"Roy?" she said in her best 'comforting mom' voice. "Roy, won't you please tell me what really happened to Cash?"

Roy just grunted. He had that same swirly blue-black that his brothers did.

"That's really the only reason I got involved here, you know," she went on. She knew that she could get through to Roy. Eugene had said he was the softy. "I just wanted to know what really happened to my friend."

Silence filled the trailer again. Hazel tried to think of other ways she could cope with her anxiety, but nothing came. She looked at Jason with desperation in her eyes but didn't find any answers in his face. He was sucking on his bottom lip in the way that he did when he was trying to figure out a particularly complex problem. The air around him was that dull tan. Maybe he would come up with a way to get them out of there.

"He was acting weird, you know?" Roy said, his voice echoed out in the silence even though he wasn't talking very loud.

Hazel knew better than to say anything else. She held her breath.

"He was arguing with Billy a lot, picking fights with him about the littlest things. And about Eugene. They were always fighting about Eugene." Roy shook his head.

"It got worse and worse, and then suddenly he got quiet. That made Billy even crazier than when they were arguing all the time. He was always reading that book you gave him, always had it in his hands. He got really calm, like a... like a monk or somethin'.

"Billy, he was getting jumpier and jumpier as Cash got calmer and calmer. Billy started carrying his gun around everywhere with him. Then one day, Cash said he wasn't going to do the job anymore. This one or the one for Mr. Mills. He said they were all corrupt, and it wasn't right, and that we shouldn't do it either. That we weren't doing our duty to Eugene.

"Billy was madder than a hornet. He was yellin' and screamin' and tellin' Cash that if he wasn't going to help the family out than he may as well just leave like all our uncles left our daddy.

"Cash said he was the only one helping the family, that he was trying to do the right thing. Billy said no way, *he* was the one putting food on the table and clothes on our backs ever since Dad died. And that Cash was an ungrateful little worm. Billy yelled at him for a while, then Cash just walked out. Billy yelled after him good riddance and he could go do the right thing somewhere else.

"We had a job that night, there was a Best Buy truck at the truck stop we could take a few boxes out of, so we all went. Billy told Danny that Cash was going to rat us out. It was usually Cash's job to do the watch. We had to pick up his slack.

"I don't know why Cash came back that night. It was... it was an accident."

Roy's voice broke, and he stopped talking. He shoved the gun back in his pocket and got up. For the first time since she had met him, the dark cloud around Roy lightened and lifted a bit. "We took him to the hospital, we didn' know what else to do, we had to tell the cops somethin'."

"You're right, Miss Hazel, it's not fair. Not fair to Cash. I think he was just tryin' to come 'pologize. He din' do nothin' wrong and if that Wallis tells the story Danny fed him, everyone's gonna think that he did somethin' awful. I can't live with it. I want you to go, you go tell everyone it was an accident. It weren't nobody's fault. Cash was just tryin' to do the right thing. I'm gonna let you go."

TWENTY-ONE

Hazel didn't dare speak or move or breathe. She didn't want to interfere with Roy's epiphany or his current course of action. Jason, however, had a few things to say.

"Roy," he spoke very slowly and softly. "If you don't want to get in trouble with your brothers for this, we need to make it look like Hazel and I escaped. I have already figured out how to untie my rope while you were talking." Jason slowly took his hands out from behind his back, the rope hanging loosely around one wrist. He reached over and began to untie Hazel.

Roy's face registered astonishment. "Billy was right! Y'all are tricksy."

"What I think we should do," Jason went on in his overly calm voice, "is you should go back over to where you were sitting earlier and you should fire a shot into the trailer wall here, right over where we were sitting. You can tell the others that you tried to shoot me when I escaped, and you missed. Then I'm afraid I'm going to have to punch you in the face. You need a big enough lump on your head to make it look like I knocked you unconscious."

Roy's face wrinkled up. "I don't know about that, sir," he said. "Don' know if I like that."

Jason thought for a minute. "What if you just give me the gun and then you can say that after you missed. I overpowered you. Hazel and I escaped while we held you at gunpoint?"

"That's much better, sir," Roy nodded. "I like that idea much better."

"Are you going to be able to lie to your brothers okay?"

Roy's face grew serious. "I'll do it for Cash," he said.

"Good man," Jason said.

They all stood back, and Roy fired a shot at the wall right above where Jason's head was moments before.

"Nice shot," Jason winced.

Roy attempted to hand Jason the gun, but he shook his head and gestured to Hazel. So Roy pressed the gun into her hands. Without a second glance at Roy, Jason headed towards the open trailer door. Hazel started to follow him, then stopped, grabbing Roy's hand for a moment.

"Your brother Cash would be so proud of you," she said.

Roy reddened. "Thanks, ma'am. I hope so."

They were about to jump out of the truck right as the ATVs, with headlights blaring, came roaring into view. Hazel and Jason froze, looking at Roy. Roy looked at them and then back to the ATVs. And then back at them. He shrugged and then immediately dove at Jason, tackling him to the floor of the trailer.

"Hey!" Hazel said, grabbing Roy by the shirt collar and trying to pull him off her husband. "You were going to let us go for Cash's sake."

"You wouldn't make it now, anyways," Roy yelled, punching Jason in the face. Jason's eyes went hazy, and he swayed. Hazel let go of Roy and dove for her husband instead. She pulled his head into her lap and slapped Roy across the face when he tried to lunge at him again.

"Can't you see he's already incapacitated?" she yelled. "My word, if only your mother had lived."

"Amen to that," Roy grumbled, rubbing his face where she slapped him.

The ATVs pulled up and Billy jumped off before Virgil had turned off the one they were riding together.

"You were right, Billy, they sure is tricksy. Mr. Dean wriggled out of 'em ropes and attacked me. I tried to shoot 'em, I surely did, but I missed, and they got the gun, but I was able to get 'em before they escaped."

Billy ignored Roy's fictitious explanation and marched up the ramp to where Hazel and Jason were crouched. "Where are their phones? Gimme the phones," he said, putting his hand out and snapping at Roy. Roy felt around in his pockets, then handed Hazel's phone to Billy.

He examined her phone for a minute, pushing the home button, then threw it down where Danny and Virgil had now gotten off their ATVs.

"You said nobody gets service out here!" Billy yelled.

Danny raised a foot and stomped on the phone decisively.

Hazel chortled. "You're going to have to try harder than that to break that thing," she said.

Danny picked it back up and fumbled, trying to take the phone out of its protective cover.

"Now what are we going to do?" Billy grumbled.

Roy was looking around at his compatriots. "What happened?" he asked, shifting his weight from foot to foot. "What's going on?"

"We've been compromised," Danny said, with that emotionless voice. "The cops are all over the cabin."

"How?" Roy asked.

"They must have told them about it somehow," Danny said. "I guess they have a better provider than I do."

Hazel's mind raced. The boys must have called the police,

like Jason had predicted. She remembered that Nora was able to track her location, but how did that work? She really hadn't gotten any service since they left the car at the beginning of the day.

"You think this is funny?" Billy spat at Danny.

"I think this is an inconvenience," Danny shrugged, his peppy turquoise was back. "We won't be able to retrieve the rest of the merchandise, but we have a half a truck full, and they don't know where we are. We can drive off and still make the rendezvous. Tie those two back up and let's go."

Billy looked more than happy to do all the tying up himself. He grabbed Hazel by the upper arm and hoisted her to her feet. Jason still looked dazed. His eyes didn't seem to be focusing.

"Oh no," Hazel murmured.

"He'll survive," Billy said.

Roy and Virgil grabbed Hazel and Jason and started to haul them into the back of the truck. This time Hazel knew that they would close it up and drive away. She looked over at her husband, who was borderline unconscious, and something in her snapped. She started to scream.

"What the hell?" Roy said, but she could barely hear him she was screaming so loud.

Hazel didn't stop screaming. She started lashing out, hitting, kicking, and abusing Virgil and Roy in any way that she could. She was frantic. Roy kept almost losing his grip on her. She kept struggling.

Hazel felt Billy grab her by the hair and drag her backwards into the truck. She screeched in pain and tears sprang to her eyes. "I've about had it with you, Mrs. Dean. We've had a strict anti-violence policy around here, but I'm seriously considering an adjustment to that in your honor."

"Anti-violence, huh? Like how Danny dealt with Cash?" Hazel spat. His threats didn't stop her from trying to wriggle out of his arms again, but he had the advantage. He twisted her arm behind her back at a strange angle, so that if she tried to move at all, the pain would become unbearable.

"Please," she said. "I just want to take care of my husband. I just wanted to help Cash. I can't be in this truck. I can't..."

Billy ignored her pleas and shoved her towards the back of the truck. She planted her feet and yelped as pain shot through her twisted arm. Jason had attempted to get her to take a self-defense class five million times since they had been married, but Hazel always resisted, saying that there was nothing to be afraid of in their tight-knit community. She had been naïve. Inspiration jolted through her. That was it, the key to all of this. And she was in a unique position to implement the solution.

"I'll buy it," she said. Her voice was suddenly calm, and she had stopped struggling.

"What?" Billy said.

"I'll buy it," she said again. "I'll pay the price for the whole trailer, all the merchandise you couldn't recover from the cabin."

"You don't have that kind of money," he scoffed.

"I do," said Hazel. "I have more money than you can probably imagine."

"I don't believe it."

"It's true," she continued. "My Uncle John got me a big settlement when my parents died. He sued everyone he could think of: the company my dad worked for, the company the other driver worked for, the driver himself, the government who maintained the roads. I have a trust fund. I don't even look at it anymore. Millions of dollars are in there. I didn't want to live that kind of lifestyle, so I just used it to build my book-shop... well, and to pay the losses on the bookshop every month. Bookshops aren't exactly the most profitable businesses anymore."

Billy blinked at her. "We were going to get a million from this trailer. You good for that?"

"Yes," Hazel said, looking at him unblinking. "Definitely."

"What are your terms?"

"Drive me and Jason home and leave us be."

"How do we know you won't turn us in?"

"You don't," she said. "We probably will. But if Danny really was the brain behind the operation, maybe your sentence wouldn't be so bad. And you'd have plenty of money when you got out."

Billy was quiet for a minute, but he let her arm relax a little bit. "The boss would never go for it," he said finally.

"You don't need permission from him, do you?" she asked.

Billy snorted.

"I mean," Hazel went on, encouraged. "What makes him the boss, anyways? Aren't you just as smart as he is?" She cringed at her obvious attempt at flattery. She couldn't imagine anyone falling for it.

Billy didn't say anything. He looked over at Virgil, Roy, and Jason. Roy was attempting to throw Jason over his shoulder and pick him up, but Jason was a big guy, and he was having some trouble. Working together, Virgil and Roy were finally able to move Jason's unconscious body back into the truck bed.

"I'll think about it," Billy finally said. "But in the meantime, I'm tying you up. I don't want Danny to get suspicious." Not overly confident in their new agreement, Hazel reluctantly allowed her hands to be tied behind her back again. Remembering the old Navy Seal trick Uncle John taught her, she stretched her hands out, splaying her fingers to make her forearms bigger while he was tying the knots. She felt that Billy enjoyed tying them too tight and causing her pain, and a hopeless despondency settled over her. Billy wouldn't make the deal with her after all. He just agreed to it so she would stop trying to hurt him.

"What's going on here?" Hazel heard a familiar voice say

from outside the trailer. She recognized the white glow of Waylon Gibbons.

"Nothing that concerns you, Waylon," she heard Danny's voice soothe. "We're just transporting some merchandise."

"I heard a woman screaming," he said, in his childlike voice. "I came over to see if she was hurt."

Roy crouched down next to Hazel and put a hand over her mouth. She attempted to keep from screaming, but the sound was muffled.

"Oh, that's just Billy's music. Terrible, isn't it? You go on home Waylon, I'll come see you tomorrow. I found a zebra wood floor someone tore out of their house. I think you could find something to do with it."

Hazel couldn't hear any more of the conversation as they walked away. After a few minutes, Billy let go of her and hobbled as quick as he could to the trailer door. She screamed, but he rolled the door of the trailer down before she could really get going. Hazel was alone in the dark with her unconscious husband, a couple of ATVs, and a couple hundred iPads.

Hazel stared into the darkness, flinching when the truck started moving. She told herself that she wasn't in a truck. That she was in a cave, or better yet, a spa. She was having some kind of new, exotic treatment in the dark. She took long, deep breaths, Jason's words from before echoing in her head. She would be safe. Yes, she would be. But it was up to her to make it happen. Her heart was still pounding. Her head was still throbbing. She had to concentrate on taking deep breaths in and out, but she began to work the rope.

TWENTY-TWO

Hazel focused on breathing and working the rope. Making tight fists, she managed to eventually wiggle her hands out, but it left her wrists sore and raw. In the dark, she crawled towards Jason, feeling around with her hands until she found him. She pulled his head into her lap carefully, trying to cushion him from the rumbling of the trailer. He groaned.

"Jason, Jason, are you okay?" she asked, choking on her own voice. He didn't move a muscle or even groan.

The darkness was intense and closed in around her. Her eye had swollen so much that it shut on its own. Gingerly, she probed Jason's head, looking for the wound that knocked him out. She found a large lump, but it didn't feel like there was blood. She choked back a sob and did what she always did when she felt overwhelmed: she began to talk to her mom.

"Momma, are you there?" she said into the darkness. "Momma, I'm so scared. Jason is hurt. I'm hurt, and I don't know where we're going. Jeremiah and Elias are going to wonder where we are. Oh, Momma, what am I going to do?"

Hazel gently put Jason's head back on the floor and felt her way towards the trailer's door, exploring it by feel. Didn't they have to put some kind of emergency handle on the inside so someone could get out if they were accidentally shut in? Or was that just for car trunks?

The truck bounced and jerked as they drove down the road. Soon she heard the sounds of highway traffic. There were a lot of different handles and levers, but Hazel worried that if she pulled one of them and did end up opening the door, she would fly out onto the highway. The thought made her flinch, and she felt her way back over to Jason.

"Jason?" she spoke loudly, shaking him. "Jason, can you hear me?"

He didn't move. Hazel put her finger on his neck and leaned over his mouth. She could feel his breath on her cheek and a heartbeat under her fingers. Hazel didn't know how far they were driving to meet the client, but she knew that by then, they would have decided what to do with her and Jason. Her mind raced over a dozen different possibilities, but the only conclusion she could think of was that they would decide to kill them. Her only hope was that Billy would decide that her offer was too good to pass up and that he would let them escape.

After what felt like hours, she heard a police siren wail somewhere nearby. She didn't dare hope. It was probably just a routine traffic violation, some little sports car speeding by them.

She still couldn't believe it when the sirens got louder, and the truck came to a stop. She heard voices blasting over a bullhorn but couldn't make out what they were saying.

Moments later, the door to the back of the trailer rose, and a spotlight blinded her.

"They're here," she heard Uncle John's voice call over the bullhorn. "We've got them." He jumped into the truck and enfolded Hazel in his arms.

"Hazel, are you alright?" he asked urgently.

"Jason," Hazel cried weakly. She didn't even have the energy to stand. She just lay there, waves of relief washing over her, making her shiver. "He's hurt."

Uncle John gently tilted her face towards him. "Oh, Hazel," he said. "I'll never forgive myself for this. I should have thrown you in jail. I could have kept you safe there."

"We found it," Hazel sobbed.

"I can hear all about it later," he said. "Right now, let's get you fixed up. Your lips are cracked. We'll find you some water." Hazel felt like a little girl again. Uncle John lifted her up and carried her out of the truck and sat her in the front seat of a squad car. "I have to take care of some things," John said, handing her a water bottle. "I'll be back in a little bit."

A half dozen policemen were milling about the trailer in no time, and her friend Officer Brandon came over to assess her condition. He shook his head.

"You're not looking so great, Mrs. Dean," he said.

"Brandon," she said breathlessly. "Jason is hurt, he's unconscious. Can you help him?"

"They'll take care of him, ma'am." Brandon said. He got out a little flashlight and shined it in each of her eyes. "I think you need to be taken care of too. An ambulance is on its way. Are you up to seeing your boys?"

"What?" Hazel didn't understand. Her mind wasn't working very quickly. Brandon pointed, and she saw her sons rushing towards her.

"Jeremiah! Elias! What are you doing here?" she asked, panic welling up inside her throat. "It's not safe."

"Watch your mom," Brandon said. "She's hurt."

"No, I'm not," she started to say.

"Mom, your face!" Jeremiah said. "What happened? Did you get in a fight with a bad guy? Does he look worse than you do? What about Dad, was he there? Did he beat up the guy that did that to you?"

"Give her some space, boys," Brandon said. He gently pushed them aside and wrapped a gray flannel blanket around her shoulders. He frowned at her water bottle. "You need more water."

"I'm on it," Elias said, turning on his heel.

Jeremiah hovered around Officer Brandon, waiting to be allowed to interrogate her again. "Why are my kids here?" she asked him. "I wish you hadn't let them come."

Brandon shrugged. "It wasn't my call," he said. "They were helping us search for you. We didn't realize that it was going to become a high-speed chase."

"It was awesome, Mom," Jeremiah enthused. "Uncle John was all talking through the radio and he told the other car to pull in front of the truck, and then they had to stop. And Uncle John got on the bullhorn and told them to surrender. It was like in a movie! I mean... I knew Uncle John was hard core, but I had no idea. He's like... like an old, fat Tom Hardy or something."

Elias handed Hazel another water bottle. She noticed he was a pale green color, like before he took a test at school and squeezed his hand.

"When it got late, your sons got worried about you and came down to the station," Brandon explained. "Elias showed us that he had your location tracked on his phone and saw the spot where you disappeared from service. We probably would still be searching if it wasn't for that hermit guy. He showed us where the truck was and told us he heard a woman screaming. Captain Tate kind of went wild then. We were rushed out of there in a few squad cars, Elias and Jeremiah included. They were really worried about you... no one had time to argue with a couple of belligerent teenagers."

Brandon stepped aside and her boys crowded around her again. "Are you okay, Mom?" Elias asked.

"I'll be fine," she said. "Can you do me a favor? Can

someone check on your dad? I'd like to be near him." Elias disappeared without a word.

Minutes later, he returned. "I found him," he said. Hazel allowed him and Jeremiah to support most of her weight and they helped her over to a makeshift stretcher where Jason was lying until the ambulance got there. He was still unconscious. Hazel had her sons settle her onto the ground next to him.

"Can you get Uncle John for me?" Hazel requested. "I need to tell him some things."

John didn't have time to talk to Hazel right away. He radioed police officials in several different precincts and contacted the Feds. The semi-truck robberies had been bothering him for several months, and the case had just cracked wide open. Hazel worried that the ambulance might arrive before she would be able to talk to him. She wouldn't be parted from Jason. She would have to call John later and tell him about Danny. But the ambulance didn't get there right away, and finally, John came to sit with her.

"How are you feeling, Hazel?"

"Much better now that I've had some water," she said.

"I was so worried when that man told me they put you in the back of a semi-truck."

Hazel turned her hands palms up. "I made it," she said. "What else could I do? Jason helped me at first, but then they knocked him unconscious. I had to get through, there was no other way."

"You've grown up to be a strong and capable woman," John said. "I hope you can forgive me for letting things play out the way they did. My hands were tied."

"I don't want to talk about it right now," she interrupted. "I need to tell you about some things I saw. Danny, the receptionist, was behind this whole operation."

"Oh, I know," John said. "It took the McCleary boys about thirty seconds to turn on him." He narrowed one eye in Hazel's direction. "Something tells me that you and Jason weren't just out for a leisurely hike. Didn't you learn your lesson the other day?"

Hazel cringed. "Eugene McCleary gave us some information we felt we needed to act on immediately."

"Hazel, we probably never would have found that cabin if you hadn't done what you did."

"Yes, but how exactly did you find us?" she asked.

"I believe you recently met a fellow, name of Gibbons?" John said, scratching the back of his head.

"Of course," Hazel said.

"He bumped into us in the woods and told us what he saw. He suspected that they might've had you in the back of the truck. He even remembered the license plate number so we could track you down easily."

Hazel smiled, then winced, her hand flying to the swollen side of her face. "I should really visit him again," she murmured.

"You're going straight to the hospital," John instructed her. He got to his feet. "You need immediate medical attention. I've got to get back. We're still trying to find Danny. He was driving ahead of the truck. The McClearys told us where the rendezvous is supposed to be, but I expect Danny might be a tricky one to catch."

"Wait," Hazel said. "Did the McCleary boys tell you that he's the one that killed Cash?"

Uncle John had turned to go, but he whirled back around. "No, they did not."

"Roy told us it was him. The McClearys will back it up now that their operation has been exposed. You'll finally find those casings you've been looking for at the cabin where you found the stolen goods."

"But why would Wallis confess?"

"I think that the McClearys didn't realize that police scrutiny of the hotel construction site would get Chris Mills into all kinds of trouble. I think Danny arranged for Chris Mills to blackmail or bribe Wallis into confessing so that he wouldn't get into trouble for whatever shady things are going on at the hotel."

Uncle John stroked his stubbly beard, nodding. "That would explain why that trailer mysteriously went up in flames."

He stared into the middle distance for another five seconds, making connections. "I'd better get to the bottom of this."

"One more thing," she said, patting his arm to get his attention. "Roy said Cash's death was an accident. I think that's suspicious since Danny just found out that Cash was planning on turning them in. I'd ask Roy about it."

John nodded and rushed away.

"Wow, Mom," Jeremiah said. Hazel jumped. She hadn't realized that her sons had been listening to her whole conversation. "You're pretty good at this stuff."

Minutes later, an ambulance pulled up. The paramedics hopped out and loaded Jason in.

"Is he going to be okay?" she asked, hovering. She repeated her question several times before anyone responded.

"He's going to be fine, but we're going to take him in just to be sure."

Hazel nodded, feeling a little dizzy. The paramedic scrutinized her. "You aren't looking so great yourself. I'd like you to come too if you don't mind."

"Try to stop me," she said, climbing in and settling beside Jason.

Brandon leaned into the ambulance. "Do you have space for a couple of teenage boys?" he asked. "We don't have space for them in the squad cars anymore now that we've got some arrests."

The paramedic shrugged. "We have one extra seat up front

with the driver. Not exactly playing by the rules, but we can take one of them."

Brandon frowned. He sized up the boys. "You better take Elias. I think we can squeeze Jeremiah in with John."

Elias clambered into the passenger's seat in the front of the ambulance. Brandon slammed the back doors shut, and the driver turned on the siren.

"Hold on," one of the paramedics said. The ambulance made a wide U-turn and took off back towards Red Gap.

THE PARAMEDICS WERE able to revive Jason on the way back to the hospital. They gave both Jason and Hazel IVs for dehydration and in ten minutes Jason was groggy but awake.

"What happened?" he croaked. "I thought we were dead."

"My new friend Waylon Gibbons informed the police of our whereabouts," Hazel said. "Don't worry. You're going to be fine. We're on our way to the hospital."

Jason lifted a hand tentatively towards her. "Your face..." he said.

"I'm okay," she soothed.

"And your hair, it's still blue," he moaned.

She smiled. He was going to be okay.

It took her most imperious tone of voice to get the paramedic to take the IV out of her arm and not admit her. She was going to be fine. She had more important things to worry about than her face.

Leaving Jason to the competent care of the hospital's ER doctors, Hazel headed towards Eugene's room. She couldn't move as quickly as she wanted and often had to put a hand on the wall for support. When she got there, she was surprised to see a large woman around her own age, wearing a gray suit, sitting in a chair by Eugene's bed. Hazel noticed the CPS ID in a lanyard around the woman's neck. She exuded a muted watermelon, and Eugene had that familiar swirl of black, brown and midnight blue.

"Here she is," Eugene said. "This is my temporary foster mom."

The woman blinked at her, taking in Hazel's battered face. "Really?"

"Hazel Randolph Dean." Hazel tried to smile and put out her hand to shake. "I was just out hiking, and my face got hurt." She tried to explain without offering too much information.

"I was just letting Eugene know what happened to his brothers," the woman said. "Have you been informed?"

Hazel nodded. "That's why I came after hours."

"How would you feel about staying with the Deans a little longer, Eugene?" the woman asked.

Eugene smiled weakly and nodded. "I can't think of anywhere else I'd rather go," he shrugged.

"You don't have any other family you could stay with?" the woman asked.

"Not that I know. Not nearby," Eugene said. "I think my dad had some brothers up in Ohio somewhere, but we never spoke with them much."

Hazel interjected. "He has an aunt and grandparents in Tennessee."

Eugene's eyes widened as his swirling cloud paled. "I what?" he tried to sit up in bed and winced.

"Oh, Eugene," Hazel said. "I have so much to tell you."

The CPS agent glanced from Eugene to Hazel. "Can I see you outside for a moment, Mrs. Dean?"

Hazel signed some paperwork, explained the estranged family situation briefly, and accepted the woman's card with a promise to deliver the letter she found in Cash's truck as soon as she could. "I remember their last name is Reeves," she said. "I think they would be happy to have Eugene."

The agent thanked her and left her to make her explanations to Eugene. Hazel walked back into his room and sat down, taking his hand in hers.

"What's going on, Miss Hazel?" he asked with the patience that only children are capable of.

Hazel sighed. "Where should I start?"

"Why are my brothers being arrested?" he asked.

Hazel looked at him sharply. "Not for killing Cash," she promised. "No, they were involved in a series of robberies."

Eugene nodded, unsurprised.

"Cash didn't want to participate in the robberies," Hazel went on. "He was also worried about some shady things they were doing in their construction business, cutting corners and stuff."

Eugene nodded again. "I know, I heard Cash and Billy argue about code and safety violations a lot."

"Eugene, why do you know so much about drugs? After watching *Jeopardy* with you, I thought your brothers must have been into trafficking."

Eugene snorted and half-shrugged. "I watch a lot of TV."

Hazel laughed. "I should have known," she murmured. "I knew Cash was worried about you," Hazel explained. "He wanted you to have wholesome, honest family to take care of you." She squeezed Eugene's hand. "He was going to take you and leave, to go live close by your aunt and grandparents."

The furrows in Eugene's forehead disappeared and understanding dawned in his face. "That's why he started talking about traveling? He wasn't leaving me. He was going to take me with him." Eugene's countenance darkened again. Hazel patted his hand.

"Yes, after you mentioned that his truck went missing, I went and found it. He had letters from your aunt, your birth certificate, some money, and everything you would need to restart your lives. I don't know when he was planning on leaving, but it was soon."

"After football season," Eugene murmured.

Hazel smiled. "Maybe."

They sat in silence for a few moments.

"Eugene," Hazel said gently, "Don't you want to know what happened to Cash?"

"No," Eugene said in a very small voice, wrapping his arms around himself.

"It's okay," she said, leaning towards him. "You'll feel better if you know. It was a man that was in business with your brothers. Apparently, it was an accident."

Eugene stared at her in silence. The hurricane of emotions inside him evident in swirling colors that grew to encompass the room. Hazel rethought the wisdom of sharing this news with Eugene after all. "Eugene?" she said. "Are you okay?"

"Danny didn't kill Cash," he whispered. "I did."

TWENTY-THREE

Hazel stopped breathing. Dizziness returned with a vengeance. She reeled. She could feel herself lean away from Eugene, then hated herself for it. She forced herself to lean in again. "What happened?" she asked. She tried to make her voice soothing, but it came out hoarse.

Eugene exhaled and stared up at the ceiling. His eyes filled with tears. They ran down from his eyes and into his ears. Hazel bit her lip.

"I didn't know..." he started. "I didn't know anything." He suddenly lurched upright, grabbing her hand. "I'm so sorry. I'm so sorry," he repeated it over and over again, sobbing. Hazel couldn't imagine that this young man was really responsible for his brother's death. It must have been a terrible misunderstanding. She patted his back, knowing 'it's alright' would not be an appropriate thing to say at the moment, so she just let him cry. Finally, hiccuping, he let go of Hazel's hand and leaned back into his pillows.

"Billy told me they needed me. He said Cash was abandoning us. That he was too good for us and he was going to leave us and go make a new life in Atlanta. They had a job, and

Cash wasn't going to do his part. I think... I think that they were extra worried because they didn't know what Cash was going to do, if he was going to turn them in or what. Billy took me with them in the truck. We drove down some back roads to where they had some ATVs parked. We rode the ATVs down to that cabin in the woods. I had heard Billy and Cash argue enough that I knew they were involved with something illegal, but I didn't know what it was. Danny was there. I had never met him before, but I could tell that my brothers were working for him. They explained that Cash wasn't going to be there anymore, but that they brought me, that I would help. Danny was skeptical. Billy handed me a rifle and told me to shoot anyone that came around."

The swirl of color around Eugene picked up speed and expanded. Hazel flinched, worried that she would be caught up in the anger, shame and guilt. Eugene's face contorted with anger.

"I was actually proud of myself," he spat. "I was anxious to show Billy that I was old enough to help, that I was a man. That I wasn't afraid. They left me there alone. They said they had to run an errand and that they would bring something back soon. I would be able to tell it was them because I'd hear the ATVs. Then they left." Eugene swallowed. "Have you ever been out in the woods alone at night, Miss Hazel?"

Hazel nodded, heartsick at what she was hearing. Nausea churned in her stomach.

"It was so dark and there were so many noises and movement. The woods were *alive*. I've never really seen them like that before. We've had a couple of bonfires and things, but usually there's a lot of people around. I guess it keeps the critters away. Now there was no one, just me, and I got spooked. I couldn't wait for Billy to come back, but I didn't want him to know that I had been scared. I tried my best to do what he asked me to do. I got the rifle all ready to shoot, and occasionally I held it up to practice or pretend, or I don't even know. I was such a *kid*." He glared at his old self.

"I didn't see Cash, really. I just heard something moving around the side of the house. I was jumpy, and I started firing. I emptied the clip. I had terrible aim, but one shot got him and that's all it took." His voice cracked, and the tears came again. "I still didn't recognize him, not until he stopped moving and I put the gun down to go check it out. When I..."

"Oh, Eugene," Hazel said, when he couldn't continue. Tears were streaming down her cheeks. She did the best she could to keep her reactions in check for Eugene's sake. He gulped for air and did his best to continue his story through his tears. It seemed that now he was telling it, he wanted to get it all out.

"When I saw it was Cash, I couldn't believe it. I don't know much of what happened after that. I sat with him there for a while. He couldn't speak, but he was breathing. I know he suffered because I watched him. I don't know how long we sat there, but eventually Billy and the others came back. They put Cash on the ATV somehow and took him back to the truck and then drove him to the hospital. They didn't know what to tell them about how he got hurt. Billy said he overheard Danny talking on the phone with Mills about some drug thing he and Wallis Trudgeon were involved with. I think Danny was helping them cover their tracks. Billy just made up that Wallis had shot him on the spot. Top of mind, I guess. None of us felt too bad about ruining Wallis' life. He's just a dirty Trudgeon after all." Hazel flinched. "Sorry, ma'am," Eugene muttered before continuing.

"Things got out of hand from there. I *saw* Cash," Eugene shuddered. "I did, several times. I knew he was haunting me. My brothers never said that they hated me, but I knew they did. Cash was always everyone's favorite. Even Billy, even though they fought all the time. I think Billy was actually really proud of him. I couldn't sleep. I couldn't really eat. Then you showed me that letter, and I felt even worse. I let Billy convince me that Cash didn't really care about me, but I could tell in that letter that he did. I didn't know what to do. I decided I'd better pick up where Cash left off. Then maybe he'd stop haunting me."

"I overheard you and Mr. Dean talking about evidence, and I knew what the message in the book meant, so I was going to go find some evidence for you. That way Cash would be at peace. But then I busted my leg. I knew you would do it though, Miss Hazel. Nothing would stop you. I'm glad they arrested Billy and Roy and Virgil and Danny. Maybe now things will be okay. I can stay with you or that aunt you mentioned."

"Eugene," Hazel said, a sob catching in her throat. "I don't know what's going to happen now."

Eugene stared past her, a look of fear crossing his face. Hazel whirled around and saw John standing in the doorway.

"Well, son," he said, with his hat in his hands. "Is there something you need to tell me?"

Hazel jumped up and pushed Uncle John out into the hall. "He just told me the whole story. I don't want him to have to go through that again."

"Oh, Hazel," Uncle John shook his head at her. "The rest of us have learned to check our feelings at the door. You're too tender hearted to be wrapped up in this kind of thing."

"How did you find out?"

"Roy spilled his guts. It's nothing but tragic, but we can't just let Eugene walk away. He made some very serious mistakes."

"He is a child," Hazel exclaimed, throwing her hands in the air. "He was influenced by his good-for-nothing brothers. How can he be responsible for his behavior?"

"Don't worry, Hazel," John soothed. "There's plenty of blame to go around. We're going to charge Billy and maybe the others with involuntary manslaughter. I don't know what charge Eugene will get yet - the lawyers are still working it out - but he will definitely be charged with something."

Hazel's hand flew to her mouth. "God bless that poor boy," she whispered. "Hasn't he suffered enough?"

Uncle John enfolded her in his arms, and she began to cry. She buried her head in his chest and sobbed. She let him stroke her hair and murmur comforting things to her, but she didn't feel any better. She had found out what happened to Cash and proved that Wallis was innocent, but it was a hollow comfort.

TWENTY-FOUR

"Tell me they decided to let you do it," Hazel demanded when Jason hung up the phone. The boys had already left for school. She and Jason were getting ready for their day when Jason's phone rang with the call from Judge Proust they had been expecting.

"They don't *let* me do anything, Hazel. I do what I want, but after consulting with the district judges and some of my other colleagues, they believe that it wouldn't be inappropriate for me to represent Eugene. At least not in Georgia."

"What a relief," Hazel said, putting her earrings in. "You'll be able to get him into that good facility then? And with the minimum sentence of one year?"

Jason smiled, tying his tie in a double Windsor. "I think I can even get him out of there early if he behaves himself."

"Of course, Eugene will behave himself," Hazel said. She clapped her hands together.

Hazel had been on the phone and researching options for Eugene for a week. His reaction to his grief, particularly his hallucinations of Cash, would be enough to get him into a treatment facility instead of a juvenile detention center. Jason thought that at the end, they would be able to get his aunt custody.

"I've got to run," Hazel said, kissing Jason goodbye. "I've got that community service sentence."

Jason smiled, suppressing a laugh. "Ah yes, of course."

"Stop it," she said. "I actually don't mind it at all. I think I'll keep going after I've served my time."

"See you at Elias' game later?" Jason asked.

"Of course," she said. "Try and stop me." A stab of regret pierced her heart when she thought that Eugene wouldn't be able to play in the game that night. Hopefully next year he would be back to playing football like normal.

HAZEL OPENED the door to her shop and stepped in. She felt a flood of emotions and anxiety rush out of her to be replaced with a deep sense of calm and peace. The stories on the shelves seemed to whisper that everything would be okay. She surrendered to an intense need to be in the stacks, sorting her books, opening one or two of her favorites to peruse her favorite passages.

Hours later, she sat in an aisle, lost in a copy of Les Miserables, when she heard the bell on the front door jingle. She made her way to the end of the aisle to observe her visitor. She usually tried to let her new customers discover the bookshop for themselves if they seemed like they would start exploring on their own. She was surprised to see LaShay Trudgeon standing at the front of the shop, taking off her gloves.

"LaShay!" Hazel cried, stepping into the lobby. "I'm so glad you came in."

"Hello Hazel," LaShay said. As when Hazel first met her, she had a twinkly violet essence to her. "What a beautiful shop. I can't believe I didn't know it was here."

Hazel waved her hand. "It was a dilapidated old structure for decades. I just fixed it up a few years ago."

LaShay nodded. "I went to see Wallis," she said.

"I'm so glad," Hazel said.

"He didn't kill the kid after all, but I think that you knew that. You were somehow involved in finding out what really happened?"

Hazel felt her cheeks get hot. "LaShay, I have to tell you something. Why don't you come back to the café and I'll make you some chocolate?"

"Alright," LaShay said, following Hazel past the stacks to the cozy chairs in the back of the building. "Oh!" she gasped. "How lovely." Hazel smiled with satisfaction. Building out the conservatory style wall in the back of the building cost a fortune, but Hazel wanted her customers to be able to see the breathtaking mountains while curling up with a book and a treat. She couldn't imagine anything more healing.

Today the fog clung to the windows, enshrouding the little shop in a cocoon of white. Trees with blazing colors poked through in surreal vividness. The mountain could be seen looming above them out of the fog.

Hazel sat down in her favorite chair. "LaShay, I knew Cash McCleary. He came into the shop just before he died. That little boy, Eugene, came to tell me about his murder, and I was like a woman possessed. I had to find out what happened. I wanted to help Eugene. At all costs. I'm afraid..." she paused, but LaShay just waited, her color unchanged. "I'm afraid that I came in to get my hair done because I wanted to find out more information about Wallis. I'm so sorry."

LaShay laughed, like a little jingling bell. "You're sorry that you thought my son was innocent and tried to clear his name?"

"Well, I don't feel like I was completely honest with you..."

"Oh Hazel, I don't mind. I understand why you did what you did." She leaned back in her chair. "After that boy confessed to what he had done, the police were able to go to the real scene of the crime and find the casings they needed. There was quite a bit of evidence that backed up the boy's story, so they let Wallis go."

Hazel nodded. She had heard this before from Jason. "I'm so glad to hear it," Hazel said.

"Unfortunately, they're charging him with obstruction of justice because he made a false confession. And he's in a bit of trouble for the drug sales he was involved in with Chris Mills. But his defense lawyer is trying to work out a deal if he's willing to testify against Chris."

Hazel squirmed. "Well, Jolene's a great lawyer. He's in good hands."

"I've been able to connect more with Trudy," LaShay said, her eyes sparkling. "I'll be able to help her out with the kids if she needs if Wallis has to serve any time in jail. Wallis is... well, he's not quite ready to forgive us yet, but I think that he will, eventually. If we show him that we will love and support him and his family no matter what."

"Of course he will," Hazel said, reaching out to squeeze LaShay's hand. "Everything will work out fine now."

"I hope so," she said, her twinkly purple dimming for the first time.

"It will," Hazel said firmly. "I know it will."

"Well, I should be going," LaShay said standing up, "I just came to thank you for what you did for Wallis."

Hazel followed her back through the shelves and grabbed a paper off a display near the door. She pressed it into LaShay's hands. "I hope you'll come to the book club. I would love to see you there."

LaShay smiled. "I'll try," she said.

Hazel glanced down at Les Miserables and was surprised to see that it had taken on a twinkly purple hue. She smiled, of course a book about redemption, forgiveness, and parental love would resonate with LaShay.

"Here," she said, offering LaShay the book. "It wants to go home with you."

LaShay blinked, "Oh!" she breathed, taking the book into her hands.

"I know it's a little long, but just skip the places that get boring and follow the storyline. You'll love it."

"Thank you," LaShay said. She gave Hazel a hug then walked out the door, clutching the book to her chest.

FROM HAZEL'S KITCHEN

From Hazel's Kitchen

Chocolate Peanut Butter Fudge Cookies

These cookies are extremely rich and best served with a glass of milk

¾ c. softened butter
¼ c. shortening
¾ c. peanut butter
1 ½ c. sugar
2.5 oz. melted unsweetened or semisweet chocolate
3 eggs
1 tsp. vanilla
2 c. flour
½ c. cocoa powder
1 ½ tsp. baking soda
1 tsp. salt
Peanut butter chips
Chocolate chips

Preheat the oven to 365

Cream together butter, shortening and peanut butter. Add the melted chocolate and mix to combine. Add the sugar and beat until fluffy. Add the vanilla and then one egg at a time while the mixer is running. Scrape down the sides of the bowl and mix again.

Add the flour, cocoa powder, baking soda and salt. Mix until combined, then add peanut butter chips and chocolate chips. Anywhere from a half to a full bag of each type.

Scoop the cookies onto a cookie sheet lined with parchment. Add about ¼ tsp, a little dollop, of peanut butter on the top of each cookie then put into the oven.

Bake for 9-11 minutes. Don't over-bake.

Chicken & Biscuits Casserole

With homemade chicken stock included in the recipe, this is a labor of love over multiple days. If Hazel is pressed for time (like she was when she took dinner to the McClearys) she will buy boxed chicken broth and use a rotisserie chicken.

1 whole chicken

Salt, peppercorns, onions, carrots, celery

1/3 c. butter

1 diced onion

5 carrots, sliced and quartered

4 stalks of celery diced

8 oz. mushrooms, diced (mushrooms can be controversial. If Hazel is taking someone a meal, she will probably ask their feelings about mushrooms before she makes the casserole.

2 cloves of minced garlic or ½ tablespoon of garlic powder.

1 tablespoon of dried thyme

Salt and pepper to taste

1/3 c. flour

4 cups+ chicken broth reserved from poaching chicken

Your favorite biscuit dough

1) Poach the chicken. Put the whole chicken in a pot and then surround it with carrots, celery and onion as much as there is space. Salt generously (2 tablespoons-ish) and add whole peppercorns. Gently poach the chicken for approximately two hours. Take the chicken out of the pot onto a cutting board. Strain the broth, reserving it for future use. There will probably be enough for this recipe with enough left over to use another time. Strip the chicken of its meat and discard the carcass.

2) Preheat the oven to the temperature your biscuit dough needs to cook at (mine says 450)

3) Melt 1/3 c. of butter in a large stockpot. Add diced onion, celery, mushrooms and carrots. Season with salt, pepper, garlic and thyme. Cook down until the veggies have caramelized. Sprinkle the flour over the caramelized veggies and stir until the flour has been incorporated and the veggies are clumping together.

4) Slowly add the reserved broth, stirring constantly until the broth thickens. Add the chicken, shredding it before you put it in the sauce mixture. Stir to combine.

5) Pour the chicken and sauce into a 9x13 pan. Put the pan into the preheated oven. You want to bring this mixture up to the temperature the biscuits will cook at. That's what prevents soggy bottoms.

6) Prepare the biscuit dough

7) Once the filling has preheated (1/2 hour-ish in the oven) take it out and place your biscuits on top of the filling.

8) Place the casserole back in the oven for 20 minutes to cook the biscuits. Enjoy.

REVIEW

We hope you've enjoyed Guilt is Midnight Blue, the first of Hazel Dean's mysteries. If you did, please consider leaving a review on Amazon or Goodreads. Reviews can do so much for up and coming authors, and your thoughts would be appreciated.

ABOUT THE AUTHOR

Josalyn McAllister is a cozy fiction author whose most recent works include *Love Over Easy* and *Guilt is Midnight Blue*. Josalyn started writing character descriptions at the tender age of seven, inspired by the works of LM Montgomery. In her teenaged years she moved on to Newsies fan fiction. Inspired by National Novel Writing Month, she wrote her first novel about a child she mentored in college. She has never stopped writing. Josalyn taught middle school history before deciding she would rather spend time with her own children rather than other peoples. A restless soul, she has moved all over the country and collected an eclectic array of hobbies. Her writing has a relatable quality that will charm and entertain you.

ALSO BY JOSALYN MCALLISTER

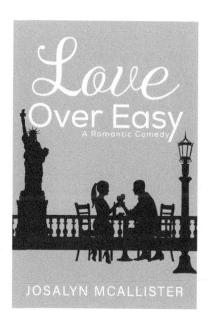

Made in United States
Orlando, FL
04 October 2022